BEN
DESIGNATED MARKSMAN

A NOVEL BY

GARY BAXTER

ACKNOWLEDGEMENTS

Writing my first solo book, in between work and other commitments, was a challenge.

This book flaunts the roles of police, governments, motorcycle gangs, and even drug cartels, but it is fiction after all.

I would like to thank Piers for his help with the police and armour terminology and Brenton Williams for researching the information from past bikie members.

Thank you to Keith and Jen for letting me use their names, although Keith is nothing like his namesake in the book.

Terry Schultz for his name as the A330 pilot.

Lachlan and Kaz, who are real film-industry wardrobe and make-up stylists.

Thank you to Vanessa, who created the cover and put up with my constant minor changes without complaining (to me anyway).

To Robert and Mandy at Hot Tree Editing for your attention to detail,

and finally, Kate from Midnight Authors, who gave me the constant encouragement and advice along the way to make this story really happen.

Gary

CHAPTER ONE

HE sunlight surrounded him like molten gold; its late afternoon heat soaked the sand. The sparse leaves of the water-starved gum tree, under which he lay, offered little shade. The faint scuttle of little creatures busy in their daily lives was the only other sign of life since he'd arrived. This was no beach resort in Bali, where a welcomed beer would arrive with the simple wave of a hand. Boy, how he would kill for that right now!

Ben Woolford was staking out a fortress that had been carefully planned, built, and dressed to look like an abandoned outback settlement. Stripped cars, broken pushbikes, and rubbish were scattered strategically around the yard. Buildings were covered in graffiti and the occasional smashed window.

A rusty-looking cyclone fence surrounded the compound, and only the intermingled stainless-steel razor wire, that was painted an ochre-brown rust colour, gave away the true security of the enclosure. Sure enough, from the air or the point of view of any passer-by, it was just another abandoned settlement. He took out his phone, opened the maps app, and took a screenshot of the exact coordinates in the event he needed to come back or share the location.

He'd been there for nearly twenty-four hours now, acting on a tip-off that a young woman who had run away from her millionaire family had been seen in the nearby outback town of Aileron, in the Northern Territory. Some bribes to the local indigenous lads had led him to this place.

Ben was ex-SAS, a retired designated marksman, or in simple terms, a type of platoon sniper. The two are different but had similar roles. He was tall, dark, and to most women, handsome. His years in the military had made him strong, and he was built like a NRL rugby player.

Compared to Afghanistan or Iraq, stake-outs like this were a walk in the park, but even then, all day in the forty-degree heat and then the freezing cold nights without moving were not what he had planned for his retirement from active duty.

The Tikka T3 sniper rifle that lay by his side served a dual purpose, a little protection should an unexpected situation arise, and an excuse should he get caught: he was just out shooting kangaroos. The Nightforce Optics NXS scope was much better than any roo shooter would actually have. It was deadly accurate for over two kilometres, and his Zeiss Victory RF binoculars were military issue. He used them both to get a detailed look at the finer points of the complex. The remote-controlled electric gate, with its super-tough magnetic lock and the carefully disguised solar panels, showed that a lot of money had been spent here. There hadn't been any movement since he'd arrived, however, just as he was starting to wonder whether he should pack up and move on, a trail of dust appeared in the distance to the south. He looked through his rifle scope to see that the two cars, a dirty white Land Cruiser troop carrier and a dual-cab HiLux ute, had pulled up maybe three kilometres away. They were too far away for him to see why they had stopped, but he kept a close eye on them.

Within a minute or two, Ben heard a drone fly past, high above him. 'Shit!' he said. He scrambled to stand, hard against the tree's thin trunk with his rifle clutched tight to his chest. The drone didn't appear to pause as it flew back towards the parked cars. He could only hope he had moved out of its sight in time. Another dust trail could be seen a further distance to the east, but that seemed to be nearer the highway, so it could be anyone. With the drone gone, he resumed his position flat on the ground with his rifle scope focused on the now-approaching car. One car, the smaller HiLux, had headed slightly northwest on a track that didn't produce any dust. It had possibly gone off-road and through the bush. *I'll still need to keep an eye on that,* he thought. His black Jeep Cherokee was parked two kilometres to the north. If they'd spotted that with the drone, it may have aroused a little suspicion, although an abandoned car around here wouldn't be that unusual. Maybe he should have left all the doors wide open, just like any other abandoned vehicle out here.

He turned back to watch the approaching troopie. It was certainly heading to the compound. The dust from the east was no longer visible, so it might have just been some campers who had stopped and found a site for the night. Ben again ran through his mind the brief from his client, Frank DeLuca, a Darwin millionaire. His twenty-five-year-old daughter, Donna, had gone missing a week ago from Darwin's city centre. DeLuca hadn't disclosed details as to why, but Ben surmised from past experience that she'd most likely run off due to some family disagreement. Her description: five foot, six inches, black hair, last seen in blue jeans, a white top, and white Gucci flat sport shoes. Just locate and report back was his brief. *Pretty easy job for the money*, he thought.

Since his retirement from the armed forces, he just did a little private investigator work to support his service pension, with a little debt collecting, finding the occasional missing person, or personal protection for high-profile people. He liked the work, it paid well, and he no longer had people shooting at him or setting off IEDs as his squadron drove through the back roads of Kabul.

The electric gate started to open as he took out his camera and turned it on. The troopie arrived shortly after and stopped in front of the slowly opening gate. *Obviously solar powered,* he thought. Two men jumped out. 'Bikies,' Ben muttered.

They each had VMC embroidered in a circle that surrounded a snake, a viper to be exact, on the patch sewn onto their denim vests, which is what bikies normally wore over their leather jackets to display their loyalty to the club, but in this heat, they just wore it over their shirts. Ben raised the camera and focused on the two men who were busy checking for unwanted guests in every direction.

'Fuck, they're armed with pistols,' Ben said under his breath. 'Are we expecting trouble, fellas?'

Ben quickly looked over his shoulder to see if there was any sign of the HiLux. Still nothing, no dust or movement. He focused back on the show in front of him. One of the armed men opened the rear door and pulled out a person who had their hands tied behind their back and a black hood covering their head. It certainly looked like a woman. The matted black hair that fell below the hood and the clothes certainly matched his brief.

This is no bloody missing person; this is an abduction. I think Mr DeLuca left out some pretty important details, he thought to himself. He clicked off a few more pictures.

Just then, two black Land Cruisers came smashing through the bush from the east, mowing down all vegetation in their path. The bikies threw the girl to the ground and started firing at them with their pistols.

Jeezuz! Ben thought. *This just got a little more interesting!* The two Land Cruisers skidded to a stop, and all except the drivers jumped out. Dressed in black bulletproof vests and armed with fully automatic rifles, they mowed the bikies down in seconds. Ben kept the camera clicking as a command was given in what sounded like Spanish. Immediately two of the men ran towards the girl, who was now on her knees, her hooded head pressed hard to the ground with her hands still tied behind her back. They grabbed her and ran to the Land Cruisers, her legs desperately trying to keep up.

Then, with a lot of wheelspin and dust, the Land Cruisers sped off in the direction from where they'd come. Ben had seen a lot of similar action in Afghanistan, but this was Australia, not some war-torn third-world country. He lay still for a moment, waiting to see if there was any movement before he risked exposing himself. *Okay, I need to get the fuck out of here*, he thought.

He gathered up his rucksack of rations, pocketed the camera, and slung his rifle over his shoulder. For a moment he thought about checking on the shot bikies, but he quickly figured that if one was still alive, which he seriously doubted, and saw him approaching, they would probably shoot at him. He stood up and looked again for the missing HiLux. Still no sight of it. He started at a fast pace back to his Jeep, trying to think of the best way to handle this situation. The sun was setting, and the light would disappear fast. There was no direct path to the car; it was bush and scrub. He needed to find his car before dark as a torch would be a giveaway, and with what he just witnessed, he didn't want to be having a chat with anyone from around here. At his first opportunity, he would call his client in Darwin to tell him that he had temporally located whom he believed to be his daughter and that this was a job for the police, or the army. Not for a part-time, one-man-show private investigator from Adelaide who now simply enjoyed collecting bad debts and photographing someone's wife who was meeting her lover in some backstreet coffee shop.

Why is this girl so valuable that heavily armed men are killing each other for her? he wondered. *It has to be drugs or a payback of some kind, or could it just be a simple ransom?*

He could now see his Jeep ahead of him in the distance, a very welcome sight, with the light all but gone. He fished out his keys and phone from one of the many pockets of his old SAS army greens from his fighting days in the Middle East, that he was still yet to return to the government. He'd unpicked the badges so as not to look too much like a wannabe soldier.

As he put the key in the door, a fat, heavily tattooed, unkempt bikie stood up from behind the car with what looked like a .44 Magnum. It was big, shiny, and particularly scary in this man's hand. It was pointing straight at his head. Ben withdrew the keys slowly and let them and his phone drop to the ground. He carefully pushed them under the car with his foot and kicked sand over them as he raised his hands above his head. Two men rushed him from behind; they grabbed the rifle from over his shoulder and threw it to the ground, oblivious of its value. They ripped off his rucksack and pulled an arm each behind his back, and with a heavy cable tie, cuffed him. Ben was kicking himself. Two years ago, there would be no way someone could sneak up on him like this.

The man with the gun came towards him and shoved it under his chin with enough force that it almost brought tears to his eyes. With his stinking tobacco breath and rotten teeth that may have never been brushed in his life, he said, 'What the fuck are you doing out here snooping around? You could get yourself killed.'

'I was hunting roos,' Ben replied without moving his bottom jaw, which was still pinned with the pistol barrel.

'That looks like a fucking sniper rifle to me. Look at the size of the fucking scope. I think he's a spy; are you a fucking spy, Mr Roo Shooter?'

'Spying on what?' Ben asked.

'Where the fuck are your roos then, Mr Roo Shooter, who's dressed in camo army greens?'

The gun now pushed harder into the soft skin between his lower jaw. He pictured the mess it would make if this idiot accidently shot him.

'No roos 'cos drought. Just getting dog food,' Ben choked out in reply.

'Well, where's your fuckin dog then?' he roared back, now pushing Ben's head back as far as he could with the gun.

'Skunk, hold him, and Bone, go get the fucking HiLux and throw this fuck in it. I'll ring Joe 'n' see what he wants us to do with him.'

The gun was pulled away from his throat as Ben thought to himself, *There won't be any answer because they are all fucking dead, you moron.* These three obviously didn't know what had just happened back at their compound.

'He isn't answering,' Ferret said in frustration. 'Let's take him back and let Joe take care of him.'

'No, Ferret! Pig said we mustn't take people there. Just let him go; he doesn't know anything,' protested Skunk, as he held tightly to Ben's shirt. Ben was a good six inches taller and much bigger than Skunk. Even with Ben's hands cuffed, Skunk wouldn't be able to hold him should Ben resist. Ben considered this but also knew that a .44 can make a big hole in someone.

Ben looked at the baby-faced lad they called Skunk. He had reasonably good skin, teeth, and no visible tattoos. He looked out of place compared to the other two.

'Or we just fuckin' waste him!' Bone said with a bit of a European accent, waving a pistol around as he walked over from the car.

Ben looked at him with a look that said, 'Really?'

Bone was a hideous-looking man with a scar that ran diagonally down his left cheek. Tattoos were all over his arms, face, and neck. His clothes were filthy, and Ben guessed he probably hadn't showered in days, possibly weeks.

'Skunk, take off your shirt and wrap it around this fuck's head. We'll take him in.' As Skunk approached him with his shirt in hand, the repellent stench of body odour hit the back of Ben's throat before the tatty fabric had got even close to his face.

Ben now knew why they called him Skunk. It was about now he decided he wasn't getting paid enough for this job.

It was completely dark as they drove the two kilometres back to the compound. As the vehicle slowed, then turned, Ben knew they'd approached their base. This was going to be a moment. He had to be ready.

'What the fuck?' Ferret yelled, as the car's headlights swung into view of the rusty-looking fence when it crested the last sand dune.

He turned to Ben. 'What the fuck did you do, roo shooter?' Ferret said slowly.

'I don't know what you are talking about,' Ben said through the stinking shirt, now getting concerned that these losers might shoot him 'just because.'

With guns drawn, the bikies slid slowly out of the HiLux. They searched in all directions as they carefully walked towards their massacred brothers.

Skunk had Ben by one arm and dragged him still blindfolded along as well.

Ferret looked down at Joe, the sergeant-at-arms of the club. He had at least six bullet wounds; they all did. Blood covered the windscreen of the troopie from the dead driver who hung over the steering wheel with half his head missing.

'The roo shooter didn't do this. These are automatics,' Skunk said as they slowly approached.

'No fucking kidding, Einstein,' Ferret replied.

'Fuuuck,' Ferret screamed out into the night.

'And they took the girl,' Bone called out as he followed the dragging footprints to where the Land Cruisers had stopped.

'Skunk, search that fuck good and throw him in the cell while I decide what to do here,' Ferret yelled.

Ben could tell Skunk was probably the smartest of the three and maybe his best chance for a little info.

'Who's the girl you were talking about?' he asked Skunk as he was pushed, still blindfolded, through the compound.

'Collateral, but don't you go worrying about that. That isn't your biggest problem, mate. Right now, you better hope I can convince these two not to kill you.'

'I appreciate that, Skunk,' Ben said as calmly as if he was

offered a refund for a cold coffee.

Skunk, who was wearing Ben's rucksack, frisked him, finding the knife that was strapped to his left leg and his camera. Thankfully he missed the Leatherman, a modern American version of a Swiss army knife, that sat in a hidden pocket near the front of his pants. For some reason, men are a little funny about frisking the front of another man's pants.

'What's your real name?' Ben asked as Skunk removed his shirt from Ben's head and pushed him still cuffed into a double-lined, free-standing tin shed. From a distance it would have just looked like a rusty old tool shed.

'Peter,' he said, closing the door and locking it with a heavy-sounding padlock.

'I hope I can return the favour one day, Peter,' Ben called out, not really knowing if he was still out there or not. Ben was grateful to have the stinking shirt off his head.

Ben could hear Ferret screaming orders while trying to contact someone on what he guessed must be a satellite phone.

The cable ties weren't too tight. Ben had clenched his fists as Skunk fitted them. He grabbed hold of the belt loop with one finger pulling his pants around his waist. He had to get the Leatherman out from its front pocket. This was one time when his big, muscly arms were not an advantage. He stretched, held, calmed his breathing, stretched a little further, and relaxed as if in a yoga class. Somehow, without dislocating his shoulder, his fingers strained to find the hidden pocket and he managed to free the tool. He heard it hit the dirt floor. His Leatherman had never been in the dirt—it was perfectly clean, sharp, and oiled—but this wasn't a time to worry about that. He sat on the ground and picked it up from behind him. He felt for which of the many options was the blade, although many of the parts would have done the job. He opened what felt like the flat blade and easily cut the plastic bindings. With a relieving flex of his shoulders, he quickly stood up and surveyed the shed, using the dim light from his watch. To his relief, the corrugated-iron sheets were tek-screwed on, impossible to remove without tools, but he had a faithful handyman with him—his Leatherman. The hex-head of the builders tek screw was designed for simple fitment with a cordless drill and socket, so it was fast, strong, and secure. It would be a slow process without the proper tools. He took out the plier option and started removing the screws, a quarter of a turn at a time. He checked his watch. It was nearly 11.00 p.m.

CHAPTER TWO

ITH the prisoner now secure in the cell, Skunk walked back to join the others in the kitchen of the main building. He found Ferret pouring himself a bourbon, and clearly not his first. 'Skunk, did you lock that fucker up?' Ferret asked as he drank the contents and banged the empty glass back on the table.

'Yes, Ferret.'

'Did you search him good?'

'Yeah, I found a knife strapped to his leg, a small camera, and his rucksack had a torch, binoculars, and some food and water.'

Bone said, 'He ain't no fucking roo shooter, I can tell you that. What roo shooter has a gun and scope like that? Ya think he's shooting roos two k's away?'

'Where the fuck is that rifle?' Ferret asked.

'I think we left it on the ground next to his car,' Skunk replied.

'Fuck, I would have liked that,' Ferret said. 'Why the fuck doesn't anyone answer their fucking phones? This is a fucking emergency!' he bellowed as he refilled his bourbon glass.

Ben had finally removed the rear internal sheet. He decided by Ferret's yelling that the door of the cell probably faced where the bikies were, so they would be less likely to see him dismantling their cell if he went out the back. The outer sheet would be much harder. He couldn't just undo screws like the inner sheets. With the light from his watch, he checked the wall for any opportunities, a bolted beam or anything to make it easy, but nothing was obvious. It really left him with only one option. The knife blade on the tool was strong and sharp, but it would still be a challenge for the little knife to cut through the tin. He folded away the pliers and flicked out the blade. He put the point against a trough in the corrugated iron. Normally he would just hit it, but he certainly didn't want to make any unnecessary noise. He pushed as hard as he could with all his weight behind it, until finally the knife pierced through the tin. Cutting it would be even harder.

He used every muscle to start slicing the metal, rocking the tool up and down as it sliced the tin at a painfully slow rate.

Ben had spent all day examining the cyclone fence, and of course, normally his tool would cut it easily, but with the stainless-steel razor wire woven through it, it could create a bigger issue. He figured the razor wire would have to be twitched with mild steel as stainless wouldn't bend, so maybe he would be able to cut the twitch and pull the razor wire back, hopefully without cutting his hands to threads. He only needed to be able to fit his body through after all. But first he had to cut this bloody hole in the shed wall. He had been in the cell for nearly two hours now; sweat had soaked his shirt.

He had cut the two verticals. He just had the horizontal to join them and fold the iron down, which was also not so easy with it being corrugated. The horizontal cut was even harder, as he couldn't use his weight: it was muscle only and the complete dark didn't help.

He eventually felt the blade give as it met the second cut. He sat on the ground and with his right foot pushed the iron out. Now, with the iron bent at forty-five degrees, he wasn't sure he had cut it big enough. He poked his head and one arm through, and with his shoulders twisted on the diagonal, he scraped his way through.

Ben had ripped his shirt and cut his back from climbing through the sharp-edged iron, but that was a small price to pay. He soon made short work of the fence to complete his exit from the enclosure. The razor wire was only held by mild steel as he suspected, an oversight by someone. He kissed his Leatherman before sliding it back into its secret pocket.

He ran to the top of the hill where he had spent the previous day and night. It was all quiet in the compound, but he knew that it wouldn't be for long. He hoped his keys would still be under the car, but he would have to find it first. From this position under the gum tree, he knew exactly where his Jeep was, but once he headed off into the dark, he could easily get lost. He pointed his finger in the exact direction he needed to go and then looked up to study the star formation directly above the horizon that he would follow. With that done, he ran off into the black moonless night.

CHAPTER THREE

FERRET was now asleep and snoring at the timber kitchen table. His head resting on his forearm and his fingers still loosely held the empty bourbon glass.

'Ferret,' Bone called out. 'Pig's on the phone, and he's not fucken 'appy.'

Pig was your typical bikie club president: bald, overweight, greying beard, and heavily tattooed. Blue ink scorpions covered his cheeks and a coloured viper curled up and around his throat. He wasn't scared of anyone or anything.

Ferret, still drunk, tried to explain to Pig, 'We split up coz when we sent the drone up and saw a car parked up norf, Joe fort it best we go and check the fucker out.'

Ferret had told Pig about the roo shooter and how he had a type of sniper rifle with a big-arse scope on it, a knife strapped to his leg, rations, and a camera.

'A camera!' Pig screamed. 'That ain't no fucking hobby roo shooter. What the fuck is on the camera?'

'I didn't fink to look,' Ferret replied.

'You fucking moron, that would have told you exactly why he was there,' Pig screamed through the phone.

'Skunk, get me that fucking camera!' Ferret demanded.

Skunk returned, camera in hand. Ferret ripped it from his hands before Skunk had a chance to try and turn it on.

Ferret fumbled with the camera. Clearly, he had no idea how to use it. 'Take it to the Roo-man and tell him to turn it on,' Ferret said as he handed it back.

Skunk headed for the door. He stopped and said, 'I think I've got it!'

Ferret yelled, 'Bring it 'ere then!'

Skunk held the camera in front of Ferret. 'Flick it here to go back and forth.'

Ferret looked in shock as he scrolled through the pictures.

Pig screamed through the phone, 'What the fuck is on there?'

'The whole fucking thing, Pig, that's what. He photographed the whole thing. Two black cruisers, machine guns. They took the girl and killed our bruvers,' Ferret said slowly, still staring at the images.

'Who the fuck are they? Do you recognise them?' Pig asked, now slightly calmer.

'No. All dressed in black. They were pros, Pig,' Ferret said, also somewhat calmer.

'Ferret, get that fucking roo shooter in there; I want to talk to him,' Pig demanded.

Ferret looked at Skunk and nodded in the direction of the holding cell.

Skunk unlocked the big padlock and swung the door open. Even though the courtyard was dimly lit, it wasn't hard to see the cell was empty.

'Oh fuck, they will fucking kill me!' he said to himself. He looked over to the fence and saw the razor wire and mesh folded back. A small part of him was happy Roo-man was free, but what he was about to face from Ferret in the next few seconds terrified him. He looked back at the peeled iron and then back again to the fence and thought, *I wish you had taken me with you, Roo-man.* He turned and ran back to the kitchen, bursting through the door, yelling, 'He's gone!'

'What the fuck do you mean, he's gone?' Ferret screamed.

'He ripped the sheets off the wall,' Skunk said.

'With his bare fucken hands? You fucking idiot, you were meant to search him properly!'

'I did,' Skunk protested.

'You two fuckwits get the fuck out there and waste that fuck before he gets to the cops, or we'll all be rooted!' Ferret yelled. Ferret told Pig he'd call him back.

'Where would we even start to look?' Bone said.

'His fucking car, you dick brain. He will be trying to get to that, otherwise it's twenty-five kilometres to Aileron. Get. The. Fuck. Going. Now!'

Ben had covered the first kilometre quickly. He knew he was blessed with the cloudless sky, and that the moon should be rising soon in the east. It would better light his way. Without the moonlight, he could easily be one hundred metres out and run straight past the black Jeep without seeing it. Ben heard the HiLux revving in the quiet of the night as it left the compound. He knew it would only take them a few minutes to get to his Jeep. He should beat them as long as he was on the exact right heading. He looked up at the stars that he was using for a reference: he was still on track.

This was one time that having a black car was not to his advantage. If they got to it before he did, they would disable it, shoot out his tyres or radiator, and then it would be a long night walking through the brown snake-infested bush back to Aileron. It was twenty minutes since he had left. He should be close. He stood still and closed his eyes, knowing that when he opened them, he would have his best chance to see in the darkness. The HiLux sounded much closer now. Ben opened his eyes and looked hard while he turned 360 degrees. There it was, behind him, he'd run straight past it. He ran back as fast as he could, knowing they would kill him if they found him. He dived under the car, feeling for his keys and phone; the lights of the HiLux were now faintly lighting the side of his Jeep. He found them both. He used the key to open the door, as the remote would flash the blinkers and show them exactly where he was.

The Jeep started instantly. He opened the door again, jumped out, and ran the five metres to collect his rifle, which was still lying there in the dirt. He grabbed it and ran back to the Jeep, reaching it just as the first bullet flew past his head. He jumped in and, without even closing the door, slammed the car into gear and dropped the clutch. A side window exploded as he sped off into the dark—the HiLux was now in close pursuit. The shooter would only have the .44, probably without a spare mag, he hoped anyway. Ben would count the shots as best he could, guessing the shooter should only have six bullets if it was the same gun that was jammed under his chin a few hours ago. The HiLux was possibly better in this terrain, as he tried to think where the Jeep might give him a slight advantage, but little was presenting. He needed to find a road or at least a track, as the Jeep may just have a better top speed. He continued swerving through the bush, not only to avoid bullets, but trees, rabbit warrens, and any other major depressions that might just appear out of nowhere and get him stuck.

He remembered the road to Aileron was to the north. The moon had risen slightly now and helped immensely with his vision. Knowing the moon would be in the east, he steered the Jeep ninety degrees to his left, now sure he was heading north towards the dirt road that he needed to find desperately. He briefly looked up and saw the star formation he'd followed from the compound, which confirmed he was right. Dirt road to the north in front of him and the Stuart Highway some twenty kilometres to the east. He knew where he was now.

Two more bullets flew past him, one taking out his side mirror. He finally burst onto the dirt track, overshooting it slightly, and turned right towards Aileron. In second gear, the Jeep slid sideways with the rear wheels spinning for nearly twenty metres as he snaked up the dirt road; the little V6 was screaming. It was almost 2:00 a.m., so there were no visible lights from the town. Ben now felt he had that small advantage. The shooter should only have two more bullets left in that gun. His petrol Jeep was faster in a straight line than the diesel HiLux, but not enough that he could just drive away. He needed to think of a plan and fast.

He slowed slightly and kept to the left, luring the bikies to come along on his right side, and they did. *Like flies to a shit, you idiots,* he thought.

Ben slammed the brakes on. He knew the driver's reaction time would be over a second in these conditions, and as predicted, the HiLux sailed past. As its taillight reached the Jeep's front wheel, Ben released his brakes and swerved hard to the right, hitting the HiLux in the left-hand rear quarter. The HiLux was turned sideways at over 120 kilometres an hour. Ben slammed his brakes back on as the HiLux hit the embankment violently, rolling at least twice in the air, before hitting the ground, where it rolled at least four more times down the middle of the road directly in front of Ben's Jeep.

The shooter in the passenger side was thrown from the car, clearly not having his seat belt on. Ben came to a skidding stop, his lights revealing the bent, steaming HiLux as the night breeze slowly carried the dust away. He reached for his rifle. He could now see Bone lying motionless off to the side of the road. He went to him and felt for a pulse. None. He could see his wallet protruding from his top pocket and removed it from his shirt and slid it into his own. He stood and walked slowly to the Toyota that was sitting upside down in the middle of the road, steam pouring from the engine bay. He approached from the rear and called out, 'Anyone alive in there?'

'Yes,' came back faintly. Ben recognised Skunk's voice.

'Please get me out of here before it goes up,' Skunk begged.

'It's diesel,' Ben called back. 'It's very unlikely to catch on fire, so crawl out with your hands up, Peter.'

'I can't, my arm is broken and maybe my leg too. I can't undo the seat belt. Get me out please.'

Ben knew he would be vulnerable climbing into the car, but he had no choice. He couldn't just leave him there. He leaned his rifle against the car, took out his Leatherman, and climbed in through where the front passenger door used to be. The Jeep's headlights filled the HiLux's interior with light, and Ben could see Skunk's arm was clearly broken.

'Put your good arm down onto the roof, and when I cut the belt, you will fall like a pile of shit. Be ready for that; it's going to hurt. Are you ready?' Ben said.

Skunk nodded.

Ben flicked out the Leatherman's knife blade and reached for the seat belt. It took an effort to cut, now that the blade was blunt from slicing the galvanised-iron wall of the cell. Skunk fell, screaming as he landed on his head and broken arm. Ben waited for the wailing to stop before reaching under Skunk's armpits and pulling him out through the passenger side.

He picked up his rifle, slung it over his shoulder, and put Skunk's good arm around his neck. Skunk's right leg might just be badly bruised, as he was putting weight on it, but it was impossible to tell at this stage. Ben opened the passenger door of the Jeep and helped him in, fitted the seat belt around him, and walked quickly around and jumped into the driver's seat. The Jeep was still running, and as he started to move off, he noticed the silver .44 lying in the middle of the road. He stopped. 'I can't leave that there for the local kids to find.' He jumped out and, with a stick, poked it through the trigger guard, raising it up and placing it under the seat of his Jeep. He jumped back in and said to Skunk, 'It's going to hurt like hell for the next hour until we get to the bitumen. This is not a good road.' He drove as slowly as he could, trying to miss the bumps that had Skunk occasionally groaning in pain. Skunk cradled his broken arm with his good one, but it still must have hurt like hell. Other than the painful outbursts, they travelled in relative silence, both desperately searching their thoughts for solutions to their current situations.

Finally, Skunk looked over to Ben and said, 'Why did you stop to help me? We were sent to kill you.'

'Let's just say we are even now, Peter. Hey, I'm guessing you were the drone pilot.'

'Yes,' Skunk replied.

'What can you tell me about the girl, Peter?'

'We snatched her in Darwin, 'cos her father owes us a lot of money. Millions, I think. I don't know any more, honestly.'

Ben thought about that. It made a lot more sense now.

'Peter, I will drop you at the Alice Springs Hospital. It's still another two hours down the road; the sun will be almost up by then. I will notify the cops anonymously about the accident so they can go and collect your dead friend.'

Skunk looked at him. 'He's not my friend. He was an arsehole.'

'Yeah, I noticed,' Ben said.

Ben pulled into the emergency-department driveway at the Alice Springs Hospital at around 5:30 a.m. He jumped out and went to help Skunk out of the car. He grabbed a wheelchair that was one of three sitting at the emergency entrance. He lowered Skunk slowly into it and wheeled him up to the counter.

A middle-aged lady looked up over the top of her reading glasses as they stopped in front of her. First thing she noticed was the tall man in army greens, shirt ripped and covered in dirt. She looked down at Skunk, who was just as filthy, wearing a bikie vest. His face and hair were red from the desert dust after the rollover.

'So, what's happened here then?' the nurse asked.

'I found him wandering down the road and gave him a lift. I think he has a broken arm.'

'I see,' the nurse replied, handing him a clipboard with paperwork to fill out.

Ben wheeled Skunk away from the counter, out of earshot,

and said, 'Right, it's up to you from here on, mate. Get away from that band of criminals. The only future for you there is jail or dead.'

Skunk looked up at him from the wheelchair and said, 'Thank you, Roo-man.'

Ben walked back towards the Jeep. He stopped to look at it, with its smashed window, shot-up mirror, dented front guard, and two bullet holes in the tailgate.

He needed to get cleaned up and maybe some sleep. He would also need to inform the cops about the rollover. He was buggered; it had been a long night.

'Oh, shit, that bloody Magnum is still under my seat, I don't need to be caught with that,' he said to himself.

He found a motel just up the road from the hospital on Stuart Highway, checked in, and showered. He slept for two hours and dressed for the long drive back to Adelaide. He'd wrapped the gun in a plastic shopping bag and, with it, headed down to the Todd mall to find a public phone and a bite to eat. There were always police stopped in the mall in the mornings, moving on the homeless people that had slept there overnight. He approached a police car that still had the engine running and both front doors open, while the two constables were chatting to two hungover men that had just been woken up on the grass. Ben dropped the plastic bag containing the .44 on the police car's passenger front seat as he walked past.

He found a public phone and called the local police station. A pleasant-sounding young lady answered. 'Alice Springs Police, Constable Reed speaking.'

'Hi, I want to report a motor-vehicle fatality,' Ben said without any emotion.

'Can I have your name please, sir?' she asked, changing her relaxed tone to a more official one.

'No, I'm sorry, no names,' Ben replied.

'But I can't file a report without a name,' the young constable replied.

'Just put down John Smith if you want, but here are the details.'

Ben told her quickly about the rollover and the driver being thrown from the car, and then a brief account of the three dead bikies that were gunned down at a secret compound hidden in the bush. He gave her the exact coordinates of the compound from the screenshot from his phone. Before she could ask him another question, he was gone.

The police car and the .44 were gone when Ben walked back through the mall towards his beaten-up Jeep. He refuelled the car, turned on some soft music, and was ready to head south back to Adelaide when he thought, *I had better call DeLuca before I am out of phone range.*

CHAPTER FOUR

DONNA DeLuca had finally stopped crying. Now she was angry. She knew that, somehow, this must have had something to do with her father and his questionable dealings. His business had given her the lifestyle she enjoyed, but why was *she* tied up in all of this?

It must be a ransom? she thought. The DeLucas lived in the biggest house in Cullen Bay, on the Darwin foreshore. They were rich, very rich, and Donna loved it. Her last birthday present was a brand-new Audi, and her parties were the talk of the town. She was the only child of Frank and Maria, who both lived very separate lives, and that, to be honest, suited them both. Her mother would fly to Sydney to meet a lover, or Melbourne to shop, and then flaunt her wares at the Darwin tennis and golf clubs.

Donna wasn't quite as scared any more. The bikies were rough, but this new bunch of criminals were treating her respectfully. She'd been terrified when the changeover happened out in the bush, being sure she was going to die there, but now, she had her own room and bathroom, and the takeaway food was pretty good too. She was sure it was much better than whatever the Viper Motorcycle Club had planned for her. The guards were mean-looking men who spoke very little English. Spanish, she'd thought. Either way—her father would be there soon to rescue her. That, she was sure of.

'Frank DeLuca speaking.'

'Ben Woolford here, sir. I need to talk to you about the job regarding your daughter.'

'Did you find her? Where, where is she? Who has her?' DeLuca asked in desperation.

'I saw a woman fitting her description just north of Alice Springs, but I no longer know where she is,' Ben said.

'What do you mean?'

'Well, Mr DeLuca, this is not a conversation for over the phone, but I can tell you I can no longer be of service to you. Your daughter is in serious danger, and you need to go to the police.'

'Well, I can't go to the police. It's complicated. Can we meet? Can you come here to Darwin and explain it all to me?' DeLuca said, deflated.

'Mr DeLuca…'

'Ben, I will pay you another five thousand dollars to come to Darwin and discuss this with me,' DeLuca said in desperation.

'Okay, I will try and get on the next flight,' Ben said reluctantly, as he hung up the phone and turned the Jeep around and headed for the Alice Springs airport.

Ferret woke, still in the chair he was in when Bone and Skunk had left to go after the roo shooter. On the table next to him was an empty bottle of bourbon, Ben's camera, the satphone, and an overflowing ashtray.

'Bone! Skunk! Where the fuck are you two?' he called out. There was no answer. He went outside, the door of the cell still wide open, with a man-sized hole clearly visible in the rear wall. He looked out through the locked front gate, the troopie and the three dead bikies still lying where they had died.

'Where the fuck are those clowns?' he said out loud. 'I can't be expected to clean up this fucking mess on my own!' Flies were already swarming over the bodies. He really couldn't deal with that. He went back inside and dialled Pig's number on the satphone. 'Pig, can you get someone up here to help me clean up this fucking mess? I sent those two fuckwits after the roo shooter, and they haven't come back. He must have killed 'em.'

'Look here, Ferret. This is your fucking mess, so clean it up. Get those bodies out of sight before the cops are all over us.'

'I can't. Bear has his brains spread all over the fucking dash, and the bodies are already starting to stink,' Ferret protested.

'Get it done, you lazy prick. Clean it up, lock it up, and get your arse back here to Alice.'

'But—'

Pig had already hung up.

Rebecca Reed knocked on her sergeant's door. She was a pretty, light-skinned redhead, with blue eyes and very thick, curly shoulder-length hair tied back in a ponytail. She was an intelligent girl and always in the top three at the academy where she had graduated about six months earlier. She was fiery and short-tempered though, and some of her superiors were a little concerned about her carrying a gun with her fearless nature. She wanted to be a detective one day.

'Hey, Sarge, I just had a call from a John Smith about a fatal rollover on a dirt road just west of Aileron. He also said there was a shoot-out between two gangs where three bikies were shot dead at their secret compound near that same area. He gave me coordinates. What do you think?'

'John Smith, hey?'

'He wouldn't give me a name,' the constable replied.

'Do you think it's legit or another hoax call?' the sergeant said.

'He had no emotion at all, but the description was very accurate, and he didn't sound like the normal hoax caller.'

'Well, I guess we still have to check it out. Call the airport and see if they have a chopper free, and go and have a quick look. Don't waste any time on it; if it all looks okay, come straight back,' Senior Sergeant Jones said. 'Check the rollover as well, and if it's true, call us on the HF radio and I'll send Jackson out there in his car.'

Tim Jones was a career cop. Sixty-two years old and with quite a tummy, he had balding grey hair and a friendly smile. He had been on the job since his early twenties, working his way up the ranks since those tough days at the academy in Darwin all those years ago. When he was promoted to senior sergeant, he took up the unwanted post to run the Alice Springs police station and serve out his time till he retired in another twelve months. Then, it was back to Darwin, fishing and playing golf and settling down with his wife of thirty-five years.

'Yes, Sarge. On it,' Reed replied.

Ferret had tied a rope around the leg of the first dead bikie, Joe, the second in charge of the club, and dragged his body into a spare room in the compound. He did the same with the second body. Bear's body was still in the troopie and slouched over the steering wheel. Ferret had to get him out before he could tie the rope to his leg. He decided to get into the passenger side and kick him out through the driver's door. That worked, and Bear's body fell in a pile next to the car. The dashboard and steering wheel were covered in blood and brain matter, that made Ferret dry retch.

He jumped back out, tied the rope to Bear's leg, and dragged him through the compound. He was halfway across the yard when a helicopter appeared overhead. Without thinking, he took out his pistol and shot at the chopper. The chopper veered away violently as a bullet went through the rear of the cabin. The pilot sped away to a safe distance as fast as he could.

Ferret dropped the rope that was attached to Bear's dead body and ran back to the troopie. He slid into the seat, the steering wheel still covered in Bear's congealed blood. He turned the key, and thankfully it started, which could have been doubtful given the number of bullet holes in it. He backed the car up, selected first, and roared off towards Alice Springs as fast as it would go. He wiped the blood from his hands onto his shirt and pants, trying to dry the steering wheel enough that it stopped slipping in his hands.

Reed grabbed the police radio, 'Helo one priority, shots fired.'

'Helo one, go ahead!' Jackson said, running to the Sergeant Jones's office with the handheld radio.

Jackson burst through the door and said, 'it's Reed, Sarge. Shots fired.'

'Coordinates as reported. Solo male, possibly small-calibre weapon, handgun. We've climbed to three thousand feet. It appears we've been hit, stand by for update,' Reed said.

'Are you able to stay airborne?' Jones asked.

'It appears so. We are remaining out of range but will keep him in sight.'

The flight to Darwin gave Ben plenty of time to think about how to approach DeLuca. He already had a pretty good idea of what was going on here. His best guess was a big drug deal gone wrong. That would explain the first kidnapping with the bikies, but the second, with so much firepower and ruthlessness, didn't quite make sense. First, he thought maybe it was another group that DeLuca had hired to recover his daughter, but if so, *What the hell am I doing here?* That group could have kidnapped the prime minister with the firepower they had. Either way, it wasn't a job for him, not anymore.

He'd arranged to meet DeLuca at a public bench that overlooked the marina in the little sandy cove at Cullen Bay. Ben stood as DeLuca approached; a bodyguard ten steps behind him was constantly scanning the area. 'Let's walk and talk,' DeLuca said.

Ben told DeLuca how he found the bikie compound and how, when they arrived with Donna, there was a shoot-out and that Spanish-speaking people took her, killing all the bikies.

'I am in a very difficult position, Ben. My business, let's just say, isn't a corner deli.'

'Mr DeLuca, I don't need to know, but what *you* need to know is your daughter is in the hands of some very nasty people.'

'You think I don't fucking know that!' DeLuca yelled. DeLuca's security guard jumped to attention at the sound of DeLuca's raised voice. 'Sorry… Sorry, Ben. I am really worried about her.'

'I am sure you are, Mr DeLuca,' Ben said, holding a hand up towards the security guard, suggesting he stand down. 'So, who are these people?'

'Ben, okay. Let's just say, I sell potatoes. For years, I have had the farmers grow them exclusively for me. They sell them to me at a good price, and I then distribute them to all the restaurants in town. I have had a monopoly on the potato market for the whole of the Northern Territory for the last ten years. Then, one day, I am approached by someone saying they are from McDonald's and want me to supply potatoes for their french fries for the entire country, worth billions of dollars. How could I say no? I then needed to find a big farmer, multiple big farmers to supply them, and I did. Trouble is, Mr McDonald's turned out to be Mr McDud, and now I have truckloads of potatoes and can't pay the farmers.'

'I see,' Ben said. 'So, the farmers want security to ensure that they are the ones that get paid back first.'

'Correct,' DeLuca said.

'How long will it take to sell these vegetables to your current restaurants?' Ben asked, looking down at the five-foot-eight Italian man next to him.

'Years,' he replied slowly.

'Can't you just return the goods?'

'That isn't possible. Most of it has come from overseas; Mexico, in fact.'

'Ah, well, that's who has your daughter then. Can't they just wait for the money?' Ben asked quietly.

'Yes, of course, with 20 percent interest,' DeLuca said.

'Hell, who are they, Mastercard?' Ben said, looking back at him again.

'Per month,' DeLuca said, looking up from the ground.

Ben looked back at DeLuca, thinking, *This chap is in serious trouble.*

'Mr DeLuca, you will need an army or the cops to get your daughter from these people. They are professional killers; I've seen them. You will need to contact them and work out a solution because when you run out of money to pay the interest, they will kill her and probably you and maybe your wife as well. This is not a job for me; I am a one-man show. I'm truly sorry. I wish I could help.'

Ben turned to DeLuca and held out his hand to suggest the end of the meeting. DeLuca paused, before reluctantly returning the handshake.

Before Ben walked away, he said, 'Sir, I really would help if I could but you need to call the police.' He knew he would only get himself killed trying to save her; the poor girl may well be dead already.

CHAPTER FIVE

DONNA DeLuca was in the shower when the two guards stormed into her room. They marched with purpose straight into the bathroom. They momentarily looked at her nakedness and smiled as she screamed and desperately tried to cover herself with the plastic shower curtain. She quickly realised this wasn't an accidental occurrence. They ripped the shower curtain from her and dragged her kicking and screaming from the bathroom, through the door, and tossed her onto her bed. One held her tight as the other dropped his pants.

The man holding her yelled something in Spanish that she couldn't understand.

She fought as best she could, but the more she struggled, the more he hurt her. The first man had soon forced himself inside her. The pain was excruciating. Donna was no virgin; she had had many lovers, sometimes at the same time, but this felt like someone taking a knife and stabbing her soul with each thrust. She soon became numb, surrendering to the realisation that for the first time in her life, her father would not be there to save her.

It wasn't long before he had emptied himself into her and the two men swapped, and she was assaulted again. Before the second man had finished, the door burst open, three more men entered, yelling a myriad of Spanish. Her second assailant quickly removed himself from her and pulled up his pants from around his ankles. Donna dived off the bed and huddled into the corner of the room, naked, crying, and shaking like a wounded animal. One of the three, who appeared to be the boss, pointed at her and then turned to the two men behind him, yelling an instruction in Spanish. One of his men ran to the bathroom and returned with two towels. He passed them to her and quickly moved away. Without moving from the corner, she wrapped herself and buried her face and tears into the towels.

The boss man, Manuel, spoke to her in poor English. 'I am much sorry, lady. You my guest. These animals not do this again.' He pointed to her shamed guards. He took out his gun and shot them both, quickly silencing their individual protests. Donna screamed with each shot, and Manuel immediately instructed for the bodies to be removed and the floor cleaned up.

'Why are you doing this to me?' she said, looking up at him in words of tears.

'I am sorry. Hopefully fixed soon and you be free to go,' Manuel said, turning to walk out of the room.

Donna again dropped her head back into the towels and sobbed. She now wondered whether her father would be able to save her at all. The door opened again, and a man walked over to her, and as she looked up from her huddle in the corner, he took a photo of her.

As Ben sat, waiting for his flight in the Darwin airport departure lounge, he welcomed the phone call that distracted him from the DeLuca situation. The international beeps surprised him.

'Hello,' Ben said. He never gave out his name in case someone was trying to find out who he was from previous calls.

'Hi, Ben. Greg Sheppard here. I need a little favour. Do you have a minute?'

Greg Sheppard was a major event coordinator and producer of films and TV commercials. He was a very successful car and motorcycle racer in his day and still loved to live on the edge. He had used Ben's services a few times, mainly to help others.

'Of course, Mr Sheppard. How can I help? It sounds like you are overseas?'

'Yes, Dallas, Texas. Now, Ben, if you needed to find somebody and all you knew was their Christian name and the city they are from, how would you go about it?'

'You are, if nothing else, Mr Sheppard, an interesting man. So, it's not Miss Gilbert this time then?'

'No, it's another one,' he said laughing. 'I met her on a cruise out of Miami.'

'And all she gave you was a Christian name?' Ben asked.

'No, but that's all she told me.'

Ben smiled, the first one for a while. 'Well, start by telling me everything you know about her, however minor it may seem. One piece of a jigsaw puzzle tells you nothing, but the more pieces you join, the clearer the picture becomes. Give me everything you can remember,' Ben asked, taking a notepad out of his pocket.

'Her name is Jennifer. Husband is Keith, rich, cattle, I think,' Greg said.

'There must be lots more. Think about every conversation, any visual references, brand of clothing, anything.'

Greg told him everything he knew, which wasn't a lot more, and finally Ben said, 'I will get back to you as soon as I can.'

It was only half an hour later when Ben called Greg back.

'Mr Sheppard, I think I found them. Keith and Jennifer Madison, big cattle ranchers near Wichita Falls, worth millions apparently. They also have a place in Dallas, 1210 Valentine Street. You may need to be careful, Greg. Word is, he isn't someone to mess with and has some very nasty acquaintances.'

'Thanks, Ben, you are absolutely amazing. I will catch up with you when I return.'

'Be careful,' Ben said, hanging up.

Ferret's face, shirt, and hands were now covered in Bear's blood. He couldn't see the chopper, but he knew that it would be following if it could. He was sure he'd hit it, but he didn't see any smoke, just that it darted away. It was only a white hire aircraft without any signage. He had no way of knowing if it was the police. He now regretted shooting at it, but hell, he was dragging a dead body. How was he going to explain that to anyone?

He knew a back way, a dirt road all the way to Alice Springs.

If the chopper had gone down, they would never find him. If it was following him, that introduced another significant problem. Once he was close enough to Alice Springs, he called Pig on his mobile phone, as he had left the satphone on the table back at the compound.

'What!' Pig snorted as he answered. 'You had better have all of that shit tidied up at Aileron, Ferret.'

'Pig, I think a fucken chopper is chasing me!'

'What do you mean? Cops?'

'I don't know. They saw me dragging the bodies, so I shot at them. I'm comin' to you now.'

Pig yelled back, 'Don't bring them here, you fucking brainless moron! You'll get us all locked up.'

'Then what do I do, Pig?'

'Go to the underground car park at the supermarket, grab a trolley or something, and try to blend in.'

'But I'm covered in blood,' Ferret replied.

'Buy a fuckin' shirt then, you idiot.'

'Sarge, we are about a kilometre behind him. He is heading south and staying off the highway,' Reed called over the police radio.

'Roger that, Reed. We have spikes and cars blocking every road we can think of that he could get through. Keep us informed.'

In the distance, Ferret could see the flashing police lights scattered along the highway at every two-wheel track that deviated off the road he was on.

'You bastards won't catch me,' he said out loud. He glimpsed the helicopter in his side mirror for the first time and then a police car not far behind him that was gaining on him fast. He decided he only had one choice now and that was a little two-wheel track that cut through the west MacDonnell Ranges that would bring him out on Larapinta Drive. He could slip into town the back way. Ferret knew the road well. It was tight and wound through the rocky cliff faces, and although the troopie had a high centre of gravity, he slid it well through each corner.

Ferret was nearly there. One more corner and he would be just another white four-wheel drive on the highway into Alice, albeit with a few bullet holes.

He turned the corner to be greeted by three police cars. He hit the brakes, locking up the front wheels and skidding to a stop. The police car following him had now stopped a little behind him. The two police officers were now hiding behind their open doors, their service revolvers pointing at him through the door jambs. He was done. It wasn't going to be much of a shoot-out; he only had two bullets left in his gun. He reluctantly dropped the gun out of the window and stepped out with his hands up.

The police sergeant called Reed on the radio.

'Reed, I think this is sorted here. Ask the pilot if he has enough fuel to take me to that compound.'

'Yes, Sarge, we have plenty.'

'Come and get me then. I want to have a look and let's see if

Jackson has got to that rollover yet.'

'Sorry, Sarge, I forgot to call Jackson about the rollover. I was a little distracted,' Reed said.

'I've already sent him. See you soon,' Jones said.

Ben boarded the Qantas flight from Darwin back to Alice Springs. He would collect his poor beat-up, shot-up, and dented Jeep and cruise back to Adelaide with a clean slate of work completed. He could go back to debt collecting and surveillance. He would now have no one shooting at him, hand cuffing him, or sticking .44 Magnums in his face.

However, by the time the plane had touched down, Ben had changed his mind, deciding to head back out to the bikie compound. He wanted to have a good look around and maybe get his equipment back. He doubted that any Viper members would still be there; they would be ducking for cover. If anything, the police might be there, and if that were the case, he would just wait for them to go or just turn around and head home. He jumped into the Jeep. It started first go, not even the slightest protest, which was surprising given what he had put it through in the last two days. He turned out of the airport car park and drove back out to Aileron. He turned west onto the dirt road and out towards where the rollover was. He slowed as he approached the HiLux. It was still in the middle of the road, and the dead bikie still lay where Ben had seen him last. He drove on past. This time he parked a little closer to the compound. He grabbed his rifle and headed on foot. He reached the mound where he had spent twenty-four hours the night before. He lay down, aimed his rifle, and with his scope searched the compound for any activity. There was none, just a dead body with a rope tied to one of its legs in the middle of the compound near where the cell was that he had been locked up in. The automatic closing gate was open, a piece of wood activating the sensor that prevented it closing on you as you drove through. The troopie was gone, and by the look of the skid marks, it may have left in a hurry. He stood up and slowly walked towards the compound gate, his rifle held low and loaded. His every step was slow and precise, his senses on high alert. He passed the fence where he had cut the wire to escape only twelve or so hours before. Ben went to what looked like the kitchen; the door was wide open. His camera was on the table, and his rucksack leaned against a wall.

'I'll have those back, thank you,' he said quietly as he put the camera in the rucksack and slung it over his shoulder. He looked at the satphone and decided to take that as well.

He had a walk around the compound. There were heavy locks on most of the shed doors. He lifted the first unlocked garage door and found six black Harley-Davidsons parked in there; stolen, he guessed. He'd decided he had had enough and shouldn't push his luck anymore when he heard the helicopter landing in front of the main gate. 'Shit!' Ben said as he pulled the garage roller door back down, covering him in darkness. He didn't need to be found here and have to explain how he'd been working for a Darwin drug dealer whose daughter was kidnapped by a Mexican drug cartel that killed three bikies, except for the one he killed when he ran them off the road.

He lifted the door slightly so he could see underneath. There was a pilot, a chubby sergeant, and a young redhead female constable, probably Reed, the one he had spoken to on the initial call. It wasn't a police chopper, so the pilot wouldn't be armed, but the other two certainly were. The female cop had her gun drawn. Maybe, it would be a quick look around and then report back for detectives to come down from Darwin to tear the place apart. Or they might decide to have a good look now in every shed they could open.

'I found the other two bodies,' Reed called out, her hand covering her mouth either from the smell or to prevent throwing up or both. 'I guess that's our three that the caller reported,' she called out again.

With the little light he had, Ben turned around the first Harley so it faced towards the shed door. He reached in behind the instrument cluster and felt for the wiring loom that led to the back of the ignition switch. He followed it to a plug and pulled it apart. He took out his Leatherman and cut a short length of wire that led to the front blinker. He spliced each end. Now he needed something that would hold the wire into the terminals of the electrical plug. With the door slightly up, it lit the floor enough for him to see what he'd hoped to find. *Yes—there are cigarette butts strewn everywhere—so dead matches have to be easy to find. They would be perfect*, he thought. Sure enough, he found just what he needed. With the wire in the plier option of the Leatherman, he quickly tried to find which two of the four wires he needed to join to get ignition. A big spark on the first try suggested he had found the power and the earth. The second attempt brought on two lights on the dash and a whir from the fuel pump. He forced the two half-burnt matches into the plug to hold the wire tightly in place. He didn't need it falling out ten metres from the shed and stopping in the laps of the two armed cops. He pulled the choke fully on, needing it to start instantly. He would drop the clutch as soon as the second cylinder fired. He put on a helmet that was hanging on the mirror of another bike and a pair of black wrap-around sunglasses from a small bench at the back of the shed. *Not a bad disguise,* he thought. He lay back down on the ground, watching till the two police officers had disappeared into the kitchen where Ferret had slept at the table. He pulled on his rucksack and slung the rifle over his shoulder with the barrel facing straight up behind him. He quietly lifted the door, jumped on the bike, and hit the start button.

CHAPTER SIX

DELUCA'S phone beeped as a message arrived. He reached for it, praying that Ben had changed his mind and would help him get his daughter back. Manuel Gonzales had sent him the picture of Donna huddled in a corner naked and crying. He screamed with a pain that only a parent could understand, his heart bleeding for his poor daughter who was being abused by these barbaric mobsters. His sorrow soon turned to anger as he yelled at the top of his voice, 'I will kill every fucking one of you fucking arseholes with my bare… fucking… hands.' He fell back against the wall and collapsed onto the floor where he stood, crying for the daughter he adored.

Once he had calmed, he forwarded the picture to Ben Woolford with a message that read, 'Please, Ben, you are her only chance.'

It was nearly 7.00 a.m. in Texas as Greg ran out of his hotel, fumbling for the keys to his rental car. He put the address into the GPS and headed for downtown Dallas. He found the house easily and parked out the front. There was no actual driveway, so there had to be a rear access somewhere. He hopped out of the car and walked to find the back lane where two large garage doors matched the house. He then repositioned his car to be able to watch the lane and the front door at the same time.

Greg Sheppard soon saw the Cadillac pull out of the rear garage and drive slowly away. He remembered the man, her much older husband that he had seen on the dock with her as they disembarked the cruise liner. The husband of the woman he had made love to in the early hours of the day before, the woman he had instantly fallen for, and she for him. They had a connection that neither of them had ever felt before, pure love and overwhelming passion. She had been in his thoughts, every minute since the first time he saw her at the pool bar on the ship. And now, she was right here, in the house that he was now standing outside. She was probably all alone and also desperately missing him as well.

But what if she wasn't? he thought with a little pain in his chest. *What if it was just a fling to her, two ships in the night? I can't provide what she has here or anything like it; they are billionaires.* An explosion of sensibility now consumed him. He felt stupid and foolish. 'What am I doing?' he said as he kicked a seed pod of a Texan elm along the ground. He turned and headed slowly back towards his hire car, his head hanging low. 'This was such a stupid mistake; she is married to a billionaire for God's sake,' he lamented out loud.

Jennifer lay in her bed, again, staring at the ceiling, imagining that the man she'd met on the cruise would just come and take her away from all of this. She wasn't happy; this was not a life she wanted anymore. She was married to a man that didn't love her, he just loved what she represented: a beautiful younger wife to hang off his arm. Greg had started the engine that was her heart and revved it to the limit, each piston, each valve, sending electrifying pulses of lust through every nerve in her body. She would never forget him; he gave her feelings she knew she would never feel again. That man who stole her heart.

The maid brought in her morning coffee at 8.00 a.m., as she did every day. She asked if she had any plans for today. 'No, Libby, just another—*normal* day.' She managed to stop herself from saying 'boring.' Libby smiled, left the room, and closed the bedroom door. Jennifer's mind slipped quickly back to that day when she was standing at the bar on the ship, her eyes meeting his, and she knew in that second that something magical was happening. She knew he felt it too. She started to feel aroused as she pictured him above her in the moments before she sinfully gave herself to him and how beautifully they had made love, not like strangers but like two heavenly beings melding into one. She reached for her bottom drawer and took out her little stick of pleasure that she had enjoyed regularly since the cruise, but before Jennifer had a chance to enjoy any physical pleasure from her arousing thoughts, Libby returned, knocking on her bedroom door. 'Ma'am, there is a man at the door asking for you.'

'Really? Tell him to come back later. It's only eight o'clock, and I'm still in bed!' she said, a little annoyed at being interrupted from her special time.

'Yes, ma'am. I will tell him, sorry,' Libby said, easily recognising the frustration in her voice.

CHAPTER SEVEN

SKUNK now had his arm plastered up; his leg was badly bruised, but X-rays showed there was no damage. He needed to call Pig or Ferret and update them on his situation. His phone was flat, so he found a public phone that was mounted on the wall in the hospital foyer. He tried Ferret's number first, but there was no answer. He then reluctantly called Pig, who answered on the first ring.

'Yes?'

'Pig, it's Skunk here.'

'Where the fuck have *you* been?'

'I've been in hospital, Pig! I've got a broken arm from the crash that Bone and I had chasing the roo shooter.'

'Where is Bone?' Pig asked in frustration. Bone was a favourite of Pig. He was a founding member of the club. Pig believed that he could one day take over as president.

'Dead. He died in the crash.'

'Fuck! What hospital are you in?'

'Alice,' Skunk said, knowing what was coming next.

'How the fuck did you get there?'

'The roo shooter brought me here,' Skunk said quietly, thinking that saying it softly would make a difference.

'So, you chase this fuck, try to kill him, you crash, Bone dies, and you and him become buddies and he gives you a ride into town?'

'Yes, Pig—I mean, no, no, not buddies. I would have died if he had left me there; I couldn't get out; the car was about to blow.'

'Where the fuck is that roo shooter now?'

'I don't know. He didn't tell me. He just dropped me and left.'

'Get here to the clubhouse and make sure you aren't followed,' Pig said and hung up.

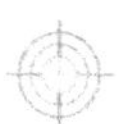

The Harley fired instantly, and before it even had oil pressure, Ben dropped the clutch. The back wheel was spinning, and the back of the bike slid sideways and then snaked through the compound as he headed straight at the chopper that was parked in front of the open gate. The pilot looked up in shock to see the black Harley speeding towards him, dirt and rocks flying from the rear tyre. Ben swerved around the chopper as he reached the gate and roared off towards his Jeep. The two police ran out from inside the building, Reed still with her gun in her hand, raised, aimed, and fired at the disappearing rider. It fired at the same time as Jones knocked her arms upwards.

'Hold your fire!' he yelled over the gun's report. 'Reed, you can't just shoot a man in the back. It doesn't matter how much of a scum they are. And you could have shot our bloody pilot as well!'

'Sorry, Sarge, it's just that—'

'It's just that nothing! You aren't Rambo Reed, and this isn't some American movie. That gun is to save your life or that of an innocent citizen, not to try and wipe out anyone who might be a baddy. What it also tells us is, there might still be more of them here. Let's get the hell out of here and call this in.'

'Shall we chase him in the chopper, Sarge?' Reed said with excitement.

'Are you crazy? Did you see that rifle on his back? He would shoot us out of the sky before we even saw him.'

'Of course, you're right,' Reed replied with a sigh, disappointed that she couldn't get another one of the bikie scum.

Jones walked further out into the compound and watched the cloud of dust disappearing to the north. He placed his thumb and forefinger on his chin and said to himself, 'He didn't look like your average bikie, and that rifle was a long-range weapon, not the sort of thing these fellas would normally have. Reed, I think we may have just briefly met your John Smith. Call up Jackson and tell him to keep an eye out for a man on a black Harley heading his way, armed and dangerous, and get an update on that rollover.'

Ben had reached the Jeep in quick time and hid the Harley under a bush. He packed bits of scrub around it, being extra careful that nothing touched the red-hot exhaust pipes that might start a bush fire. Ben fired up the Jeep and roared off back to the road that led to Aileron. He knew it was only a matter of time before the cops attended the rollover, and he hoped that he could pass it before they arrived. He reached for his rifle, slipped out the magazine one-handed, and slid it under his seat. He then reached over and placed the rifle gently on the rear floor, covering it with his jacket that was on the front seat next to him.

'Jackson is there, Sarge. A dead male, Viper member, thrown from a dual-cab HiLux that's in the middle of the road, upside down. He said there was something strange about it, though.'

'What's that?' Jones said.

'He said the driver's seat belt was still plugged in, but the belt had been cut. There may have been another person or persons involved.'

'Radio the station and ask them to call the hospital, and if someone comes in with a MVA-type injury, to let us know straight away.'

Ben could see the flashing lights of the police car from a long way off, and chances were that the cop could see his dust as well, so turning around would be suspicious. And if they had decided to look for him in the chopper, he wanted to be as far away as possible. As long as they didn't see the stashed Harley, they would still be looking for someone on a bike. He decided to stay with the roo-shooter story should the police ask; he didn't want to stop to hide the rifle.

As Ben approached, the police officer held up his hand, signalling for him to stop. Ben pulled up and lowered his driver's window. The officer approached with caution noting the dented mudguard, broken mirror and side window.

'There's been an accident, sir. Can I ask where you have come from?'

'I'm a professional roo shooter, and I'm just having a look to see how much the drought has affected the numbers out here.'

The police officer took a step back. 'Are you armed, sir?' he asked.

'Just a rifle. I have a licence.'

'Is it loaded?'

'No, sir,' Ben replied.

'Can I see some ID please?'

Ben took out Bone's wallet and handed Jackson the driver's licence and gun licence.

'I think you need a new licence. This photo is unrecognisable,' the officer said.

'I'm ex-military,' Ben said, ignoring the statement.

'Oh, okay,' Jackson said, Ben noticed him appear a little more relaxed with that information. The officer handed back the licences and said, 'Thank you, Mr. Bukowski. Just be careful getting past the HiLux please.' Ben was impressed that Bone had a gun licence. That really did come in handy.

Ben could see there was now a blue tarp over Bone's body as he drove slowly past.

It was getting dark, and it had been a very long day. He was desperate for some sleep. He drove back into Alice Springs, checking his phone for service as he got closer so he could call ahead to book a motel room. He was nearly there when he heard the ping of a message. He grabbed the phone, ignoring the message, and called the motel that he had stayed at that morning. He managed to book a room for the night. He decided to call into the local Chinese restaurant and get the first meal in days that didn't come out of a packet. He got a chow mein because it had lots of vegetables, however over-cooked they might be. He was still covered in dust from the bikie compound. He decided he would shower, then relax with his meal and get some much-needed sleep. The shower was a godsend, but his hunger forced him to keep it brief. He dried off, turned on the television, and sat down to his meal. He was halfway through it when he remembered the text message. He reached for his phone and opened the message from Frank DeLuca.

'Jesus Christ!' Ben said as the horrid vision of Frank's towel-clad naked daughter filled his screen.

CHAPTER EIGHT

WELL, *that's it then*, Greg decided as he walked away from the door. He was going back to his hotel, packing up, and booking the next flight back to Australia. He felt like a fool. Kara, his best friend and part-time lover, had encouraged him to chase her. She knew he had fallen for this woman, and she only wanted what was best for him, knowing that no matter what happened he would always be her best friend. He dialled her number, despite knowing it would be midnight there, but he needed to talk to someone. The drive back through Dallas was a lot slower now that the traffic had doubled. 'Hello, stranger,' Kara said as she answered. 'How's it going?'

'It's a disaster. Do you remember Ben Woolford, the PI?' He quickly realised she wouldn't, as it was Kara herself that he'd organised Ben to track down for him, he quickly moved on. 'Anyway, he found her address for me, I sat outside the house until her husband left, and after toing and froing, I knocked on her door. The maid answered and told me I should come back later; she couldn't see me now.'

'Did you tell the maid who you were or your name?'

'No, I just said, "It's okay; I probably won't come back. I need to catch a plane, sorry to bother you." But anyway, I can't give her a lifestyle like that! You should see the place, and she's probably happily married and just wanted a little fling while she was away.'

'You know that wasn't the case. It was more than that, a lot more,' Kara said sternly.

'Well, it doesn't matter now. I'm coming home; I've made up my mind. Three seventeen-hour flights in three days. What an idiot I am!' Greg said.

'How will you feel when you are back here knowing that you were so close, and you gave up? That's not like you, Greg,' Kara said.

'I will hate it, I know I will, but it's for the best. I'm trying to think with my head and not my heart.'

'I actually think it's a mistake. Have a bit more of a think about it, but whatever, it's okay. I'll see you when you get back. Whenever that is,' Kara said.

'Good night. Sorry to wake you, if I did,' Greg said, hanging up the phone.

Who was that at the door, asking for me? Jennifer wondered. *No one comes here asking for me.* She had lost the urge to play now and had put the little toy back in the bottom drawer. She threw back the covers, reached for her dressing gown, and walked quickly towards the window. She slid the curtain back slightly and could see a man crossing the street diagonally. There was something familiar about him, but it wasn't until he turned and looked up towards her window that she saw who it was. Her hand went to her mouth, her legs turning to jelly. 'No, no, no, come back, come back!' she said as she watched Greg drive off.

'Libby, Libby, come here!' she screamed out and ran to open her bedroom door. Libby was already running down the passage. 'What is it, ma'am?' Libby said, nearly out of breath.

'That man, what did he say?'

'I told him what you told me, ma'am, that you couldn't see him now and that he would need to come back later.'

'What did he say? Hurry, Libby, tell me!'

'He said, he was sorry to bother me and he wouldn't be able to come back; he needed to catch a plane.'

'No, no, no, get the driver here as quick as you can… Please, I'll be ready in ten minutes.'

Jennifer ran back to her room to dress.

'Oh God, my make-up. I can't have him see me like this.'

She dressed in three minutes, which gave her seven minutes for make-up.

She looked up at the mirror, deciding it would have to do. She was an exceptionally beautiful woman anyway; even without make-up she would turn any man's head.

'The driver is out the front,' Libby called, standing outside her bedroom door.

Jennifer walked up to Libby and clamped her two hands on her shoulders.

'Libby, would you recognise the man if you saw him again?'

'Yes, ma'am.'

'Right, well you are coming with me then. Let's go!'

Libby reached behind to untie her pinafore apron as she chased Jennifer down the stairs.

Jennifer was already in the car when Libby closed the front door of the Madison mansion.

'Airport please, driver,' Jennifer instructed. 'Now, Libby, this man is very important. I really need to see him.'

Jennifer turned to face Libby, who was still somewhat daunted by her first ride in a limousine, let alone how confused she was with what was going on.

'This is just between us. Do you understand, Libby?' Jennifer said softly so the driver couldn't hear.

'Yes, ma'am.'

'If you were flying to Australia, what airlines would you fly on?' Jennifer asked the driver.

'Qantas would be the most likely if he flew with the OneWorld Group, or Delta, United, or Singapore, if he was with Star Alliance.'

Okay, too much information, she thought. *I have another plan.* Jennifer took her phone from her bag and called her travel agent.

'Hello, Linda, this is Jennifer Madison.'

'Yes, hello, Mrs Madison. What can I do for you?'

'I need to know all the flights that are leaving for Australia from Fort Worth in the next three days. Please call me back when you have that information, thank you.'

Common sense was starting to come to Jennifer. He wouldn't be on a flight today, surely. It would most likely be tomorrow or the day after, but she felt better if she did everything to block the door of his escape. He had found her; all he knew was her first name, and yet still he found her. She knew that if he left, there would never be another chance. If she had to sit at the gate of every flight to Australia for the next week, she would do it.

Her phone rang: it was the travel agent. Linda had started to tell her the flights that were direct, ones with stopovers, and so many with connecting flights. There were nearly a hundred different scenarios.

'Okay, thank you so much for all that, but could you please text me all the direct flights and most commonly booked to get to Australia?'

'Yes, Mrs Madison, but to tell you the truth, Qantas has an A380 that flies direct to DFW from Sydney and back, three times a week, and certainly most Australians would be on that.'

The list came through shortly after, and Jennifer was deciding a plan of attack. There were no real serious options today.

'Driver, can you take us back home please?'

'Yes, ma'am, of course.'

Ben couldn't finish the chow mein. The picture of Donna horrified him, simply filling him with anger.

He had to sleep, having only snatched a few hours in the last forty-eight.

His sleep was unsettled, broken with dreams of tortured women and people drowning that he couldn't save. He did sleep though, and surprisingly right at 7.00 a.m., he awoke as a fresh, newly determined man. He made himself a cup of tea and then called Frank DeLuca.

'Ben, did you see that fucking photo? I want them dead,

Ben, fucking dead! Every one of those fucking slimy Mexican bastards dead.'

'I did. Mr DeLuca.' He paused, before asking, 'What's my budget, sir?'

'Unlimited, I can get however much you need,' DeLuca replied without hesitation.

'All right. Send two hundred and fifty thousand to my account, and then, I need to know everything you know about them. Don't leave out a single detail. Your daughter's life depends on it. I want you to write it out on a piece of paper and send it express post, so I should have it by tomorrow morning. Here is my address in Alice Springs.' Email would be so much easier, but he knew DeLuca wouldn't want to have such delicate information where someone could hack it or trace it back to him.

'Ben, thank you, you will have that money tomorrow. You're the only chance she has.'

'I will do my best, sir.'

Ben hung up, then took out his camera and Ferret's satphone from the rucksack.

He was going to need help; this was not a one-man job.

He turned on the camera and looked through the photos he'd taken that night from the mound. He studied the men. There were eight of them. More than enough to shoot a few bikies and kidnap a girl. He wondered, *Could there be more? Probably not,* he concluded.

Then he studied the cars, the two black late-model Toyota Land Cruisers. It was hard to imagine they would have hired those in Alice Springs or even Darwin. They may have been a special order and were freighted in, but the Mexicans would have most likely flown into Australia through Sydney, so possibly they hired or bought them there and drove them to Alice. He certainly couldn't make out the rego number, as it was almost dark and too far away, but he could see that the six digits were on black-on-yellow plates. New South Wales for sure. So given their business was with a Northern Territorian, he guessed they were probably still in the region somewhere, and most likely still somewhere here in Alice Springs.

Next, he looked at the photo of Donna that DeLuca had sent, to see if there was any info there. He enlarged the photo to maximum and could see signs of red dirt on the floor, a window to her left with a sheer curtain, and what looked like a steel mesh screen behind it, probably fitted from the outside. He could dimly make out an old rusty fence and no neighbouring houses, but nothing else stood out to him at this stage. He closed the picture and dialled a number.

'Dan speaking.'

'Dan, Ben Woolford. How's things?'

'Good, mate. How's it hangin'?' Dan said. Daniel Potter was a fellow SAS, who served with Ben in Afghanistan. He wasn't anywhere near as tall as Ben but certainly a tough stocky little character, with dirty-blond curly hair and quite a baby face. He was the type who could be sure to find something funny to say at the worst possible times. Like asking a fat lady when her baby was due, something Ben had seen him do.

'Mate, I'll cut to the chase. I'm in Alice, and I need you and a couple of boys to give me a hand with a job. Good money, a little hazardous. Can't talk details on here, but would you be interested?'

'Maybe, well yes. Tell me a little more, and I'll make a couple of calls.'

'Okay, remember the extraction job we did in Kabul?'

'The media girl?' Dan said.

'Yes, exactly the same as that. Serious bods and probably better funded than the Taliban.'

'Shit, mate, what have you got yourself into? I thought you were retired,' Dan said.

'It was just a simple job that turned to shit, big time. It should take a week or two, $30K each. What do you think?'

'Jesus, let me make some calls, but I'm in.'

'Great, talk soon,' Ben said as he hung up.

Ben went through Ferret's satphone and wrote down some of the interesting contacts, in case he had to ditch the phone. He got to Skunk's number and hit Call.

'Who is this?' Skunk asked suspiciously.

'Can you talk, Peter?'

'Maybe, who's this?' Skunk replied.

'The roo shooter,' Ben said.

'I'm at the clubrooms; it's not safe to talk here. How did you get that phone?'

'Don't worry about that now. Is your arm okay?'

'Yes, but the rest of me will be fucked if they catch me talking to you. Pig is really pissed you told the cops 'bout the compound. He wants you dead!'

'Yeah, I bet he does. Now, Peter, if you would like to make some easy money, call me on this phone. I just want a little info and a little job I know you would be good at.'

'I can't do that, bro. I know I owe you, but these blokes are my brothers.'

'The info I need is not about your club; it's about the girl. The Mexicans will kill her, and I need you to help me save her.'

'I can't, man. Sorry, I gotta go.' And Skunk hung up.

Greg had called Qantas and managed to get on a flight the next day at 5:00 p.m. out of Austin, which was about three hours down the road from Dallas. The flight would be via LAX but only a very short stopover. He spent the rest of that day visiting the typical Dallas 'must do's when you are there,' including tours of the JFK assassination museum and the Cowboys' stadium. The food shops were so richly Texan, simply meat, meat, and more meat! Oh yeah, and BBQ sauce on everything! He would spend the night in Dallas and drive the three hours down to Austin tomorrow. Greg's mind as expected was constantly thinking of what could have been. *What would really have happened if she had opened the door herself? Would she have grabbed me, rushed me upstairs, and made love?* He shook his head. *Of course not. It would have just been awkward. She more likely would have thought I was a stalker and had me thrown from her steps by some big bodyguard. Grrrrr, love is so frustrating,* he thought. *Why can't it be simple? Just find the love of your life and run off together?*

Maybe I could ring her? Kara had told him not to give up, so perhaps that might be a good compromise. Just make a phone call. If he was just a fling to her, he'd be able to tell by the conversation, and then that would be it. No awkward moments, it could just end there—with a polite 'See you later.' But if she did feel the same way as he did, he would know that as well. *Yes, that's a good idea,* he thought. It was late afternoon in Dallas, so morning in Australia, and Greg after exhausting every option he could think of, decided to call Ben again to ask for advice on how to get her number.

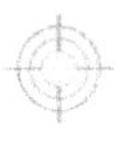

Donna DeLuca had been in the shower for nearly an hour, desperately trying to wash away the trauma she had just endured. It somehow made her feel better, but she was terrified at the feeling that leaving the warm water would bring. She told herself she was tough, took a deep breath, and turned the taps off. She dried herself, dressed into the only clothes she had, and curled up in her bed. She pulled the blankets to her chin and softly said, 'Daddy, please come and get me.'

The next morning, there was a knock at the door. The man who had taken her photo the day before unlocked the door and was standing there with a pad in his hand.

'Excuse, ma'am. Mr Manuel would like you to write what you like from shop please.'

Donna reached for the pen and pad and said, 'Give me a minute.'

'Yes, ma'am.'

Donna closed the door and heard the lock click from the outside. She sat on the bed with her legs crossed, not knowing if she would ever be the same again. Her period was due to come any day soon—well, she hoped it would. She had quite a list by the time the Mexican returned. She tried to imagine him buying the underwear and sanitary products she'd requested. That did put a little smile on her face for the first time in a while.

Ben had woken early and checked his bank account, which showed the funds from DeLuca had been deposited. He just needed the call back from Dan to confirm he had a team, and then it was action stations. Ben started to make a list of what he would need.

'Come on, Dan. Tell me we have them,' he said to himself as he wrote out his armoury shopping list. The phone rang, and Ben answered on the first ring.

'Dan?'

'No, it's Greg Sheppard, in Dallas. Sorry, mate. I'm sure you are busy, but can I ask one more question?'

'Hello, Mr Sheppard. Yes, I am a little busy just at the moment, you know, life-and-death stuff, but what can I help you with?'

'Mate, how would I find her phone number?'

'That's easy. Leave it with me, and I'll call you back.'

Ben hung up the phone, a little frustrated, and then paused for a second, 'Well, that is actually my real job,' he said to himself.

He then thought about the fact that Greg worked in the film industry and another idea came to him.

Ben called a mate at the telecom exchange in Sydney with Jennifer's details, who promised to call him back as soon as he could.

The phone rang again as soon as he hung up.

'Ben, I have Steve Morris from Melbourne, ex-Army, a real tough cookie. Can we get away with three of us?'

'Yes, I think we can but I do have a plan for the fourth,' Ben said. 'Okay, the two of you get your arses up here ASAP. It's all go from this end.'

'We are both ready to leave today, mate.'

'Good, I will arrange everything this end. See you soon.'

Ben's phone rang again; it was his mate from the exchange. 'Ben, I have that US number for you. It was a little tricky, as it was an unlisted number.'

'I appreciate your help, mate,' Ben said.

The satphone rang.

'Hello,' Ben answered.

'Hey, Roo-man. It's Skunk, or rather, Peter. I'm interested to talk.'

'Great, Peter. I will call you back with a meeting place shortly.'

'Okay. Bye.' And Skunk was gone.

Ben still had no idea whether he could trust him or not, so he decided he'd wait till the other two arrived before he set up the meeting. After all, he knew nothing would impress Skunk's club president more than if he could bring Ben to him, delivered on a plate.

Greg packed the little rental car and headed for Austin. He was feeling better about his decision to walk away. He still had a little pain in his heart, but hell, he had been there before.

He was almost to Austin when he received the call from Ben.

'Greg. I have that number for you.' Ben read it out, and Greg wrote it down, not sure whether he really wanted it now.

'Greg, you might be able to help me.'

'Sure, anything, Ben.'

'In the film industry, you would have an armourer to supply the weapons, uniforms, and other gear?'

'Yes, Mark Holland. Good fella, ex-cop.'

'Is the stuff real that they use?'

'Most of it is; we just fire blanks, though, but they are real guns. He has the lot, just about enough to fit out a platoon of SAS.'

'Perfect, would he be interested in a dry hire? You know what I mean, no chaperone. I can pay big bucks?'

'I could ask him. Send me a message of what you want. I'm guessing you aren't making a movie.'

'No, not really, but it might end up on TV though. Thanks, Greg, I will send you my shopping list.'

Once Greg hung up, the butterflies hit him again. With the push of a mere ten buttons, he could talk to her. His flight wasn't for another four hours. He pulled over, put his head in his hands, and asked himself, 'What do I say?'

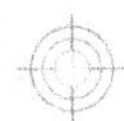

Jennifer and Libby had planned their day. First, breakfast, and then to DFW airport to watch the Qantas flight to Sydney board. She knew it wasn't like a domestic flight where you can watch each passenger all the way to the gate. They would have to loiter around the baggage check-in because once through customs and immigration he would be gone and out of sight. Then she thought that maybe he might only have carry-on luggage. They both searched the departures until the flight had long closed. Jennifer couldn't believe it; she had been sure her plan would work.

'Let's go, Libby,' she said, dejected, when her phone rang. She looked at the number. It was an unknown international number, so she just let it ring out.

CHAPTER NINE

BEN sent Greg his armoury shopping list and began to put a plan together. He would start with Alice Springs and then Darwin, and if unsuccessful, every other little town along Stuart Highway. He made a note of everything he knew. The black Land Cruisers, NSW registration, red dirt on Donna's floor, at least eight Mexicans, heavily armed. This group would need supplies, phone service, accommodation. They had to be in a larger town, because they would stick out like a sore thumb in a small one.

Ben's phone rang; it was an Adelaide number.

'Hello,' Ben answered.

'Mark Holland. I believe you would like to dry hire some gear for a… movie in Alice Springs?'

'Yes, Mark. It's a bit of a shoot-'em-up type of film, if you like. Did Greg send you my list?'

'Yes. Okay, I have everything you need, except grenades, of

course. We don't normally use real grenades in films.'

'I guess you wouldn't; I can work around that. Is everything you've got the real deal, Mark?'

'Yes. everything is ex-STAR Force or army.'

'That's great. Send me payment and pick-up details, and I will sort that straight away,' Ben said.

'You'll need to meet a road train out on the highway to receive the goods. It will be an overnight service. I will text you the pick-up details, and Ben, Greg said that he will be the guarantor on this gear, so I'm happy with that, but please try really hard not to lose anything. It's really hard stuff to get legally,' Mark said.

'Mark, we have a big budget, so include a healthy security deposit in case we do loose something,' Ben said.

'Thank you. I understand, but try not to lose it if you can,' Mark said, hanging up.

He checked his watch. Dan and Steve were arriving soon, and given that the airport was a bit out of town, he fired up the Jeep and headed off.

Dan and Steve walked out of the airport, both with military duffle bags. He shook their hands as they jumped into the battered black Jeep.

'Looks like you started the fun without us, Ben,' Steve said, looking at the car.

'Yeah, just a warm-up so we can have the big fun later,' Ben smiled in reply. Then in a more serious tone, he continued. 'Now, fellas, we really need to hit the ground running here.' He swiped his phone to bring up the picture of Donna and handed it to Dan next to him.

'Nasty,' Dan said, handing the phone to Steve in the back seat.

'Who is she?' Steve asked, handing the phone back to Ben.

'Drug dealer's daughter being held as collateral.' He went on to tell them both about the shoot-out at the Viper Motorcycle Club compound and his chat yesterday with her father in Darwin. 'I think our best chance is to try and find the two black Land Cruisers. They will be the only ones in town with NSW plates.'

'How many men do you think they have?' Steve asked.

'Not sure. I've seen eight, so there is at least that number, but if you think about it, eight fully armed men should be enough to abduct a young lady, wouldn't you think?'

'I agree, more than enough,' Dan said.

'I've gotta fella with a drone who may help us; he's one of the bikies who tried to kill me, but he sort of owes me now. I want to meet him today, but I don't trust him yet, so I will pick a public place, and I'll need you two watching my six.'

Ben pulled up at the motel and handed Dan and Steve keys to the adjoining rooms he had organised earlier for them.

'Meet me back here at my room at thirteen hundred,' Ben said.

'Roger that,' Steve confirmed.

Ben took out the satphone and called Skunk.

'Hello,' Skunk said quietly.

'Peter, can you meet me at Sportie's Bar in the mall in sixty minutes?'

'Yes.'

'Peter, I can trust you, right?'

'Yes, I owe you.' And with that, Skunk hung up.

Ben briefed Dan and Steve with the plan for the meeting.

'I want to use this fella to get his drone up nice and high and see if he can find those cars. Meanwhile, I thought we could each get a scooter, dress as locals, and ride every street in this city. Chances are, they aren't in the middle of the city, so I suggest we work from outside in. Our arsenal will arrive tonight at a little town just a few kilometres south of here, with our suits, radios, night-vision googles, handguns, and semi-autos. Let's hope we don't need to shoot anyone.'

Skunk was already there with a beer in front of him when Ben arrived. He would have preferred it was the other way round, but it was what it was.

'How's the arm, mate?' Ben inquired, looking at the sling.

'It throbs a bit, but the doc said it should mend perfectly. You said I can make some cash to help you find the girl; how much we talkin'?'

'$10K. Do you still have the drone?'

'Phew, no, it's fucked. It got shot up. It was in the troopie when those arseholes filled it with holes.'

Ben slid a piece of paper and pen over to Skunk and said, 'Write down what you want, and I will try to get you another one or something better. I will meet you here at twelve o'clock tomorrow, okay?'

'Sure,' Skunk replied. He finished the rest of his beer and left.

Ben walked to the doorway of the bar and looked to his left. He received a nod from Steve, then to the right, and the nod from Dan had them all on their way back to the car park. The three of them headed off in the Jeep. Ben pulled up outside a workshop, and Dan looked at him.

'What's this place? A front for gunrunners, or counterterrorism maybe?' Dan asked.

'No, scarier; a mechanic. I want to get my window fixed before the cops pull us over and start asking questions about the bullet holes. They are going to replace the mirror as well and put little black vinyl stickers over the bullet holes. No questions asked. The dent I can live with. Now, while I'm sorting the Jeep and picking up the truck, you two head around the corner and grab the three Yamaha scooters I booked. They're paid for under the name of Bukowski.'

Ben handed them each a map of where they would go to prevent doubling up on the ride.

'I will meet you both back at the motel at nineteen hundred,' Ben said, as Steve and Dan headed off to collect their scooters.

Ben ordered the best drone money could buy and arranged for it to be sent up from Adelaide on a plane overnight. It was then into the Avis hire office to pick up a little truck. He'd used Bone's licence and ID that he'd swiped and paid cash for the rentals just in case. While they looked nothing alike, the photo was really bad, and it really could have been anyone. He needed the little truck to collect the military hardware tonight out on the highway that should already be on its way up from Adelaide.

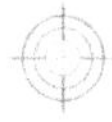

Jennifer and Libby arrived back at the Madison mansion after hours wandering around DFW airport. Libby went back to work, and Jennifer crashed face down on her bed. She had made herself up to look so nice for him; her make-up was perfect. She wore a tight-fitting bodycon dress and matching shoes that she hated to wear. She lifted herself onto her elbows and opened the phone. No messages, just a missed call. She looked at it and saw the sixty-one start. *What country is that?* she wondered. She googled the country code, and it said 'Australia.' Her heart missed a beat. He must have tried to call her. She called the number back; it went straight to a message. Greg's voice thanked her for the call, and that he would call her back if she left a message. She froze and hit end. *What would she say?* Her day hadn't been wasted after all—now they had each other's phone number.

Greg was on the American Airlines flight from Austin to LAX, knowing he would only have forty-five minutes to get onto the connecting Qantas flight to Sydney. He sat back and thought rationally. There were many reasons as to why she wouldn't answer his call. He closed his eyes and let himself drift back to their brief time together. You never know, maybe one day he would send her a text when he was sitting at home alone and see if she replied. It didn't really matter now, and he resolved that this brief chapter in his life was over. He needed to get back to work. He'd been away for over two weeks now, first on the five-day cruise and then this crazy trip back to the USA chasing a woman whom he didn't even know, but who'd stolen his heart. *Oh well, I don't really need that heart anyway, do I?*

The Boeing 757 had landed at LAX, and because the flight was domestic and the one to Sydney was international, that meant he had to collect his bag and head to a completely different terminal for the Qantas check-in. His bag was carry-on, and he was soon on the shuttle to the new Thomas Bradley terminal. The check-in went like clockwork, he already had the boarding pass, and it was just the immigration check. Boarding wasn't for another fifteen minutes, and he decided to let Kara know where he was. His phone was still on flight mode. He turned it back on, and a message came through as he started to dial; the number was the same one Ben had found for him. He clicked on it.

> Greg, I can't believe you found me! I'm so sorry—I didn't know it was you at my door. You are all I think about. I would really love to see you. J x

He sat there stunned, reading it over and over, his heart pounding. *She does feel the same way, my God!* The feeling of lust and love flooded over him as he again imagined her with him, holding him tight as she did that night. They called his flight. 'Shit, do I forfeit the flight and return to Texas or continue home?' he asked himself. He watched the queue as the five hundred passengers worked their way slowly onto the largest passenger aircraft in the world. He couldn't decide, so, he called Kara.

Kara answered, 'Where are you?'

'LAX', he said, 'I made one last attempt as you suggested, and I called her. She just messaged me back, right as I'm about to board the plane for home. She wants to see me. What should I do? I know I'm not thinking straight, but I am desperate to see her.'

'She got in touch with you? That's amazing! It sounds like you've achieved what you wanted to, since you found her and made that connection. Perhaps come back to Australia, let it build, and decide from there.'

'That's why I called you. That's sensible. I'm coming home. I'll see you tomorrow. Thank you so much.' He hung up and joined the queue for the flight. He thought hard about what to say in reply to

Jennifer. He was grateful knowing that he'd have a window seat; his gold frequent-flyer status ensured that. Once finally seated, he took out his phone, thought for ages, before eventually typing his reply.

> Jennifer, thank you so much for your message. I can't describe how it makes me feel. You stole my heart the night we made love. I just had to see you again. I thought you must not have felt the same way. Greg x

The call came over the speakers, indicating the front door was closed and all electronic equipment must now be turned off. He looked at the message, reading it over and over till the flight attendant asked him to please turn his phone to flight mode. He hit send and slowly turned the phone off while it sent. Closing his eyes, he imagined that beautiful woman there with him, his heart now warmed by knowing that she felt the same way.

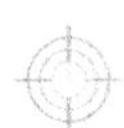

At nineteen hundred, Ben, Steve, and Dan met at Ben's motel room. Ben handed them each a beer, and they sat down with their maps and crossed off the roads they had covered.

'Okay, I was sure we might see something today, but let's get some sleep and tomorrow we'll have the drone as well. Let's hit the road at zero seven hundred and convene at Sportie's at twelve hundred, as we did today. We will set Peter up with areas to search, and we'll have a good feel with how it's going. In the afternoon, I want you two to go and sit at the two big supermarket car parks and keep a watch out for those black cruisers. I will get our tactical gear tonight, and the new drone will be here at the airport in the morning.'

While they finished their beers, Ben continued to tell them how he thought it might play out, but ultimately, for now, they had to find her first.

It was midnight, and Ben was parked in the little truck he'd hired, waiting in the darkness outside Stuarts Well Roadhouse. A set of lights flashed through his cab as the Northern Road Freight B-double pulled in.

Ben jumped out of the little Mitsubishi and walked over to the big Kenworth to meet the driver. 'Hi there, you have a delivery for Woolford?'

'Yes, must be expensive stuff, all locked tight with padlocks and all; they look like gun cases,' the driver said.

Ben smiled and said, 'Everyone says that. It's just camera gear, very important for my work.'

Ben checked off each case in his head, knowing exactly what he'd ordered. He thanked the driver and headed back to Alice Springs, leaving the semi driver to close up the Tautliner's curtains.

Next morning Dan and Steve continued their scooter rides, searching for the black Land Cruisers. They worked their way closer in towards the city centre, continually checking the supermarket car parks until it was time to meet Ben at Sportie's Bar. Dan and Steve again kept watch outside, while Ben met with Skunk, bringing the new drone. Ben felt safe with them on lookout, just in case, as he still wasn't sure if he could trust Skunk completely.

Ben placed the large aluminium box in front of Skunk, whose eyes were bursting with excitement. 'This is a Matrice M300, my God! This must be worth ten grand.'

'Twenty' Ben said without flinching. 'It has the longest flight time and a thermal imaging camera included. There are two spare batteries in there as well.'

'There is a ready-made business sitting right here,' Skunk said.

'Here's the deal, Peter. You help us rescue the girl, and it's yours. Only condition is, you get away from the Vipers and start a new life.'

Skunk agreed with only a nod as he turned the fifty-millimetre thermal-imaging camera over and over in his fingers.

'Okay, we need to get to work,' Ben said as he opened a large map and spread it across the table. Ben had to push the drone aside to get Skunk's full attention.

'We have been searching these areas looking for these vehicles.' He produced six A4 printouts of the photos from his camera.

'Where did you get the photos from?' Skunk asked.

'From my camera that you took from me.'

'But I took it. Doesn't Ferret have it?'

'Not anymore,' Ben said.

'But how…?'

'Don't worry about that now,' Ben said. 'Let's find that girl, and I can tell you all about it later over a beer.'

Ben pointed to a section on the map that he wanted Skunk to search, which included farmhouses with long driveways that you couldn't just ride the scooters down for a look.

Skunk packed up the drone with a gentleness that matched its value.

'Can you start straight away?' Ben asked, looking him in the eye.

'Yes… what's your name anyway?' Skunk asked.

'Call me roo shooter or Roo-man for now,' Ben offered. 'Ring me on Ferret's satphone if you find anything at all.'

Dan and Steve went into Sportie's Bar as they watched Skunk leave with his big new alloy case.

'How did that go?' Dan asked.

'Good, I think. I'm still not sure how much I can trust him, but if it all pans out right, we save the girl and we save him from stuffing up his life with those bikies. The drone should do a dual purpose: he can get up really high, so not only will they not hear it, they won't see it either, unless of course they have binoculars and are expecting it; it also has thermal imaging so we can see how many there are inside, and on the day, he can monitor movements inside the house or whatever it is that they have her in. If she is in a cave, we will be stuffed, but from the picture from her father, the room is sunlit with a light curtain, some kind of mesh on the windows. At this stage that will probably be our best way in.'

Ben continued, 'I received a note from her father this morning detailing everything he knows about them. Mexican drug cartel, as we know, out of Mexico City. The drug lord is Manuel Gonzales, now a part-time gunrunner as well. DeLuca couldn't believe he came out here in person to run the show. It must be big bucks he's owed. He doesn't go anywhere without two armed men by his side; I'm guessing he's in for about twenty mil. He believed his daughter would be respectably treated, until the photo arrived, and that's clearly not the case, as we can see.'

'How do you want to tackle it, Ben?' Steve asked.

'Ideally, no one gets hurt, but I will be surprised if that's the outcome. Let's make sure it's not one of us. When we find the location, we spend twenty-four hours on surveillance visually, and with Skunk on the drone, we see how many there are, check their movements and what their security detail involves. We go in at night, if we don't see a better window during the day. I can't imagine them having any sophisticated alarm system, but we can't just assume. In our twenty-four-hour visual, we will need to learn as much as we can. Park the scooters for now. I think the drone is our best chance from here. Let's go back to the motel and sort the equipment that came in last night, check that it all works and is ready to go.'

CHAPTER TEN

BEN called Skunk at 6:00 p.m.

'How are you going with the drone?'

'Still learning how it all works. It's far more sophisticated than what I had before.'

'Will you be ready to go by the morning?'

'Yes, definitely. I have already done several test flights, and it went really well. It's fast.'

'Are you confident we can keep it out of sight and still achieve what we need?'

'Yes, it has a massive zoom and the camera is ten megapixels.'

'Do you have the thermal imaging sorted?'

'Playing with that now, will be right by the morning.'

'Great, work on those areas I gave you and report back as soon as you see something.'

'Will do, Roo-man.'

Ben hung up and looked over at Dan and Steve, who were now fully dressed in the black tactical coveralls, ballistic load-carrying vests, balaclavas, night-vision googles, a gun belt fitted with an Austrian-made Glock pistol that securely hung low in a thigh holster, and an ArmaLite AR-10 semi-automatic rifle slung over their shoulders, all of which had come up from Adelaide the night before.

'Well, fellas, you look the part. Let's hope we're overdressed for the party,' Ben said.

It was late morning when Ferret's satphone rang.

'Roo-man, I think I've found the cars.'

'Where are you?' Ben asked with an instant rush of adrenaline.

'I am south-west of Alice, just outside an Aboriginal community called Amoonguna.'

'I'm on my way,' said Ben.

Ben knocked on the doors of Steve and Dan, calling out, 'Let's go, we might have them.'

Within thirty seconds, the Avis truck with three big men across the front left the motel. Amoonguna was about twenty minutes east of the turnoff for The Gap. Ben pulled up behind Skunk's borrowed Commodore station wagon, and the three of them rushed to the drone operator.

'What can you see, Peter?'

'I've circled the farmhouse and spotted a black Land Cruiser under a loose-fitting tarp. I'm guessing the other is in the shed.'

'Great work, Peter. That looks like one of the cars all right.'

'Any movement outside?'

'Just one fella came out for a piss, nothing else. But look at this: looks like two graves,' Skunk said, zooming in on two little mounds of dirt in the backyard.

'Yeah, it sure does. Let's hope one is not our asset.'

'What do the thermal images tell us?' Dan asked.

'It's a little hard through the double brick walls, but I guess five or six men, and I would think the girl is in this room here at the back. There're bars or something on the windows and what appears to be a separate bathroom to that of the house, sort of like a granny flat.'

'What's the red light flashing?' Steve asked.

'Battery is flat. I need to bring it back and change the battery.'

'Sure, excellent job, Peter,' Ben said. 'Bring it back, change the battery, and let's start some planning.'

The drone landed, and as Skunk started to change the battery, Ben, Steve, and Dan discussed the situation.

'We need a way in. It's a long way off Ross Highway, so let's get the drone up and work out the best way in, and more importantly, the best way out. It probably won't be the same route. We need to know where each of them sleeps, who's awake, and where they are. We need to get a good look at the window of that room and of course make sure it's definitely her in there. I don't want to be tapping Mr Gonzales on the shoulder saying that we are here to rescue him! I would love to disable the two Land Cruisers, but if they are locked, we can't really do that without making any noise.'

Ben turned towards Skunk and asked, 'Have you got that map I gave you, Peter?'

'Yes, Roo-man.'

'I want you to send the drone out again and log every road in and out as best you can, also the condition of them. Once you have done that, I want stills of the house from every angle and from above so we can work out the floor plan of the house, and with the thermal imaging camera on, I want to know where each man is, particularly at 3.00 a.m.

'I will need hard copies of those stills as soon as you can in the morning. If all goes well, we go in tomorrow night. Can you be at my motel by zero nine hundred?'

'Will do, Roo-man,' Skunk said, turning back to changing the drone's battery.

'Here's the address, and Peter, put some black tape over those Nav lights. We don't need those standing out tonight.'

'Okay, boss.'

Ben, Steve, and Dan sat around Ben's table in his motel room once they returned from Amoonguna.

'We will know more tomorrow, but a loose plan is, we will hit at 3.00 a.m. tomorrow night. We sneak in from behind Amoonguna and approach from the rear; I don't think they will expect that. We drive in with night vision, no car lights, and disconnected brake lights. We park as close as we can, without them hearing the car, and walk in.'

'We really need that forth person to be in the car, ready,' Dan said.

'You're right. Let me think about that for a minute,' Ben replied slowly.

'Dan, you will go around the front and watch the front door. Steve, you help me get the bars off the window, which should be easy from the outside. They would have been purposely fitted to stop someone getting out, not in. Steve, I think it will be quickest for you to go in. I am hoping the window is unlocked as I don't want to have to wake her to open the window. If all goes well, we reverse out the way we came. If it turns to shit, I will run with the girl while the two of you provide cover and back out the best you can.'

'We definitely need a driver, Ben. We have a spare suit and full kit,' Steve said.

'I know; I have an idea. Okay, rest up and get some sleep. I'll see you both here at zero seven hundred.'

The Qantas flight from LAX landed at Kingsford Smith airport in Sydney at 5:20 p.m.

Greg was soon on the connecting flight to Adelaide by 7:00 p.m. His head was spinning from all that had happened, and then the message from her just made it worse. As soon as the flight landed, he quickly collected his bag, and as promised, Kara was there to meet him. With a big warm hug, Greg felt welcomed home and prepared to get his busy entrepreneurial life back on track. He had been putting off meetings with potential new clients to rush back to the US to chase a love.

Kara dropped him home, he thanked her, and they agreed to have lunch the next day so he could run her through the events of his past seventy-two hours. Kara drove off as he stood at his townhouse doorway, fumbling with his keys one-handed, when his phone rang.

'Greg?'

'Yes,' Greg replied, dropping his bag and swapping his keys to his now spare hand.

'Ben Woolford. Can you talk?'

'Yes, Ben, and thank you for all your help. It was invaluable.'

'Are you in Adelaide?' Ben asked.

'Yes, just landed. Did you want me to pay you now?'

'No, but, I'm in need of your help. I need a driver, a good driver, a fast driver.'

'Sure, I'm not too bad at driving.'

'I have checked you out. Two racing championships, lap records at almost every circuit in Australia. Impressive. What I really need is your off-road skills and ability to perform under pressure.'

'Okay, send me an email with all the details; I'd be more than happy to help.'

'The only problem is, it's tomorrow and I need you in Alice Springs tonight. There is an A330 freighter leaving Adelaide in forty-five minutes for Singapore. It stops in Alice and Darwin on the way through. I have you a spot in the jump seat; the pilot is a mate of mine. You should only be gone two days if it all goes to plan. Ten grand if you can leave right now.'

'If what goes to plan?' Greg asked, bewildered.

'I can't tell you any more than that now. Are you up for it, Greg? I need someone I can trust, and you are the only one I do.'

'Sure, what the hell! Okay, text the details. I'm on my way.'

Greg quickly dialled Kara.

'Kara, where are you?'

'Just around the corner at the Royal Oak Hotel, grabbing a bottle of wine. Why… want me to come back over and…?' she said with a sexy voice.

'No, I need a very quick lift back to the airport.'

'What! Are you crazy?' she said.

'Yes, I think so. Now can you get me there ASAP?'

'Okay, crazy man, I am on my way,' she said and hung up.

Greg ran inside, grabbed a handful of clean clothes, stuffed them on top of the dirty ones in his bag, and locked the door behind him just as Kara pulled up.

Greg threw the bag onto the back seat and jumped into the front next to Kara.

'What are you doing? You aren't going back to the US, please tell me that?'

'No, just to Alice Springs.'

'Just to Alice Springs! What the hell for? What's so urgent?'

'I actually have no idea. Ben called and asked if I could help and be there tonight. He's got me a flight on a freighter, and if it goes to plan, I will be back in two days.'

'If what goes to plan?'

'I don't know, a driving job, I'm guessing a limo driver for a VIP. He wouldn't say.'

'Did you get clean clothes while you were home for all of ten seconds?'

'Just undies. Most of my clothes are still clean; we didn't wear much on that cruise, remember!'

'You're insane; you haven't been home for nearly three weeks now. What about your work?'

'I think I have that sorted. I'll probably just be sitting around, bored, waiting for some fancy polly to have lunch, and then drive them back to the airport. Then I deliver the car back to wherever, and I fly straight back. I will just FaceTime the clients while I am sitting there. Besides, he's paying me ten thousand bucks.'

'Phew, he must be pretty important. Maybe it's the prime minister?'

'Maybe. I thought that too; he does do security for people

like that.'

The instructions had arrived from Ben. Greg needed to go to the general aviation terminal.

> Ask for Terry Schultz, don't say anything to anyone. If anyone asks, you work for Singfreight.

Kara pulled into the little terminal at the far end of the airport, wished him luck, and headed home again for the second time in two hours. As Greg watched her drive off, he wondered what the hell he was getting himself into.

A short, dark-haired man wearing a flying jacket with four bars on his epaulettes and holding a flight case met him with his hand out as Greg walked up the three steps into the little freight company office.

'Mr Sheppard, Terry Schultz; nice to meet you. Thank you for getting here so quickly. We need to leave straight away,' Terry said, shaking his hand and handing him a high-vis vest that had Singfreight printed across the back.

Greg followed Terry to the big Airbus freighter, the pilot's head turning from side to side as they crossed the tarmac. Greg marched up the stairs, doing his best to keep up with the pilot who took two steps at a time. Terry pointed to a spot just outside the cockpit for him to drop his bag. He noticed the first officer was already halfway through the pre-flight checklist as Terry offered a little fold-out seat just inside the cockpit door.

'That's yours, Greg. I'm afraid it's not business class, but it is the third-best seat on the plane. This is Alan, my FO.' Alan waved with half a smile as he quickly returned to the pre-flight.

Greg took out his phone and sent Kara a message to thank her as he heard the port engine starting. He could hear the pilots talking into their mics, probably to the tower. The starboard engine was winding up now as well. Terry reached into his bag and pulled out a spare headset and handed it to Greg. It was noisy now, and he pointed to a headset jack on the panel above his head. Terry waved to someone outside on his left that Greg guessed must have moved the stairs away and closed the cabin door. He immediately heard the tower as the lead clicked into the jack. 'Clear to taxi, Niner Victor Mike Foxtrot Charlie.'

Terry repeated the clearance back. Greg was a private pilot a few years ago but was still mesmerized by all the screens, switches, and levers. It appeared Alan would be flying this leg. As the taxi clearance came through, Alan advanced the throttles slightly to move the aircraft. Within a minute or so, the plane came to a stop at the hold point, and Terry called, 'Mike Foxtrot Charlie ready for take-off, runway twenty-three.'

'Mike Foxtrot Charlie, cleared for take-off runway twenty-three; do not delay.'

Greg looked out the pilot's side window to see what he imagined was a 737 on final approach. Terry responded back to the tower with his call sign. Alan advanced the throttles slowly to full as the large aircraft turned onto and then roared down the runway. Alan pulled the stick back, and they lifted off into the clear, black night sky. 'Gear up,' Alan called.

'Mike Foxtrot Charlie, climb to and maintain one zero thousand on a heading of two seven zero; contact Adelaide control on one one eight decimal two. Good evening,' the tower said.

For Greg, it was a calm, uneventful flight that didn't seem to take long at all before they were on the descent into Alice Springs airport.

The aircraft pulled up away from the main terminal. A vehicle arrived with stairs that were built into the chassis and extended over the roof of the cabin. Another vehicle arrived to unload freight. Greg thanked Terry and was quickly ushered to a small car park, where Ben was waiting by the Avis truck. He now doubted he was actually a legal passenger.

'Thanks for coming, Greg. I really appreciate it,' Ben said, shaking his hand. 'Jump in. I have a lot to tell you and a lot, for your safety, I'm not going to tell you.'

'My safety?' Greg said.

'It's a dangerous job for us, but you will only be needed to drive us away fast if there's trouble.'

'What trouble?'

'That's the part I can't tell you yet.'

'I thought maybe I would be driving a high-profile person somewhere?'

'You will be, Greg. It's just that there is a small group that doesn't want us to.'

'A small group? A small group, like cops?' Greg asked.

'No, quite the opposite.'

'So the cops are on our side?'

'No, not really,' Ben said. 'Greg, I can tell you that a young girl has been kidnapped, and we are going to collect her and return her to her parents.'

'Why aren't the cops doing it?'

'That's the part I can't tell you.'

'So some paedophile has kidnapped a girl, and we are going to punch him in the nose and take her home?'

'Not a ped, a Mexican drug cartel.'

'A fucking what?'

'It's cool; you will be away from the action. You just need to drive us to safety once we collect her.'

'I see. How many of us is 'we'?'

'You make us four.'

'And them?'

'Possibly eight.'

'Okay, I said I'm in, so I am, but can you try not to get me killed please? I have a girl I am dying to see.' *Did I just say that?* he thought.

Ben smiled. 'Yes, I know. I will do my best, I promise you.'

They arrived at the motel, and Ben handed Greg a key to a room. 'You can't tell anyone anything, okay?'

'Sure, I understand.'

'Get some sleep, mate. Tomorrow is going to be a big day. Meet here at my room at zero seven hundred, sorry, 7:00 a.m.'

'I know what zero seven hundred means,' Greg mumbled to himself as he put the key in the door.

Greg dropped his bag on the floor, took out his phone, and sent a text to Kara.

> I'm here in Alice, if I'm still alive tomorrow night I will see you the next day. Good night x

> What the hell do you mean by that?'

Kara sent back immediately.

It's all secret squirrel stuff, I'll tell you when it's over.

Greg opened his bag, got out his toothbrush, and cleaned his teeth, wondering if the brush would still have an owner in twenty-four hours' time or if some forensic cleaner would be throwing all his stuff into a collection bag.

He slept well, jumped out of bed, and had a much-needed shower, realising that the last one he actually had was back in Texas. That all seemed so long ago. His mind drifted to the beautiful Jennifer and how he hoped one day he would be able to kiss those sweet lips and hold her tight again. He decided to send her a message.

Hello Jennifer, I would love a picture of you so I can spend every minute of my day staring at it. Love Greg.

Greg looked at his watch. It was time.

Ben's door was open when Greg arrived, and he walked straight in.

'Greg, this is Steve and Dan. This is Greg, our driver for tonight.'

There were hellos all round, and they all shook hands.

'Peter should be here around nine with all the maps of the house and roads for you, Greg.'

Ben laid out a large map of the Amoonguna area and showed Greg where they would enter and exit from, should it all go to plan.

Greg was fascinated and engrossed as each option of exit was discussed.

'What about this track should it turn bad?' Greg said, pointing to a two-wheel track that followed the creek all the way back to Alice Springs.

'That's a great idea. Let's see what Peter has for us when he gets here. It's hard to tell how rough it is.'

'What car will we use?' Greg asked.

'My Jeep is due back this morning from the workshop. It's a Cherokee; will that be okay?'

'Should be fine. Three in the back seat on the way home will be cosy.'

'Let's *hope* we have three in the back seat on the way home!' Dan said.

Skunk arrived at 9:30 a.m. with a bundle of pictures, videos, and thermal images.

They spent two hours planning each option and everyone's position at each moment. Skunk would be parked on a mound at Amoonguna, monitoring the whole event from the air and communicating to them all via radio. When they were happy with the plan, they all went and stepped out the whole thing for real on the motel's tennis court. Greg smiled at the end, as the four of them trotted off, making out they were driving the Jeep away through the bush.

'Dan, can you fit up Greg with his gear, all but guns; he shouldn't need one. I will go and pick up the Jeep. I'll disconnect the brake and interior lights when I get back.'

What have I got myself into here? Greg thought.

Greg looked the part in the black tactical kit, bulletproof vest, night-vision goggles—the works.

'You will need to go out tonight, mate, and practice driving with the goggles. They take a bit to get used to,' Dan said.

'Will do,' Greg said, starting to feel a real integral part of the team.

When Ben arrived back, he instructed everyone to get some rest if they could.

'Greg and I will go out at twenty-two hundred and practice with the night-vision goggles, and we will all move out at zero one thirty.'

Greg quickly adjusted to the goggles; it was like playing a video game in 3D. It was all about just trusting what you see. Greg drove down the full length of the creek road to test for speed and any hazards. He did his best to note bumps, dips, and sharp corners.

At 1:30 a.m. the team of four met at Ben's room all suited up, guns checked and loaded and the Jeep with all the repairs done, packed and ready. Skunk was to meet them at Amoonguna. They would all start from there.

When the team arrived at Amoonguna, Skunk had the drone all set up, all batteries charged and ready to go. They went through the plan again, keeping in mind the drone battery would only last forty minutes, so that was the maximum time, and there would be a dead spot of five minutes while he changed the battery. Ben picked up the small toolkit that hopefully would have what he needed to get the security screen off the window. If the window was locked, he would try and wake her, but that created another problem.

Ben looked at Skunk and said, 'You are our eyes, Peter. Tell us everything you see.' Ben shook his hand; however, Skunk didn't look him in the eye, giving Ben a little pang of concern.

It's nothing, he convinced himself. *Probably just nervous like the rest of us.*

'Final radio check, and let's move on out.'

'Alpha 2,' Dan said.

'Alpha 3,' Steve said.

'Alpha 4,' Greg said.

'Alpha 5,' Skunk came back.

'Alpha 1, and good luck, gentlemen. Let's get the asset home safe.'

Greg started the Jeep, and the drone went up. The Jeep proceeded around the back of the Amoonguna compound with its lights off. Greg drove in a high gear to keep the engine revs low and noise to a minimum. On the night-goggle test run, they worked out that you couldn't hear the car from a hundred and fifty metres away at idle.

'How is it looking, Alpha 5?'

'It's all quiet. Two sitting awake in the front room, probably watching TV. Looks like four others asleep in separate rooms. Girl asleep in her bed, I think facing away from the window, over.'

'Roger that,' Ben called back.

Greg pulled up at the agreed spot, a hundred metres from the rusty corrugated fence that bordered the property's backyard. Greg turned the Jeep around, ready for the getaway. The three men quietly hopped out of the car, closing the doors on the first catch only. They reached the fence, and Ben press his mike button. 'Update, Alpha 5.'

'No change, Alpha 1.'

Ben made a signal to go. Dan ran to cover the front door of the house while Ben and Steve went to what they hoped was Donna's window.

'Alpha 2 in place.' Ben already had the first screw out, when Dan's message came through. There were only six screws, and within forty-five seconds, Ben handed the screen to Steve.

'We have movement in the front room, one heading for the front door,' Skunk called.

'Alpha 2, I have him.' Dan could see the red glow of his cigarette as he stood and relieved himself in the warm night breeze.

Once the Mexican was back inside, Ben tried the window with a small lever. It moved, with a slight squeak. The last thing he needed was for Donna to wake and scream. He moved it another inch, then another. There was no counterweight on the window, and he had to hold its whole weight as he lifted it. Steve was helping lift the window squarely so there was minimal noise from the timber dragging up the frame. It really was a delicate job. The window was now high enough, and Ben signalled for Steve to remove his rifle and go in. He was the smallest of the three and would be quicker getting in and out. He was to cover the girl's mouth as soon as he could and whisper in her ear that they had been sent by her father to get her. Steve stepped like an angel onto the timber floor; there was a small squeak, but all stayed calm.

Greg was staring into the rear-view mirror, desperately wanting to see the team appear from around the iron fence. His hand was holding the gearstick, and his foot rested on the clutch, ready to put it into gear and either sneak off quietly or flat out, depending on how it all went. He was starting to shake with adrenaline when his phone beeped: a message had come through.

That will be Jennifer's picture, he thought, now a little distracted from the job at hand.

Steve looked over at Donna. Her long black hair completely covered her face. Steve had to decide how best to approach her, and fast. *Do I pull her hair back and reach for her mouth, or just try and cover her mouth with a hand full of hair and maybe miss her mouth altogether?* He decided the first option best; he would pull her hair back with one hand, expose her mouth, and clamp it tight. After he'd barely slipped a finger through the hair, Donna's heightened sense of danger jolted her and she screamed for at least half a second before he could cover her mouth. She struggled like a wildcat, her nails looking to gouge whatever they could.

'Donna, it's all right. Your father sent us,' Steve said. She stopped thrashing, instantly calmed at the sound of her name.

'Alpha 3, we have movement. Both men from front room heading your way.'

'Shit! Donna—we have to go.'

Ben called, 'Donna, I will help you out of the window, but we must go now or we'll have to leave you behind.'

Steve held the window as Donna dived headfirst into Ben's arms, and he was off, running with her tucked to his side as if she was a toddler. It would be quicker than her trying to run through the yard that was covered in thorns and prickles with her bare feet. The bedroom door burst open as Steve jumped out, grabbing his rifle that was still leaning against the wall. The window dropped with a huge smash, and the glass exploded.

'All occupants moving now.' Skunk called over the radio.

Dan had already started running and had caught up with Ben and Donna. Gunshots rang out through the night, and bullets rattled off the iron fence.

Greg put the Jeep into gear as he saw Ben and Donna tuck in behind the corrugated-iron fence.

'Alpha 4, back the car up! I'll count you down.'

Greg changed from first gear to reverse and dropped the

clutch. The Jeep roared back towards the opening in the fence.

'50, 40, 30, 20, stop!' Ben called out.

'Alpha 3 is down!' Skunk called out.

Dan had now tucked in with Ben and Donna behind the fence. The shooting had stopped.

'Stay here with her, Dan.'

Ben ran to the passenger side of the Jeep. 'Greg, spin the car around and let's get Alpha 3, sight him, put the car between him and them, and then get your head down as you drive. Put him outside my door and be ready to go.'

The Mexicans didn't see the Jeep come back straight away or expect them to be coming back for a team member. In Mexico, you don't go back for anyone. Greg dropped the clutch, and the back slid around in almost a car length. It wasn't until he had stopped next to Steve, that the bullets started again: only one gun probably, because the Land Cruisers had now started to move. Greg's head was down near the gearstick when all the windows on his side of the car exploded. Ben threw Steve and himself into the back seat as he yelled, 'Go, go, go!'

Greg again dropped the clutch and spun the car around as the first of the Land Cruisers' headlights appeared in the distance behind him. He stopped at the fence, and Dan and Donna jumped into the back seat, basically on top of Greg and Ben. Greg was off before the door was closed.

'Donna, climb into the front seat, get the seat belt on, and keep your head down,' Ben called out over the noise of the back window shattering. It sent glass splinters over them all. Donna didn't hesitate.

Steve had been hit in the leg and was losing quite a bit of blood. Dan had wrapped it tight with a bandage that was standard equipment in their suits.

'Alpha 5, what can you tell us?' Ben called. 'Alpha 5. Come in, Peter. Are you there?'

Skunk had gone. Ben quickly thought about it. The drone battery would have been flat by now anyway, or so he justified it to himself. With both the Land Cruisers in hot pursuit, Greg turned on the headlights, as they could see him anyway. He would be much faster without the night-vision goggles. He knew there was no way he could outrun the twin turbo V8 diesels that the Land Cruisers would have under their bonnets, so he had to outdrive and outsmart them. The tighter the road, the better chance they would have in the short wheelbase Jeep. There was a corner he remembered where the road did a sharp ninety-degree turn to the right; straight on was into the creek. As he approached the corner, he flicked down the night-vison goggles and flicked off the lights, so the Mexicans wouldn't see him turn. As he approached, he pulled the handbrake on, the back of the Jeep slid perfectly into the corner, and he dropped the handbrake and powered out. The first Land Cruiser had arrived at the corner with far too much speed and went over the edge, tipping the three-tonne car onto its side and resting in the dry shallow creek bed. Ben looked back to see the Land Cruiser's headlights vertical. The other cruiser was too far back to see where they'd gone and was now wandering along the creek track as Greg headed for the main road.

'I think we lost them,' Ben said.

With the car back on the bitumen, it was easier to talk, although it was noisy with most of the windows gone.

'Great driving, Greg. How are you going, Steve?'

'Just a flesh wound, boss,' Steve said, grimacing with pain.

Greg parked the Jeep around the back of the motel and out of sight, in the position they had all agreed earlier.

'Let's get Donna safe inside and see what we need to do with Steve's leg,' Ben said calmly.

Greg jumped out and ran to help Ben get Steve out. As Donna hopped out, she screamed as she saw about fifty Viper Gang bikies approaching with guns pointing at them.

Ben and Greg were both holding Steve, one of his arms over each of their shoulders; they looked up in shock. Dan was still sitting in the Jeep; the AR-10 on his lap.

The only unarmed man of the group walked forward from the middle of the wall of bikies. He had a man either side of him pointing automatic rifles at them. He was probably sixty years old, tall, and his fat, ugly face and bald head were covered in tattoos.

'So you're the Roo-man,' he said casually. 'You've caused me a lot of trouble, young fella, cost me a lot of money, but you did save my stupid nephew, so for that I will let you live—for now. I see you have something that was taken from me.' His demeanour changed instantly. 'And I want her fucken back!' Pig yelled.

Ben didn't answer, and no one moved. Ben knew there was no option for him; his men would be cut down in seconds. Ben looked at Greg and said, 'You got him?' Greg nodded, and Steve transferred his weight onto Greg. Ben walked forward and stood next to Donna.

'I want you to guarantee me she will be treated fairly. She doesn't have anything to do with this.'

'I don't need to guarantee you shit, Roo-man.'

Ben leaned down to whisper in Donna's ear, and he could see she was crying. 'Be brave, my dear. We won't give up. We will have you back within a couple of days, I promise.' He put his arm around her, and despite feeling her resistance, he walked her to Pig.

Pig was nearly as tall as Ben, and with him now less than a

metre away, he looked into Ben's eyes and said, 'The next time I see you, Roo-man, I *will* kill you. It would be in your best interest to make sure that doesn't happen.' Ben knew the only reason they were still alive was that they didn't want to have a shoot-out here in a public place and have cops everywhere.

Ben watched Pig turn with two of his men holding one of Donna's arms each. The fifty guns were still pointing directly at him. Ben walked backwards towards his team as he watched the bikies retreating into the bushes, and within seconds, they were gone and so was Donna. He heard the starting of their cars, vans, and bikes that were in the side street. He stood there in disbelief as their engines faded into the distance.

Ben was angry.

'Fuck, let's get Steve inside,' he said.

Dan stepped out of the car, the ArmaLite still in his hand.

'Ben, can you tell me what the fuck just happened?' Dan said as he and Greg helped Steve inside.

'That fucking Peter double-crossed us, that's what happened.'

Greg had already started to take Steve's pants and boots off to check the wound.

The bleeding had slowed, but it needed to be checked.

Dan came over with a bowl of warm water and cleaned the bullet hole that was halfway up his thigh.

'I'm no doctor, but it doesn't look like it hit a bone, and the slug has gone right through,' Dan said.

'What would you like to do, Steve?' Ben asked.

'We can't go to the hospital; the cops would be there in two seconds flat. Let's just wait a few hours. The sun's coming up soon, and if I need to, I'll say I shot myself cleaning my gun.'

'Okay, let's get a couple hours' sleep and regroup here at eleven hundred. And Greg, we are all trained for this, you aren't, but you did a bloody amazing job under fire, and we couldn't have done it without you.' Dan and Steve agreed with soft acknowledgements and a shake of his hand.

Greg just nodded, appreciating the compliment.

CHAPTER ELEVEN

PIG started shouting orders to his senior members as soon as the big gates were closed at the Viper fortress. It was known to them, of course, as the Viper Motorcycle clubrooms. They were situated just outside Alice Springs proper, not far from the town's airport.

'I want that girl secured so tight that it will take the US Marines to get her out. We haven't seen the last of that little team of heroes, and then there's those fucking Mexicans. They will think it was *us* that took her from them… and they will be pissed.'

Pig called Jarrad Stone over, his new sergeant-at-arms.

'Stony, I want four men on the roof, armed at all times, twenty-four seven. Everyone sleeps in shifts. Those fuckers will be back, you can mark my word on it. They aren't the type to give up that easily.'

'Yes, Pig. I'll have it done.'

Skunk felt bad for what he had done, but he had no choice. His uncle was so unbelievably pissed at him for not searching the Roo-man properly in the first place. Pig now blamed him for everything that had happened: losing the girl, losing the compound at Aileron, his sergeant-at-arms being killed, his good friend Bone dying in the crash, and of course Ferret being in jail. He lay in bed contemplating his options. If he had done what the Roo-man suggested and left the Vipers to become a model citizen, the bikies would have hunted him down and killed him. It's what they did; you don't leave. Once you were in, you were a brother, for life. Pig might've spared him, given that he was his brother's son, but he doubted it. He desperately wanted to say sorry to the Roo-man's team. He was one of them. He was Alpha 5, and they'd accepted him, they'd trusted him with their lives, and he just handed them over on a plate. And the poor girl. Whatever happened to her would be all his fault as well.

Greg was busting to tell Kara about the ordeal but decided to leave that for another day. Just a simple text would do.

Greg had trouble sleeping as his mind replayed the last few hours. He wondered how close some of the bullets must have been from hitting him. Almost every window was smashed, taillights smashed, bullet holes in every panel. He awoke before the alarm and headed for the shower. He stood there again, hearing that sound of bullets peppering the Jeep, the glass exploding, a window at a time. Steve could so easily have died out there. They all could have. If he'd crashed the car, the Mexicans would have been all over them with no prisoners taken.

He dressed and was walking out his door when he nearly tripped over the large alloy box that sat at his doorstep with a simple note, which read, "I hope this helps. Alpha 5." At that moment, Greg realized it was the drone. He took the handle and lifted it, and only then did he notice the manilla folder that was under it. He opened it to discover that it contained a detailed floorplan of the Viper clubhouse. It showed where the girl was, where the guards were, and the best way to penetrate the complex.

'Well, I'll be,' Greg said, collecting it up and walking into Ben's already open door.

'Greg, what have you got there?'

'The drone, I figured.'

'It could be a trap, a bomb that explodes when we open it. We can't trust them,' Dan said.

'Then why would he give us this?' Greg handed the folder to Ben. Ben opened it slowly and flicked through each page, placing them on the table as he read each one. Everyone studied a page at a time.

'Ben, are you seeing what I am seeing?' Dan said.

'Yes, I think I am. What do those four numbers mean?'

'Not sure, but I guess we'll find out.'

Greg turned to Steve. 'How's the leg, mate?'

'All right, I think. I won't be doing any marathons for a week or so though.'

'Great to hear.'

Ben turned to Steve and said, 'Mate, do you think you could fly the drone?'

'With a bit of practice, I'm sure I could. I do have one.'

'You have six hours to practice, ol' mate,' Ben said.

They all looked at Ben.

'Tonight?' Dan said with a sense of shock.

'They won't be expecting us back this soon,' Ben said.

'Do you have a plan?' Dan asked.

'Not yet, but I will,' Ben said. 'Are you going to hang around for part two, Greg? I understand totally, if you want out.'

'Do you need a driver?' Greg asked.

'Yes, but we'll manage if we have to,' Ben said.

'But what about getting there and back? The job's not finished… No, I'm still in,' Greg said with purpose.

Ben smiled back at him. 'Good on you, mate. Glad you will be with us.'

'Greg, can you take Steve in the truck somewhere out of town so he can familiarise himself with that drone?'

'Sure thing.'

Greg helped Steve into the truck and loaded the drone into the back while Dan and Ben headed back inside to plan out the rescue for that night.

Ben had a call to make first.

'Reed!' Sergeant Jones called out.

'Coming, sir.'

Rebecca Reed walked into her sergeant's office with a 'Yes, sir?'

'Reed, I want you to have the report done by the end of today regarding that Viper incident at Aileron. Jackson can do the report for the rollover.'

'Sir, in relation to that, the hospital called and said a tall man dressed like a soldier dropped off a lad who had injuries that could have been an MVA. He had a broken arm and bad bruising, claims he got drunk and fell over. His report said zero alcohol in his blood.'

'Name?'

'Fake, sir.'

'Not much good to us, then. Any detail on the man who dropped him off?'

'Claims he saw him wandering along the road and picked him up, then left straight away.'

'Any info on the gun that just appeared in the mall ranger's car?'

'Forty-four Magnum, filed-off serial number, had been recently fired, one bullet still in the chamber,' Reed said.

'No one saw anyone put it there, no mall cameras?'

'No, sir.'

'Sit down, Reed. Let's go through this. A man calls up, gives the name John Smith. He gives the coordinates to a secret bikie compound where three bikies are found dead, a mass of stolen Harleys and a meth lab. Then details about a fatal crash site, where another is dead; then someone drops a badly injured person to the hospital and disappears. Then someone who looks more like a sniper than a bikie roars out of the compound while we were there, and a .44 Magnum ends up in a police car in the mall. What the hell is going on here? Do you think this John Smith is involved in it all?'

'I'm not sure, Sarge, but I feel we haven't seen the end of it.'

'I agree, and that's what worries me. Okay, get that report to me ASAP. I want to get some heavies down from Darwin before this blows up in our faces.'

'Yes, Sarge.'

Rebecca met Constable Jackson halfway down the hallway. 'Phone for you, Bec.'

'Thanks, Will,' she said, taking the cordless phone from him.

He watched her with adoring eyes; she was so cute when in full police mode.

'Constable Reed speaking.'

'Rebecca, it's John Smith. Thank you for not shooting me in the back the other day, I assume that was you out there?'

She turned and marched quickly back to the sergeant's office, he looked up as she pointed to the phone she was holding.

'That was some pretty crazy riding, John.'

'Yeah, now listen carefully. There is going to be a shoot-out at the Viper bikie clubrooms on Maryvale rode tonight with another gang; do you know where that is?'

'Yes. I know where it is, near the airport.'

'They are heavily armed. Are you able to get help from up north and maybe the AFP?'

'How do you know this? I can't just go to my sergeant and expect him to rally the Australian Federal Police from all over the state on an anonymous call.'

'You can trust me, Rebecca, this will be an international incident.'

The phone went dead.

'What did he say?' the sergeant asked.

'A shoot-out tonight at the Vipers' clubrooms.'

'Do you believe him, Reed?'

'Yes, sir, of course; why wouldn't we?'

'I can't just get the Territory Response Group down here from Darwin on a tip-off. All right, get everyone you can locally, call the AFP at the airport and see if you can get a couple from there. If two bikie gangs want to shoot the shit out of each other, we aren't going to be standing between them. Reed, this is your baby.'

'Thank you, sir.' Rebecca turned to leave, a big smile on her face. This was just what she had dreamt of.

'Jackson, what time are you finishing tonight?'

'Six o'clock.'

'Not now, buddy. Call everyone you can, even if they are on holidays. We need all hands on deck tonight.'

'What's going on?'

'Shoot-out at the Vipers' clubhouse tonight.'

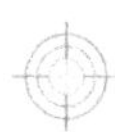

Ben jumped onto one of the scooters and rode down to the Domino's Pizza shop.

'Hello, can I please have a pizza box delivered to a farmhouse just the other side of Amoonguna?'

'Just a box?' the sixteen-year-old attendant asked, almost laughing.

'Yes, just a box with an invitation inside. Would two hundred dollars cover that?'

'Yes, sir,' the attendant said, coming to attention. 'I would deliver that myself. When would you like it done?'

'Would you take your delivery van with the sign on the roof?'

'Would you like me to?'

'Yes, that's very important. I would like it done straight away. Do not read the note, just hand the box to the man at the door and leave straight away. Do not wait for a tip, do not answer any questions, do you understand?'

'Yes, mister, sure.'

The attendant took a box down from the top of the oven and opened it. Ben took the folded note and two hundred dollars from his pocket. He put the note inside the box and closed it. He then looked up at the attendant and handed him the address and the money.

'Robbo, I will be doing a delivery. Can you cover the front for me?' the attendant called out to the other sixteen-year-old lad cooking the pizzas out the back.

'Yeah, I guess.' The boy looked confused, likely as he hasn't made a pizza for him to deliver.

Ben rode back to the motel and parked the scooter.

Dan was still running over scenarios: A, B, and C.

'What do you have, Dan?' Ben asked.

'The tunnel is at the rear. The entrance is in that deep bush to the south. Plan A, the cops and/or the Mexicans distract them from the north-facing front gate, while we go in through the tunnel. We park the Avis truck a couple of kilometres away on Maryvale Road—the airport is near, so it's not that odd for a truck to be around—then we ride the scooters through the bush. We go in through the tunnel, as they are holding the girl underground not far from the tunnel exit. We collect the girl and go out the same way. Greg will have his scooter running, and he will take Donna straight to the truck and be ready to leave. We leave the scooters behind and head straight to Adelaide; there is a dirt road shortcut through to Stuart Highway.'

'That's great; sounds like the most preferred way,' Ben said enthusiastically. 'What's Plan B and C?'

'I'll work on that as soon as we know Plan A's not working,' Dan said, looking up at Ben with a smile.

Ben heard the little Avis truck pull up and a door close, then a minute later a second door close. Greg walked in with Steve's arm around his neck for support.

'How did it go, Steve?'

'Really good, I think. It's actually easier than mine to fly.'

'We'll need you really high just watching our arses, mate,' Dan said.

Dan went through the plan again with everyone, and after a good many questions, everybody was happy.

Ben reminded them, 'Last thing, guys: don't forget to bring all your gear tonight. If it all goes well, we will be out of here and heading south to Adelaide.'

Ben, Greg, and Dan loaded the three scooters and all the gear into the back of the truck.

'I will drop the Jeep back to the panel shop for a touch-up, and if we win tonight, I'll get it freighted home later,' Ben said.

When the Avis truck was loaded, Ben said to them all, 'We leave at twenty-one hundred. Party starts at twenty-two hundred.'

Greg lay back on the bed and thought about Jennifer. *My God!* He'd just remembered her message during the shoot-out. He flicked back through his phone and opened the message. There she was, her hair, her smile, she just made him melt. To think only days ago, not even a week, he had made love to this goddess. His heart was aching to see her again. He sent her a message.

Thank you for the picture, you are just the most beautiful thing on the planet, I would love to see you again. Could you come to Australia?

He pushed send, his fingers shaking from the excitement. He fell back onto the bed and sighed. There was no better feeling than to love and to be loved. A message beeped, and he opened it.

Of course, I can come and visit you, anytime. When would you like?

Greg's heart was about to burst. There wasn't this much adrenaline flowing through him last night when the Mexicans were shooting at him.

I am busy for the next few days, I will let you know when I am home, I love you

I love you too

Greg dressed in the tactical gear again for the second night in a row and met the team at the truck at 9:30 p.m.

'Let's go,' Ben called.

Greg started the truck, and they headed out through the town and past the airport. He pulled up at the agreed position on Maryvale Road. They unloaded the scooters, the drone, and the last of their gear, rifles, goggles, big cable ties, and duct tape.

'Steve, send the drone up and see if there is any action happening anywhere,' Ben said.

'Roger that,' Steve replied.

The drone took off, and Ben called for a radio check.

'There are a couple of cop cars sitting two blocks away to the northwest. No sign of the Mexicans.'

'Guards?' Ben called.

'Four on the roof behind a one-metre-high brick wall,' Steve said, now sitting down with his leg up on the chair they had stolen from the motel.

'We can't go in till we have that distraction,' Ben said. 'Where are those bloody Mexicans?'

'If they don't arrive soon, we may need to create one ourselves,' Ben said.

'Here they come, Ben, two black Land Cruisers, one with the left-hand side caved in, coming from the northeast.'

'Perfect timing. Let's get going on the scooters. You're our eyes, Steve; we will see you soon, mate.'

They rode slowly with the headlights off and night goggles on, pulled up, and turned the bikes back in the direction of the truck for a quick getaway. Greg would stay with the lead scooter and rush Donna away as soon as she came out of the tunnel.

'Update, Alpha 3?' Ben asked over the radio.

'Cruisers are stationary. They are now on foot, fully armed.'

'Roger that,' Ben replied.

Ben and Dan walked the hundred metres to the little tin shed. It was about the size of an outhouse. It was completely covered by scrub and painted in a reddish camouflage style that matched the surroundings. Ben decided to use his night vision to see rather than have a light waving around should the police or cartel decide to approach from the rear as well. There was a large combination lock on the shed door, big enough to lock up the treasury. Ben took the lock in his gloved fingers; it was awkward as it sat under a covered pocket in the door that enabled it to be unlocked from either side. He put in the code that Skunk had provided. 3195. The lock popped apart with a bit of force; it clearly hadn't been used in a while. The door squeaked open, again, requiring some effort. The little shed had a couple of empty cardboard boxes scattered on the floor that would give a casual passer-by the impression nothing was in there. Ben pushed them aside and reached down to a handle that lifted a slatted timber hatch. A rusty wire at the back of the shed wall was used to twitch to the handle and hold the hatch up. Dan pulled the shed door closed behind him and followed Ben down the ladder. Ben cringed at the number of cobwebs. His head told him that the spiders that had made them would have been long dead, but somehow, the thought of a spider down the collar of his tactical coveralls just didn't appeal to him. He marched on. The entrance of the tunnel was at least fifty metres from the clubhouse wall, and from the maps, it went another twenty under the building.

They reached the end of the tunnel where an aluminium ladder rose to another hatch. Ben climbed up and ever so slowly lifted the hatch to see if anyone was in the room. He heard a voice and lowered it softly back down.

In a whisper, he asked, 'Alpha 3, what's the sitch?'

'The movie is about to start, Alpha 1,' Steve came back.

A gunshot was just audible from where they were, then noise exploded from the room above them, with running footsteps and chairs falling over on the timber floor.

'Mexicans just dropped one on the roof, over,' Steve said through the crackly radio.

Ben again lifted the hatch and checked it was all clear. They lifted their night-vision goggles, and he threw the hatch back, hitting the wall with a bang. The girl would be in the second room on their left. Ben pulled a little mirror out of his pocket and slowly held it out into the hallway.

'Cops have arrived at north-eastern corner, over,' Steve said.

Ben clicked the talk button twice to acknowledge the message. He turned to Dan and held up one finger; Dan knew exactly what that meant. It wasn't dark enough to be able to sneak up on the man guarding the door. The guard was now on high alert since the shooting had started. His gun was up and finger on the trigger.

Ben really didn't want to just shoot the man, although that would have made his job much easier. With the shots now constant outside, one more inside probably wouldn't attract too much attention.

'Update, Alpha 3?' Ben whispered into his mike.

'Mex and Vipers trading shots, three bikies down, cops just spectators at this stage, over.'

Ben double-clicked the mic.

Ben did the maths: a five-metre run from a standing start, no more than a second. The guard's gun was in his left hand, slung low and facing away from Ben. He decided the guard couldn't turn it, aim, and fire in that time. Ben would be all over him, although through the mirror he couldn't see his face, he looked young and skinny and very nervous.

Ben turned to Dan and in a whisper said, 'I'll rush him. Follow me in. I'll knock him to the ground and punch him till he stops moving, and then cuff him. Hard to tell, but that could be a combo lock on that door too. Let's hope it's the same number, and if not, tell Donna to get away from the door and just shoot the lock off. We won't have time to pick locks.'

'Roger that,' Dan replied in a whisper.

Ben held up three fingers and counted them down. He rushed into the corridor; the guard didn't have any time to react. Just his head turned as a gloved fist hit him square in the middle of his face, sending him to the floor and his gun flying down the passage. With Ben now on top of the guard, he set to deliver the knockout punches.

'Roo-man!' the guard screamed through the blood that filled his mouth.

Ben held back the punch. 'Peter?'

'Now I have a broken fucking nose to match my arm. Why the fuck did you hit me so hard?'

'Sorry, mate; didn't know it was you. Now tell me, is the code the same?' Ben asked, nodding to the door.

'Yes. But tie me up before you go!'

Dan punched in the code, and the door opened.

'Grab her and go!' Ben yelled.

Within a second, Dan and Donna ran past him for the tunnel room.

Ben pulled out a cable tie and bound Skunk's good wrist to his plastered one. He took out the duct tape to cover his mouth but Skunk protested, 'You've broken my nose, so I won't be able to breath. Just go.'

Ben stood up, nodding. He collected his rifle and looked back and said, 'Thanks, Peter.'

Skunk just nodded with acknowledgement as Ben turned and ran for the tunnel. Ben caught Dan and Donna at the outside exit.

'Asset collected. Update, Alpha 3?'

'All clear between you and scooters, over,' Steve confirmed

'Dan, get her to Greg and let's get the fuck out of here.'

The three of them ran to the scooters, Donna was soon on the back with Greg, and within a second, they were off. Dan had started his bike and was not far behind Greg and Donna. Donna had her arms wrapped so tightly around Greg it looked like he could hardly breathe, but he didn't seem to mind. Ben started his bike and looked back over his shoulder to see Constable Reed walking out into the open field demanding everyone drop their weapons.

'What the fuck is she doing?' Ben said to himself.

He dropped the scooter, ran to the south-west corner, and ducked in behind the brick wall. He watched as Reed moved slowly towards the centre of the gravel entrance, calling for the shooting to stop. Ben could see the same police sergeant that was at Aileron yelling for her to get back. The shooting momentarily stopped, and it all went quiet. It was almost surreal.

'Jackson,' Sergeant Jones yelled. 'What the fuck is she doing? Get her back here.' They watched her walk out, and when her courageous effort seemed to be working, they were all stunned into silence.

But then a single shot rang out, and Reed spun and hit the ground.

As she went down, it was all like slow motion for Sergeant

Jones. He screamed out, 'Noooooo!' as she lay there motionless. As Jackson went to take off to rescue the woman he was so secretly infatuated with, Jones caught his arm. 'No, stop! You will only be shot as well.'

Then out of nowhere, they saw someone dressed in full black police tactical gear run out from the scrub, and in almost a baseball slide, slid in next to her.

'Who the fuck is that?' Jones yelled.

'Looks like TRG,' Jackson replied.

'It can't be; I didn't call them.'

'I can't breathe,' she gasped, looking into the eyes of a man in a black balaclava and helmet. Ben quickly thought, *If she has broken ribs, I can't pick her up in a fireman's lift, but I've got to get her out of here.*

Ben grabbed her hands and dragged her backwards as puffs of gravel started to burst up around them.

Dan had returned and was now watching from the same corner where Ben was positioned just before he ran to Reed. Then, all of a sudden, Ben dropped Reed and collapsed onto the ground next to her. Dan ran to them, now only five metres from the protected brick corner.

Ben yelled with a painful breath, 'Take her! I'm okay. Just get her to the truck, she might have broken ribs.'

Dan picked up Reed's hands and dragged her to safety. He turned to see that Ben was following on hands and knees; he was now covered by the corner of the building and out of range of the shooters. Dan had parked the scooter at the wall this time. He lifted

Reed onto the front of the scooter seat and sat behind her with his arms reaching around her to hold her on as he rode the bike. It was slow, but it was working. She cried out with every bump.

Ben was badly winded—a bullet had hit him square in the back. The bulletproof vest had stopped it from penetrating, but he was sure he had broken ribs. Just able to get to his feet, he hobbled to the scooter, doubled over, each step and breath a huge effort. It took him three goes to pick the scooter up from the ground. He climbed on, and it started straight away. By the time he was back to the truck, the drone had landed and was packed and everyone, including the injured Reed, was inside. Greg had the engine running and clutch in, ready to go. Ben hopped into the front, obviously still in a lot of pain.

'Are you okay, Ben?' Greg asked as he started to drive away.

'Yeah, but we need to get that stupid cop to the hospital. She's in a bad way.'

'How are we going to do that?' Greg asked. 'The cops will have closed all the roads by now.'

'Turn left, then right onto that dirt road we were going to take to leave, but turn right onto Stuart Highway and back into Alice past the Finke rally club.'

'Roger that, Alpha 1,' Greg said, looking at Ben with a smile.

Ben smiled back, a painful smile, and said, 'Glad you stayed on, mate.'

'Jackson, pull everyone back, and find out who the fuck it is that has Reed,' Jones yelled.

The gunfire was starting to calm to just the occasional shot from the Vipers' roof.

The Mexicans had gone.

By morning, the police had surrounded the fortress and were waiting for backup to flush them out. They had found the tunnel entrance, the three scooters, and where the getaway truck had been parked. For the second time this week, Sergeant Jones stood looking at tyre tracks, with his thumb and forefinger rubbing his chin at a situation that didn't make any sense.

Why did they take Reed? he wondered. *They risked their own lives to drag her to safety; it doesn't make any sense.*

His phone rang.

'Jones!' he said abruptly.

'Sarge… it's…. me.'

'Where the bloody hell are you, Reed?'

'Hospital… sir… three… cracked ribs… and collapsed… lung.'

'Jesus, Reed, thank God you are okay. I'm on my way.' Sergeant Jones was almost in tears.

CHAPTER TWELVE

B Y daybreak, they'd crossed the border into South Australia. Greg drove with Ben in the passenger seat and Donna in the little seat between them. The rough ride was tough for Ben; he felt every bump, his broken ribs a harsh reminder of the last few days. Steve had made himself a comfortable spot amongst the tactical gear so he could straighten out his leg, while Dan sat very uncomfortably on the deck chair from the motel. Donna hadn't said much, and neither Greg nor Ben wanted to pressure her with questions, even though they both wanted to ask.

'Are you all right, Donna?' Ben said softly.

'Yeah, I'm okay,' she replied.

Ben could tell that was all he was going to get from her.

'Donna, when we get to Coober Pedy, we need to call your father and tell him you are safe and find out what is best for you from here.'

'Okay' she said, still staring blankly out through the windscreen.

Greg turned the truck into the Coober Pedy township and pulled up for fuel at the truck stop's diesel pump. The little truck was surrounded by road trains, semi-trailers, and B-doubles. Greg jumped out and opened the back so Steve and Dan could get out for a stretch and maybe some breakfast. They'd changed out of their tactical gear. Ben and Greg had removed the vests and shirts but still wore the pants and boots. Steve's leg appeared to be healing well, and he was now able to get around on his own. Ben handed Donna his phone, and she walked off, dialling her father's number. He watched her during the call as she sat on a little brick wall that surrounded the service station. She was quite animated now, her free arm describing the scene between sobs, with tears streaming down her face.

Ben stood next to Greg, who was still filling the truck with fuel. While they both watched her, Ben said, 'I think this has been a much harder ordeal for her than we think.'

Greg hung up the nozzle and replaced the fuel cap as Donna walked back towards them. She handed the phone back to Ben. 'Dad wants to talk to you,' she muttered.

'Mr DeLuca,' Ben said.

'Ben, those fucking arseholes raped her. You will need to get her to a hospital.'

'Will do, sir. We didn't know, I'm sorry. She wouldn't talk to us,' Ben said, now a little uncomfortable.

'Thank you, Ben, for getting her out. I can't tell you how grateful I am. When you get to Adelaide, I want you to put her on a plane to Melbourne. She can hide there with my sister for the time being. Then I want to know where the Mexicans are. They will pay for this.'

'Mr DeLuca, I have their address, but you must try to take the emotion out of this before you make any big decisions. Anyway, I doubt very much they will still be there.'

'Ben, the decision I have already made may solve two of my problems.'

'Roger that,' Ben said, knowing exactly what he meant.

Greg had invited Donna to come into the roadhouse and get something to eat. She followed him in but just to sit. With them now having phone service for the first time since leaving Alice Springs, they were all busy texting and receiving messages. Greg had one from Jennifer.

> Greg, I can't wait to see you. Should I leave today?

> Yes, I will be home late tonight, very excited x

Jennifer's message had Greg's heart pounding. He then typed a message to Kara.

> Hey Kara, on our way home. Job went well. Jennifer leaving USA today. X

Ben told Greg what had happened to Donna, which took the wind out of his sails.

Greg said, 'If we take her to the hospital, they will call the cops and we won't have any answers for them. Worse still, they might think it was one of us and lock us all up until we tell them what really happened.'

'I know,' Ben said. 'Let's talk to Donna.'

Greg and Ben walked over to Donna, who was quietly sipping an iced coffee. 'Donna,' Ben said, 'your father told us what happened to you, and we are very sorry. He has asked me to take you to the hospital.'

'No!' Donna said, staring at him with piercing eyes. 'The men who did it are dead, and that's all that matters. Please just get me to Melbourne, and I will sort it from there.'

'Okay, can we just make sure your father is happy with that?'

Ben pulled out his phone and dialled her father. It was a short conversation. Ben nodded to Greg and said, 'Let's keep going.'

'Roger that,' Greg said.

Keith Madison had arrived home from the office in his Cadillac CT5-V Blackwing. He changed from his work clothes to take his dog for a walk. Keith Madison was a very confident man, tall and average build, sixty years old, grey and balding. He was never seen without his light grey Stetson Diamante, exclusively made for him from beaver felt and chinchilla fur. He was like a god in the cattle industry, although most people couldn't actually tell you why. His presence commanded respect, and he usually got it. He was not the man to have offside: he had the politicians and police in his pocket. If you needed a difficult government approval sorted, a drink-driving charge squashed, or a bank loan approved, he would have it done, but you would owe him, and he would collect with interest.

He could close the most difficult deal with a wink and a handshake. After all, he was the president of the Southwestern Cattleman's Association and the most well-known of all the cattle farmers throughout Texas, Oklahoma, and Kansas.

'Hello, my dear,' Keith said to Jennifer as she descended the stairs. He kissed her on the forehead, which was about as romantic as he got these days.

She asked, 'How was your day?'

'Same as usual,' he replied, heading to the front door with his golden labradoodle frantically pulling on the lead.

Keith's phone rang; it was Jerry. Jerry Stokes was Keith's right-hand man. He looked more like a recycled drug dealer than a businessman. He did the hard jobs for Keith and did them without question. When it was time for a favour to be repaid, Jerry made sure it was done.

'Mr Madison, the ten thousand head of cattle will start arriving in the morning from Oklahoma.'

'Thank you, Jerry, well done. We will probably need them for a week.'

'Yes, sir, we have them for two weeks,' Jerry said.

Keith walked his dog along the path of the William Blair Jr. Park, on the favourite loop he did each day after work as part of his fitness regime. He had an extra stride in his step now that Jerry had another cattle rancher on side. Whether by choice or coercion, it didn't really matter. He was up for re-election for the presidency of the association soon. He enjoyed the kudos that it brought him, but most of all, it was the power he could wield. If you were against him, he would make sure no one would deal with you; there would be no bidders for your stock at auction, no matter how prime your cattle were. There were only a few people who dared to stand up to his corrupt, coercive ways, but life became even harder for them to survive in the industry. He made sure of that.

Jennifer knew she was playing a deadly game, but she was in love, madly in love with a man she hardly knew. Uncontrollably, in fact. She had to see him, touch him. He had found her, and she unknowingly had pushed him away. The lust, love, or passion, or whatever it was, needed to be quelled. She'd fainted at the sight of him on the last day of the cruise, devastated at the thought of never seeing him again. But now she had another chance, and whatever the cost, she was going to make it happen.

Keith and Jennifer sat for dinner. Keith spent most of the time checking stocks and the daily finishing price of beef. Keith pointed to his wine glass for Libby to top it up, when Jennifer said,

'Keith, I might take a little holiday.'

'Sure, where to, my dear?'

'Australia, my love,' Jennifer replied.

Libby's hand shook and bumped the glass, and wine spilt onto the tablecloth.

'Libby, what are you doing?' Keith said sternly.

'I'm so sorry, sir,' Libby said, looking over to Jennifer. Jennifer looked back at her with a look that said plenty. Keith lifted the glass as Libby wiped the bottom and patted the wet tablecloth.

'Poor Libby has had a big day, my dear. It's not her fault,' Jennifer said calmly.

'Why Australia? That's a damned long way. You need to be back for the Cattleman's Association annual general meeting in a couple weeks' time. It is extremely important that I have my beautiful wife by my side when I win the presidential vote.'

'Yes, dear, it would only be for a few days. I'll buy you some of that Australian wine that you like and get some sun to top up my tan from the Jamaican cruise,' Jennifer said.

'Well, you better keep your top on this time,' he said, looking back at his phone.

Jennifer had already booked the Qantas flights, first class to Sydney, then on to Adelaide, where she would again meet the lover for whom her body was desperately craving. Just the thought made her tingle where she wanted him most.

Next morning, Libby arrived in Jennifer's bedroom doorway and told her the driver was here. Libby helped Jennifer carry the four packed bags to the car. As the driver placed them in the boot, Jennifer turned to thank Libby, when she noticed the look on her face.

'You aren't coming back, are you, ma'am?' Libby said with a tear trickling down her cheek.

'We will see, Libby. It's just between us, remember?' Jennifer said, kissing her on the cheek.

As the car moved away, Jennifer looked back to see Libby crying into her hands. Jennifer turned back around and said softly, 'I will miss you too, Libby.'

Ben had offered for Donna to take the coach that would be coming through from Darwin later that day. It would be a lot more comfortable than the little truck.

Donna, for the first time, started to show some of her trauma and said, 'Until I get on that plane tomorrow, I would like one of you with me at all times.'

'Don't worry, Donna, one of us will be with you,' Ben said. 'Steve will accompany you on the plane as well. He's actually from Melbourne, and to be honest—you might be able to help him get on and off the aircraft.'

Donna smiled for the first time in a long time. It wasn't big, but a smile all the same.

Greg fired up the little truck. The two boys in the back had bought air mattresses and a stack of food and drinks, and they were now quite happy being in their small mobile cell. Along the way, Ben, Donna, and Greg worked out a plan. When they arrived in Adelaide in the late afternoon, Donna and Steve would stay with Greg, and then he would take them both to the airport the next morning. Dan would stay with Ben. Greg said he would ask his friend Kara to organise Donna some clean clothes and shoes and possibly stay over, so there would be another woman there. Greg thought that it may be a comfort for Donna, just in case she wanted someone to talk to.

As they arrived in Port Augusta, their phones all beeped with messages again. Greg looked at his and saw one was from Jennifer. He handed it to Donna and said, 'Can you read it to me?'

'Sure,' Donna said, taking the phone.

Donna read the message and, with her second smile for the day, read it out loud.

'She said that she is now on her way and will be in Adelaide tomorrow morning at 9:00 a.m. and that her heart is bursting for you.'

Donna handed the phone back to the now blushing Greg. 'Thanks,' he said.

'Greg, I don't want to pour cold water on that ferocious fire, but you need to be careful there,' Ben said seriously.

CHAPTER THIRTEEN

REED lay in the hospital bed in the Alice Springs Hospital, an oxygen mask on her face and her eyes staring at the ceiling, thinking about how stupid she was to do what she did and wondering who the hell those people were who saved her. She briefly saw the faces of the two men that helped carry her onto the stretcher, but she was almost unconscious by then.

Senior Sergeant Tim Jones and Constable Jackson appeared at her door.

'Are you awake, Reed?' Jones asked.

She nodded and tried to talk through the mask.

'Are you doing, okay?' Jackson asked, looking desperate to comfort her.

'I think so. The doctor said the lung has re-inflated well, so I'm just being observed. I'm so sorry, boss. I know that was stupid,' she said, looking at Jones.

'Yes, pretty stupid, all right. You could have been killed. Jackson here tried to get himself killed as well when he started to run to you.' She looked at Jackson and mimed a thank-you, and he blushed. He opened his mouth to say something, but seemed to hold it back.

'Any idea who those men were?' Jones asked.

'No, I was pretty out of it, sir. There were at least four of them, and there may have been a woman with them who I think was holding my head. I don't really remember much after that; I could hardly breathe.'

'That's okay. Just relax. Good to see you are coming along; we'd better get back and do some police work, but we'll see you soon.'

Reed replayed back in her head what John Smith had told her about the shoot-out and the two gangs. Nothing made sense at this stage. She needed to get out of the hospital and solve this. She needed to find out who the second gang was and what was happening to the Vipers. She desperately needed to talk to John Smith, especially now that Sergeant Jones had called in the TRG from Darwin, and even the STAR Force up from Adelaide.

Pig called a meeting with the eight senior members of the VMC.

He banged his fist on the table. 'We are fucked. We could have talked our way out of this as self-defence, but some fucking idiot shot that cop. That changes everything, and the fucking girl is gone. How the fuck did those Mexican assholes get through the fucking tunnel and into her fucking locked cell and just walk out with her?'

'Skunk must have let them have her; he probably gave them the combination!' someone yelled out.

'If he did, it only stopped them smashing the fucking door in. They would have just shot the fucking lock off anyway. Now, the cops have us surrounded, and when they get enough of them, they will overpower us and throw us all in jail.'

'We will fight them off, Pig.'

'Till the last one of us,' someone else said.

'You fucking idiots, that is exactly what will happen. We'll all be dead. We need to find a way out of here or we fucking surrender; there's no other way,' Pig said.

Pig's mind was racing, his eyes darting from side to side as he considered his options.

'Get everyone together. Are there any injured?' Pig asked in a calmer manner that surprised everyone.

'No, Pig. Four dead, no injuries.'

The bikies assembled quickly, and Pig stood up in front of them.

'Fellow Viper brothers, we have found ourselves in a situation which doesn't leave us with a lot of options. The future of our club is greatly threatened. The way I see it is, we all walk out with our hands in the air and go to jail, or we create a distraction around the front gate area, and we rush the tunnel. They can't shoot all of us and—to be honest, if we appear unarmed, I doubt they will shoot at us at all. We will need a plan to scatter. We will need wives, girlfriends, mates, and cousins to pick us up as we run through the bush. Some will get caught, but it won't be any worse than walking out the gate and giving up. We need to vote. Who would like to surrender?'

Not a single hand went up as everybody looked around at each other.

'Those in favour of rushing the tunnel?' Pig called out.

It was unanimous, with cheers of support.

Pig started bellowing out orders.

'It'll have to be tonight, because whoever they are waiting for will be well on their way. I need someone to go to the tunnel shed and report back with what you can see. I need all the details. How many? Is the door locked? Is it our lock? Shit like that.

'You two,' he said as he pointed to the first two men in front of him, 'as soon as you can, go!'

'Pig, what will be the distraction?' one man asked.

'Well, Skunk can stay behind and create the distraction; he has a broken face and broken arm, and this is somehow all his fault anyway.'

Skunk went to protest, then stood. 'I will be pleased to do that for my brothers.'

'Done then. Everyone else dress in civvies; we go at midnight. Skunk, you come with me.'

Greg pulled the truck up at Ben's apartment. He stopped and opened the back so Dan could hop out. They all shook hands and patted each other on the back.

Ben turned to Donna. 'Good luck, my dear. Stay low and safe.'

'I can't thank you enough, Ben,' she said as she reached out and hugged him tight.

Ben's wince indicated his ribs still hurt like hell, but Greg could see he appreciated everything Donna's impromptu hug meant.

Steve had remained in the back, as it was simply too painful to clamber in and out of the truck. Donna hopped back in the front with Greg. When they arrived shortly after at Greg's North Adelaide townhouse, Kara was already there. On hearing the truck pull up, she came out to greet them. Greg introduced Donna and the injured Steve to her. Steve was now walking on his own, but still limping heavily and moving slowly. The girls hugged, then Kara escorted Donna to show her a bedroom she could use, and to offer the warmth of a shower. Donna accepted willingly and thanked her. Steve crashed onto his bed firmly, which signalled he clearly wouldn't be moving again for a couple hours at least.

'So, Greg, what the hell happened up there?' Kara asked.

'You wouldn't believe it, trust me, but, over a bottle of wine very soon, I will tell you all about it.'

'That's a definite!' Kara said.

'And did you get the message that Jennifer will be here tomorrow at 9:00 a.m.'

'Yes, I did, and you were going to give up.'

'I know. To be honest, I'm a little nervous,' Greg said.

'You may need to talk more about that too. But for now—what's wrong with Steve's leg?' Kara asked, pointing towards the closed door.

'Bullet wound,' Greg replied.

'Are you kidding? You can't just ignore it and hope it goes away,' Kara said firmly.

'I know, but you also can't just go to a hospital and say you have a bullet wound straight after probably the biggest shoot-out the town has ever seen. The cops would've been all over us.'

'Shoot-out, what bloody shoot-out? I thought you were driving the prime minister to the airport?'

'Well, it got a little crazier, let's just say,' Greg said, trying to calm her down. 'I'm sorry, Kara. So much happened that I really had no idea about. But we've saved an innocent woman here. I'll tell you all about it as soon as things settle down.'

'I want the full story! Anyway, right now, we need someone to come and at least have a look at him; he could lose his leg,' Kara said.

Greg had a thought. 'I know! Tracy, the nurse we use on the film shoots, she owes me big time.'

Greg took out his phone and called her.

'Trace, Greg, I have been working in Alice Springs and just arrived back with some of the crew. One of the guys injured his leg and needs to be on a plane back to Melbourne tomorrow morning. I was just wondering if you could do me a big favour and come to have a look at him for me, off the record, if you know what I mean?'

'Sure, send me the address. I'll come straight away.'

'I really appreciate it, Trace,' Greg said before he hung up and sent her the address.

It was only fifteen minutes before there was a knock on the door, and Kara greeted Tracy.

Greg knocked on Steve's door and woke him from his deep sleep.

'Sorry, mate, but I have a nurse here to have a look at your leg.'

'We can't!' he protested.

'It's okay, mate. She'll just have a look to see how bad it is. I can't have you die on us!' he said, trying to make light of the moment. 'She won't say anything.'

'Hello,' Tracy said. 'Slip those pants off and let me have a look.'

Steve struggled, and Tracy helped. She unwrapped the bandage that had really been on there too long.

'This looks like a—' Tracy said.

'A stick wound, yes!' Greg said, cutting her off.

'Right, yes, a stick wound.' Tracy nodded, looking knowingly back at Greg. 'Can you roll over please, Steve?' Tracy asked, and he did so carefully.

'Well it looks like the stick went all the way through,' Tracy said, glancing up at Greg with a look that said, *What have you got yourself into here?* 'There doesn't appear to be any infection, no real swelling, and it seems to be healing up pretty well,' Tracy said as she gently prodded the area. 'You should have antibiotics though. These lead-based sticks can be nasty.' She looked at Steve. 'I suggest, when you get to Melbourne, you find a busy doctor in a big clinic, tell them you were checked out in Adelaide and have a bladder infection that needs antibiotics. It might just work. Some chemists will hand them out for bladder infections without a prescription. Good luck, Steve, and try and stay away from sharp sticks from now on, hey!'

'Thanks, Doc,' Steve said.

'I'm just a nurse,' Tracy said, getting up from the side of the bed, and slowly walking towards the front door.

'I don't even want to know, Mr Sheppard. I'll see you on the next shoot,' Tracy said as she walked back to her car.

'Thanks, Trace, I owe you!' he called out.

Kara fetched a new bandage from the first-aid kit and wrapped Steve's leg.

Greg returned and suggested some dinner, as most of them hadn't slept in thirty-six hours. A quick feed and to bed was the priority.

'We need to be leaving at six thirty, as the flight to Melbourne is at eight and I have a special guest coming in at nine,' Greg said. He gulped back the mixture of excitement and nervousness that was making his heart race.

The two scouts had returned to Pig's office.

'Pig, there are two armed guards at the tunnel exit shed. It doesn't look padlocked, but the gate is closed and the bolt through.'

'Perfect,' he said. 'We will go tonight at midnight. Tell everyone to have their rides ready on the other side of the scrub, but spread them out. Don't make it a fucken car park out there! Tell everyone to know exactly where the car that's picking them up is parked.'

Pig had instructed Skunk that at the stroke of midnight, he was to start firing the gun he'd been given from the rooftop, as a distraction. 'Don't shoot at anyone, just make a lot of noise and keep your fucking head down. I don't want you dead before we are all out.'

Skunk agreed, appreciating the concern for his wellbeing, and went to prepare for his own part of the plan.

At eleven thirty, the Viper brothers gathered again.

Pig stood on a chair as the forty-six members looked up at him for the final instructions.

'Right, brothers, we need to have four of you in the shed ready to bust out just after the shooting starts. As you burst through the shed door, wave your arms above your heads, yell that you are unarmed, and run like hell in different directions through the scrub. I doubt they will shoot you in the back; you four will have the best chance of escaping.'

Pig knew that wasn't the case, but he needed four decoys for the cops to chase.

'When the next four are ready, run, and so on. I will be part of that second group.' Pig figured that was his best chance. 'Let's go, and good luck, brothers.'

At the stroke of twelve, Skunk started firing off some random shots into air. The police dived for cover, and their radios were busy with instructions. After a couple of minutes of firing, Skunk dropped the gun and, as quickly as he could with one arm, descended the ladder from the roof. He went to his room and changed into his street clothes that he had out ready, and pocketed the heavy cable tie and a large bottle of water. He went down to the holding cell that Donna DeLuca was in only twenty-four hours earlier. He punched in the code and stepped in. He pulled the door closed, and it locked heavily behind him. He hoped his plan would work. A very painful push of his broken nose soon had it bleeding again, and blood ran freely down his face and clothes. He formed the cable tie into a loop that would be his handcuffs for when the cops arrived.

The Vipers didn't know that two entire tactical response teams from Adelaide and Darwin had arrived two hours earlier, having anticipated they would try to make a run for it. They hid, scattered through the scrub, catching each and every bikie as they exited the tunnel shed. Being in groups of four had made it simple for the one-hundred-strong police. As the last of the Vipers were handcuffed and taken away, a team of twenty TRG police went in through the tunnel armed with their assault rifles.

Skunk picked up the cable tie and placed the strap into his mouth. He slid both his wrists through the loop and pulled down with his hands and up with his head until the strap was tight. He had rehearsed his story over and over until he almost believed it himself. He sat in the corner of the cell, his knees to his chest. He could hear them coming, doors opening and closing. He heard the door handle move.

'Help,' he called. 'Help me, please!'

'Who's in there?' a deep voice called out.

'Peter Watkins. They have me tied up; I am a prisoner.'

'Stand back from the door and cover your face!' they yelled back.

A short burst of gun fire, and the door burst open. A man in black rushed in, waving his gun around.

'Clear,' he called out, and two more entered the room. They lifted him gently from the floor, his smashed nose evidence of his mistreatment. One officer produced a knife and cut the cable tie. He stayed with him as the others continued through the building.

'Let's get you out of here. I am sure the local police have a lot to ask you,' the TRG officer said.

Skunk was handed over to the paramedics, who dressed his nose and cleaned up the blood from his face.

A police sergeant watched Skunk with a suspicious eye. He walked up to the back of the ambulance and introduced himself.

'Mr Watkins, can I ask why they had you locked up? Are you a drug dealer and owe them money?'

'No, sir, I was out west of Aileron with my new drone, shooting the desert landscape a couple of days ago, when this bunch of bikies beat me up and accused me of spying. I told them I didn't know what they were talking about, and they brought me here and locked me up.'

'Where is the drone now?' Jones asked.

'They took it, sir, and smashed it,' Skunk said with an air of anger.

'What was the brand and model of it?'

'It was a DroneX Pro; it was a gift.'

'We have that drone. How did they smash it, Peter?'

'They shot it with a gun, sir.'

'Mmm, do you have your licence on you or any ID?'

'No, they took my wallet.'

'What about your phone?'

Skunk took it out, explaining, 'They destroyed it. Put it in a bucket of water, sir.'

Skunk showed Jones that it didn't work, but that was because it was completely flat.

Jones made a note of his details, name, address, and a brief description of his story.

'All right, well I think these good people want to take you to the hospital to get checked out, but don't leave town, okay?'

As the ambulance officer was closing the doors at the rear, Jones grabbed it.

'Peter, one more thing, how did you get to Aileron with the drone?'

Skunk choked; he hadn't thought of that. He tried to think fast.

'Motorcycle, sir,' Skunk blurted.

'With a big drone like that, I find that hard to believe.'

'It folds up small in the case, and I tied it onto the back of the seat.'

'What sort of bike is it, son?'

'Harley-Davidson, sir.'

'And the rego number, colour, and model?'

'I can't remember. It's black, though.'

'Of course it is,' Jones said.

Jones nodded to the paramedic to close the door. Skunk relaxed back onto the gurney. That didn't go as well as he had planned, but anyway, he was the only Viper not dead or in handcuffs. He figured if the same woman was behind the counter when he arrived at the hospital as when he was there with the broken arm, he might be in trouble, and it wouldn't be long before they realised he'd given them a false name and address as well.

CHAPTER FOURTEEN

GREG was the first awake the next morning. He showered and spent more time in front of the mirror than he had ever done before in his life. He stepped back into the bedroom and looked at Kara, who had shared his bed. She was still asleep.

Wow, what a week, he thought.

He heard someone put the kettle on, and he continued to dress. He tapped Kara on the shoulder and asked her if she wanted to come to the airport. She declined but said she would clean up while everyone was gone. Greg bent over and kissed her cheek and whispered, 'Thank you.'

Greg rounded up the troops and headed for the airport in his charcoal-grey Mercedes-AMG C63, a damn sight nicer to drive than the little truck that he had just done fifteen hundred kilometres in. Steve's leg had improved further overnight, and he was even able to carry his own bag now. Greg watched Donna and Steve at the boarding gate. Donna turned and blew him a kiss, and Steve just gave a short wave as they disappeared down the airbridge. He realised he would probably never see either of them ever again. That did feel very strange.

He bought a coffee and sat, waiting for the flight from Sydney that would deliver Jennifer to him.

His phone beeped: it was Kara.

> I hope she is everything and more than you remember x

Greg smiled; Kara was one in a million. They'd been lovers before, and would still get together on the odd occasion if they ended up in the same place, succumbing to reminiscent wine and lust. But first and foremost, they were best friends. Kara had been there through thick and thin for him, and him for her. They each knew their strengths and weaknesses. When Greg's fiancée died in a freak car crash years ago, she was there by his side till he could once again face the world. He'd saved her too, from some turbulent, emotionally abusive situations. Moreover, they understood each other, and the respect was unconditional. Kara knew and accepted Greg's biggest weakness, that of his ability to fall hopelessly in love at a first encounter. She knew this was what had happened with Jennifer. After just one night of passion on that Caribbean cruise, he fell, hook, line, and sinker. Kara would always offer counsel, but never judge him, and encouraged him to follow his heart. They had each other's back—always.

QF755 from Sydney touched down and was taxiing to the gate. Greg was hit with a wave of doubt. *How do I act?* he thought. *I'll just play it cool, I guess.*

Jennifer was the first person off the plane. His mouth dropped, his heart pounding.

Her searching eyes found him in seconds, and the most beautiful smile formed on her face. Her radiance was so overwhelming in that moment. Greg thought he was going to pass out.

His feet finally registered the need to move, and he walked slowly towards her, managing a smile. She held out her arms, and he filled them. Her head fell softly against his chest. The perfumed smell of her hair brought back the vivid memories of their first kiss, shared tenderly as they stood against the rear rail of the cruise liner, their skin caressed by the warm Caribbean breeze. He didn't want to let her go, and she made no effort either. She felt so perfect in his arms. Eventually, he relaxed and pulled slowly away. His index finger slid across her forehead, pulling the hair away from her damp eyes. They had still not said a word; they didn't need to. He clasped her face in his hands and kissed her lips softly, then turned, took her hand, and they headed for the baggage carousel. He had never felt happier. He kept looking at her in disbelief, before finally saying,

'I can't believe you are here.'

'Neither can I, Greg.'

As Jennifer's four identical cases arrived, Greg said, 'So not just an overnight bag for you, then?'

'You never know. I might like Adelaide,' she said with a smile. Her American accent seemed much stronger now.

'I hope you do,' he said, looking back at her. 'Jennifer, these cases won't fit in my car. Let's put them in a taxi, and he can follow us.'

'Okay, that will be fine. It's just clothes and stuff.'

Kara was receiving Jennifer's cases from the taxi when they

pulled up at Greg's house in the AMG.

Greg jumped out and ran around to open Jennifer's door. Kara and Jennifer's eyes met. Instantly, Jennifer turned back to Greg. 'Are you sure I should be here? Isn't she the lady you were on the cruise with? I don't understand.'

'Of course you should be here. It's all right,' Greg said, as he escorted Jennifer towards his front door.

'Kara, meet Jennifer… again.'

Kara moved up and gave her a gentle hug. 'Lovely to meet you properly, Jennifer. I'm so pleased you are here.' She stepped back, offering a wide smile, then started down the path to leave. 'Greg, I'll get going or I'll be late for work.'

Greg paced to catch Kara, gave her a quick hug, and kissed her on the cheek. 'Thank you, Kara.'

As he turned back to Jennifer, he saw her still-perplexed expression. He took both of her hands in his. 'Jennifer, it's okay. Kara's my best friend, I had guests last night, and she came over to help. She was the one who encouraged me to go to Dallas to find you.'

He could feel her calm restoring as she said, 'My God—did she really?'

'Yes, she's a great friend. Now come on in…,' Greg said as he took hold of two of Jennifer's bags. Jennifer tried to help, when Greg protested and took it from her.

He looked at her and asked, 'What room shall I put them in?'

She smiled, walked towards him, and kissed him, a long passionate kiss.

As they parted, Greg nodded with a smile and took her bags to his bedroom.

Skunk was almost unrecognisable to the admissions staff with the two black eyes and the plaster that was taped to his face holding the nasal splint in place. It was just as well, because as he had suspected, the same lady was there at reception. He needed to get out between when her shift finished and her next one started.

The doctor had arrived to check on him around seven o'clock, asking about the plastered arm and what had caused the trauma to his face. He decided to give as little detail as he could get away with, in case a better story came to him later.

'I was punched,' was all he said.

'And held against your will, I believe?'

The doctor checked his wrists and was surprised to not see any marks from being in cable ties for three days.

Skunk noticed and said, 'They weren't very tight, luckily. They must have figured, with a broken arm, I wasn't much of a threat.'

The doctor nodded. 'Well, Peter, your nose will fix itself. Leave the nasal splint on for a week and come back and see us. Has the nurse done your paperwork yet?' the doctor asked.

'The forms are over there for me to fill out,' Skunk replied.

The doctor picked up the clipboard and handed it to him.

'Once that is done, I am happy for you to go. I will see you in a week, okay?'

'Thanks, Doc,' Skunk said. He quickly wrote "Thank you everyone," on the sheet, as the doctor moved onto the next room. 'Now, Constable Reed.'

Skunk knew it was now or never. He could either sneak out

now and disappear, or stay and ride out his alibi that the police weren't swallowing as well as he had hoped. He decided to make a run for it.

Greg offered for Jennifer to have a shower and freshen up, as he wanted to show her around the beautiful city of Adelaide.

Greg's phone rang; it was Ben.

'Mate, we need to get rid of that Avis truck, albeit fifteen hundred kilometres away from where it was supposed to be, and the person who hired it is dead.'

'Would you like me to run it over to you? It could be a chance for Jennifer to see what the other side looks like.'

'Haha, sure, whenever you are ready. How is it going? Was it worth chasing her around the world?'

'My God, yes. I can't even start to explain it,' Greg said.

'That's good to hear, by the way, I am going to fly up to Alice in a couple of days and grab my Jeep. Donna's father wanted me to see if I can find out a little more about what happened to the bikies, see if they are all dead or in jail. It may just help void the debt he owes them.'

'That's good for him, I guess. I'll see you soon, Ben.'

'Greg, before you go, I found out a little more about the Madisons. He is a nasty piece of work, so if this is going to be any more than just a little bit of fun, we will need to talk.'

'Got it, thanks. See you shortly.'

This was the first time Ben's warning had sunk in. If Ben thought he was nasty, he must be really bad.

Greg called his chauffeur friend Jim to see if he was free and could meet them at Ben's house.

The sight of Jennifer emerging from the bedroom cleared all those thoughts from his mind. If this was all meant to be a few days of fun before she left and headed back to her real life in Texas, he wanted to make the most of it.

'And I thought you couldn't possibly look more beautiful,' he said, shaking his head and looking at her from head to toe. 'We have a little job to do for a friend, if that is all right?' Greg said.

'Sure, I am in your hands.'

Greg smiled as he imagined just that, in a few hours' time.

He took her hand as they walked out to the dirty little Avis truck that was parked opposite his home.

'Well, I can say I have never been in one of these before,' she said with a grin.

Greg helped her step up into the truck, then walked around and hopped in the other side.

Jennifer felt like she was in another world, the freedom of no one knowing who she was, or who she was married to. No man would even look at her in Texas, as her husband would have him dealt with by Jerry. She despised Jerry; he was a horrid man, just as mean as her husband—but the only difference was that Keith didn't get his hands dirty. Jennifer knew that Jerry had made people disappear who'd owed her husband money, or worse, who'd just got in his way. She was just one of Keith's assets, a beautiful woman to have by his side. She knew she would have to return to Texas, no matter how wonderful she felt here. He would never let her go.

She craved that adorable feeling of love, intimacy, and romance. Something the man sitting next to her in this little truck gave to her on that one night out at sea. They pulled up at Ben's apartment, and Ben met them as they alighted.

A black Chrysler was already there waiting.

Greg introduced Jennifer to Ben, who greeted her with a knowing smile.

'I appreciate you dropping it back to me, Greg. Let's talk when you get a chance, hey?'

Ben shook their hands and watched them walk over to the black Chrysler, holding hands like two school sweethearts. But he could now see what all the fuss was about.

'You're playing with fire, my friend,' Ben said under his breath as the two of them left.

'Where to, Mr Sheppard?' Jim asked.

'To Glenelg please, Jim. We will have a late breakfast and then to my favourite winery at the top of Kensington Road please; you know the one.'

'Yes, sir, I do.'

CHAPTER FIFTEEN

CONSTABLE Will Jackson had asked the sarge if he could pick up Reed from the hospital and take her home. He had shared her pain from the shooting. Seeing her lying in that hospital bed tore him apart. He knew the time was approaching fast when he would need to tell her how he felt, how she would make his life complete by them being together.

Jones told him to take the police car so he could park out front.

He pulled to the side of the emergency doors, making sure he didn't obstruct the path of any ambulances. He walked in, nodding to Jan at the counter, when he remembered the sarge had asked him to check up on the lad from the bikie camp. He stopped and walked back.

'Hey, Jan, Sarge asked me to check up on a Peter Watkins that came in last night around 2:00 a.m.'

'If it's who I think you mean, he's gone. He shot through

straight after the doctor saw him this morning.'

Jackson looked a little more concerned.

'The sarge is very interested in this character. Do you have his sheet?'

'Yes, but he put his name down as "Thank you everyone,"' she said.

'Don't you have a nurse to make sure all that is done properly?' Jackson said, reaching for his phone.

'We are desperately short-staffed, Will. You know that,' Jan replied.

'Sarge, Peter Watkins is gone, walked out the door sometime early this morning.'

'Damn,' Jones said.

'Okay, Jackson, collect Reed, take her home and then get in here. I want him found. He's one of them, I'm sure of it.'

Constable Reed seemed pretty glad to see Jackson arrive and to get her out of the stale hospital room.

'What's been happening, Jackson?' Reed asked once they were in the police car.

'We got all the bikies, every single one of them. They tried to make a run for it just as the sarge said they would. We had every police tactical member from Adelaide to Darwin hiding in the scrub, and we grabbed them as soon as they came out of a tunnel that was at the rear of the building. It was like fishing in a fishbowl.'

This would have been a dream come true for Reed. Sarge had said this was her gig; she would have been known as the constable who brought down a whole bikie gang. But no, she had been lying on her back in a hospital bed sucking oxygen because she was stupid enough to do what she did.

Jackson could see her disappointment at not being part of the action and said, 'Maybe one got away?'

'What do you mean?' Reed looked over with a little more enthusiasm.

'We found a young man, twenties, face bashed in, blood everywhere, arm in plaster, locked in a cell in the back of the building. Sarge is a little suspicious of him.'

'Why, what's his story?'

'Apparently, his story goes, he stumbled across them out at Aileron, and they beat him and locked him up.'

'Where is he now?' Reed asked.

'We don't know. He gave the sarge and the hospital a fake name and snuck out this morning.'

'He must have been in the room next to me. I heard them come in in the early hours. Take me to the station. I want to follow this up.'

'No, Bec, you need to rest!'

'Bullshit, I missed the best day of my life because I was on my back in that bloody hospital. I want to get onto this.'

'Okay, but Sarge will crack it.'

'Leave that to me,' she said.

By the time Senior Sergeant Jones arrived at the station, Reed was already at the whiteboard in his office plotting out what they knew so far. The gun found by the mall patrol had fingerprints that matched the dead bikie at Aileron. A John Smith called in the crash and then told them about the compound where three dead bodies, a drug lab, and many stolen Harley-Davidson motorcycles were found. The next morning, a man presented at the hospital with a broken arm. John Smith called in again to report there would be a shoot-out between the Vipers and some other gang. Reed stepped back to look at the board. *The police were called for what? To observe?* she thought.

'Reed, what are you doing here?' Jones said as he walked into his office.

She ignored his question. 'Sarge, look at this. I am trying to join the dots together here.'

'You know they had a drone up watching it all? The airport picked it up on their radar,' Jones said.

'That means there could be a recording of the whole event,' Rebecca said. 'Do you think the dead bikie's gun was put into the police car by the person who presented with the broken arm?'

'Broken arm? Peter Watkins, or whatever his name is, had his arm in plaster,' Jones said.

'But he couldn't have placed the gun in the patrol car because he would have still been in hospital.'

'So, maybe we can assume this Peter Watkins was the driver in that rollover at Aileron?'

'So who cut the seat belt to get him out? And if he was a captive of the Vipers, why was he driving the car?'

'Reed, what can you tell me about the men that dragged you to safety and took you to the hospital?'

'There were four or five of them,' she said, trying desperately to remember. 'And there was a girl, Sarge, there was a girl in the back as well. She was helping me. I remember now. She had dark hair and was dressed in very dirty jeans and what was probably once a white shirt.'

'Why would she be there? What part would she play?' Jones said, holding his chin again.

'Sarge, I think the question is, why were they all there?'

'I think we can also assume one of those men is our John Smith,' Jones said, his fingers still rubbing his chin.

'Yes, I am sure of it,' Rebecca said, drawing lines to connect items on the board. 'Could the mystery gang that were shooting at the Vipers be part of John Smith's team?' she said.

'If so, why would he call us to be there? That doesn't make sense,' Jones said.

'What if the girl was a hostage and we were the decoys while they went in?'

'Through the tunnel,' Jones said.

'So where is our John Smith now?' Jones pondered.

'Reed, you said they took you to the hospital in a truck?'

'Yes, sir, a small one, like a hire one.'

'Check all the traffic cameras and see if you can get a rego on it, and find out who owns those scooters.'

'Great idea, Sarge.' Reed walked off to her desk to make some calls.

Jones was sitting back behind his desk, staring at the whiteboard, trying to make some sense of it all, when Reed rushed back into his office.

'I got him, sir! An Avis truck was hired by a Reuben Bukowski.'

Jones looked slowly up at Reed, who was obviously a little surprised he wasn't more excited by the information.

'What?' she said.

'That's our dead bikie, Reed,' Jones said slowly.

'Oh, he's good; I'll give him that,' Reed said, turning and walking back out of Jones's office.

'And the scooters, Reed?' Jones called out.

'Bukowski!' she called back.

Skunk knew he had to lay low for a while and, as soon as the heat was off, to get the hell out of Alice. He guessed they would have roadblocks on the roads out of town by now. He had a little unit just on the other side of the Todd River and plenty of money thanks to the $10K the Roo-man had given him to fly the drone. The supermarket would deliver, so he would just have to bide his time. He knew the Vipers were finished and doubted any would talk. If one did, he could be in trouble, although Pig was probably the only one who knew his real name. Once his arm was better, he would cut the plaster off, maybe grow a beard, shave his head, and no one would know him. He couldn't ride his bike until the plaster was off anyway. His phone was still in his pocket; it had been flat for three days now, and he might just charge it but not turn it on, just in case they worked out who he was and tracked him by his phone. He then realised that didn't make sense anyway, and he turned it on.

Ben's car would not be ready for another two days, but as he didn't have any work outstanding, he decided he might go and meet Mr DeLuca and finalise the account. Then back to Alice to see what had happened to the Vipers and collect his car. He would also love to give the new drone to Skunk to thank him for his help.

Ben booked a flight for the next day. He would leave the little truck near the Avis depot at the airport. He figured it would take them a few days to find it and then another day to tell the Alice Springs police where it was found. Ben spent the rest of the day cleaning out the back of the truck and wiping off any fingerprints and the blood from Steve's leg.

Jim picked Greg and Jennifer up from Glenelg after their light brunch. He then took them to the winery at Magill. It was Greg's most favourite place in the whole world: the cellar door was world-class, the restaurant one of the best in Adelaide, and the wine was just to die for. They did the one-hour tour, which covered the history of the founding winemakers, including a walk through the little house they lived in when they planted the first grapevines. Then it was to the cellar door for an exclusive tasting of the amazing premium reds. It was after that they were escorted to their table in the restaurant. They held hands at every opportunity, softly running their fingers along each other's.

'So, what have you been up to, Greg?' Jennifer asked.

'Well, this week, we were shot at with machine guns while rescuing a female hostage from a Mexican drug cartel, and then raided a bikie stronghold through a secret tunnel, while a shoot-out with police was happening outside.'

'Wow, that sounds so exciting. What will that movie be called?' Jennifer asked.

Greg smiled and said, 'It might just be called *Ben*.'

Greg ordered a bottle of Bin 169 to go with the seven-course, three-hour degustation meal. He asked Jennifer about her life in Texas, but he could tell it was something she wanted left for now. As each sip of 169 was consumed and each bite of food eaten, they both knew they were getting closer to the moment when, for them, the world would stop turning and they would share that exquisite erotic passion that only a true love could produce.

CHAPTER SIXTEEN

BEN arrived in Darwin to be greeted by a very happy Frank DeLuca. The little Italian millionaire hugged him the minute he walked through the gate into the airport lounge.

Ben jumped as he squeezed. 'Broken ribs, I think, Mr DeLuca.'

'Shit, I'm sorry,' DeLuca said, pulling away. 'Ben, I cannot thank you and your men enough. Donna is now safe with my sister,' DeLuca said with almost a tear in his eye, as they turned and started towards the exit.

'I will always be in your debt. And, Ben,' DeLuca said, touching Ben on the forearm to get his full attention.

Ben slowed and looked at him.

'I am a very good person to have owe you a favour.'

Ben fully acknowledged the statement, and replied, 'I appreciate that, and thank you, Mr DeLuca.'

DeLuca treated Ben like a celebrity. He gently pushed aside the driver to open the car door for him. The driver took the case from Ben that contained the drone and his rucksack, and placed them in the boot of the Mercedes-Benz S500.

Once they were both seated in the back seat, DeLuca turned to Ben and said, 'Tell me about the Vipers. What has happened to them?'

'We invited the police to watch the shoot-out between the Mexicans and the Vipers. I did hope the police would catch them all, but the Mexicans did get away. The Vipers were pinned down with really with no way out; we couldn't hang around to watch the end of the movie, if you know what I mean.'

'If the Vipers are out of action, that does reduce my potato problem significantly,' DeLuca said.

'Mr DeLuca, I will be calling into Alice on my way home. I'll see what I can find out for you, but I'm pretty sure it will be good news.'

'I will appreciate finding out as soon as you know,' DeLuca said. 'Ben, today, you are royalty to me. Whatever in your wildest dreams you would like, please tell me and it is yours. Food, wine, boat cruise, a lady or ladies—it's yours.'

Ben smiled. 'Sir, as delicious as that all sounds, I have a flight booked for Alice later today. I just wanted to run through the costs with you and return what we didn't spend.'

DeLuca looked at him. 'Ben, there will be another $250K being transferred into your account tonight, and if the Vipers are all locked up, you will be getting that amount again when that is confirmed.'

'I have already included a heathy charge for my time in my original costings.'

'Keep whatever is left over. You saved my daughter; that is a small price for me to pay.'

'Thank you, Mr DeLuca, that is very kind.'

Ben was momentarily torn by the fact that he was being paid with drug money, but he decided he would donate a good portion of it rather than just let it be paid to the Mexican cartel, plus, after all, he was technically unemployed now.

DeLuca's first thought was for Ben to get to Alice Springs as soon as he could to find out whether he was fifteen million dollars better off, but quickly decided whatever had happened was not going to change in a day. Ben Woolford had risked his life to save his precious daughter; that did need to be rewarded.

'Ben, why don't we change your flight to tomorrow? I would like to show my appreciation.'

Ben went to refuse the offer, as he hated changing plans once they were in place, but then thought, *Hell, why not?*

'I accept your offer, Mr DeLuca, thank you.'

'One condition though,' DeLuca said.

'Yes?' Ben said.

'You must call me Frank.'

'Thank you—Frank.'

'Driver, please call the casino and book the best room they have available for Mr Woolford please.'

'Yes, Mr DeLuca, sir.'

The Mercedes pulled up at the casino front doors, and two doormen opened each of the two rear doors. Ben and DeLuca hopped out. Ben only had his rucksack, which really didn't contain much, just a toothbrush, razor, two walkie-talkies, Ferret's satphone, the new charger he had to buy for it, and a simple change of clothes.

Certainly nothing to wear to the places DeLuca would be expecting to dine. The little Italian walked swiftly to the reception desk with Ben two steps behind.

DeLuca looked at the name badge of the young man behind the desk.

'James, this is Mr Woolford. I want him in the absolute best room you have available.'

'He already is, sir.'

'Thank you. He's to have whatever he wants whenever he wants it, okay?' DeLuca said, handing the young lad a fresh one-hundred-dollar note.

'Yes, sir. Thank you, sir.'

'Everything is to be charged to me. You know who I am, right?'

'Yes, Mr DeLuca, sir. Please leave it to me.'

James looked at Ben, who just shrugged and smiled back.

DeLuca turned to Ben. 'Ben, please enjoy the afternoon here. The pool bar is fantastic, and the scenery breathtaking, if you know what I mean. If you decide to walk along the beach, stay away from the water. The lizards are a little snappy.'

Ben just smiled back and nodded.

'This place has the best Chinese restaurant in town. Do you like Chinese, Ben?'

'Love it!' Ben replied with enthusiasm.

'Great, I will see you at the Dragon Court Restaurant at 7:00 p.m. Can you arrange that please, James?'

DeLuca turned and walked back to his Mercedes.

James had already come around from the desk and took the drone case from Ben.

'Please follow me, sir,' James said. 'Mr Woolford, I would like to show you three types of rooms. Please let me know which you prefer. All our suites are beautiful.'

James opened the door to a ground-floor suite. 'Here you have our best, the Mindil Lagoon Suite with private pool.'

'That is amazing, but I would really like an ocean view if I can,' Ben said.

'Of course, Mr Woolford. Please follow me.'

They took the elevator to the top floor, and James opened the door to the Grand Suite.

'This is perfect, thank you, James.'

James placed the drone case on the floor and asked, 'Will there be anything else, sir?'

'Actually, I might need some clothes for tonight. Where do you recommend?'

'Either Casuarina or Smith Street Mall, sir. I can have a driver ready in ten minutes.'

'Let's make it thirty minutes, thanks, James,' Ben said.

'Yes, sir, thirty minutes.'

Ben watched James close the door behind him and then walked out onto the balcony. He stood facing the sea. The warm tropical breeze teased his hair and chilled the perspiration on his brow. He took in a deep breath and thought back to only a week ago, when he was lying on the hot desert sand, staking out a bikie compound under a gum tree in the middle of nowhere. What a week it had been. He thought of Dan and Steve; he hoped his leg would make a full recovery. He thought of Greg, just a local businessman out of Adelaide who put his own life on the line without question to help save Steve, who was lying injured, stranded in the crossfire. And Peter, the pretend bikie. He was probably in jail now with the rest of them. He went inside and took out Ferret's satphone and sent Skunk a message.

Ben went back out to the balcony, pulled out a chair, and with his feet up on the second, dialled the Alice Springs police station.

'Alice Springs Police, Constable Reed speaking.'

'Rebecca, John Smith. I would like to meet with you if that is possible?'

'Ah, Mr. Smith, you have been busy, and thank you for saving my life by the way.'

She wasn't completely sure that it was him, but his response would confirm it.

'My pleasure, Rebecca. I see you are all better, so it wasn't too serious then? You didn't look too good the last time I saw you.'

'It was just a collapsed lung and cracked ribs in the end, and some very serious bruising. You should see it.'

'I'd like to see that,' Ben said.

'That's a bit naughty, Mr Smith."

'I would like to meet. Just you and me, off duty, off the record. I can help you with information and, maybe you could help me with a little as well?' Ben said.

Reed was straight into police mode. She could trap him, lock him up, and close this case with all the perpetrators in jail. She would be commended by the commissioner for sure, and make first-class constable in her first year. But then she remembered this man did risk his life to save her. He was even shot, she recalled.

'You were shot as well, weren't you?' Reed asked.

'Yes, my vest saved me. Broke a rib or two, though.'

'I'm really sorry about that. Where would you like to meet?' Reed asked.

'Let's say Sportie's, twelve o'clock tomorrow. Give me your number, and I will call you.'

Reed's police ear could hear people at a pool in the background, splashing and yelling, also the music from the outside speakers. *There is only one place in Alice he could be, The Gap Hotel,* she thought.

'It's a date,' she said back and gave him the station's mobile phone number.

'Rebecca, I can trust you, right?'

'Yes, of course. I will see you tomorrow.'

Ten minutes later, two police officers rushed in through The Gap Hotel's front door. The officers had a good description of who they were after, but no one was even close to fitting the bill.

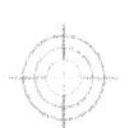

Ben went to the mall and bought some casual clothes and a pair of shorts to wear at the pool bar. He ordered a light lunch before the driver took him back to the Casino Resort. He took them up to his room and checked the satphone for a reply from Skunk. Nothing. He must have been caught. *Too bad,* he thought. *He could have made something of himself.*

He realised then that he had probably dragged the drone across Australia for nothing. *Oh well.*

He put the satphone away and headed for the pool bar. James spotted him and rushed from the front reception.

'Mr Woolford, sir, our special guests can sit in this exclusive area if you would like?'

'No, thank you, James. Just by the main pool will be fine.'

James waved to an attendant to bring over a lounge and umbrella.

Ben ordered a drink and lay back against the chair. Mr DeLuca was right; the scenery was magnificent. It did remind him that it had been a while now since he had had a woman. It'd been all work and no play for Mr Woolford.

CHAPTER SEVENTEEN

GREG Sheppard awoke to see her lying there, her soft golden-chestnut hair partially concealing the side of her beautiful face. Her naked body was shadowed by the grey Egyptian cotton sheet. *Could anything possibly look more beautiful?* he thought. An explosion of warmth pulsed through his body from his heart to the tips of his fingers and toes. He exhaled as he felt a wave of contentment shroud him. Then the little pang of guilt as he knew he had made love to another man's wife, but somehow in this moment that didn't seem to matter so much. He knew he was on a runaway train, but as long as she was in his arms when it crashed, he didn't care.

As the transition from her blissful sleep to the real world filtered through, the realisation of where she was enveloped her, and it was the most wonderful feeling. Last night she had given her body and soul to a man she hardly knew. He had penetrated them both to the depth of her inner being. She had felt love before, but nothing like this. She knew now, she could not return to Dallas. She slowly opened her eyes to see his deep brown eyes smiling back at her. A smile burst onto her face, and she quickly pulled the sheet over her head to hide. Greg gently pulled it back and softly moved away the hair that covered her face.

'Good morning,' he said as he ran his fingertips gently down the side of her face.

'How do you feel?' he asked softly.

'I might still be a little drunk,' she said with a shy smile.

'You know what I mean,' he said with an even softer tone.

She did know what he meant. She hesitated while the right words found her lips.

Her look changed as she took his hand in hers.

'I am so deeply in love with you, Greg Sheppard,' she said softly.

He drew her into his arms and held her tight. Uncontrollable tears filled their eyes. Neither of their worlds would ever be the same again.

They showered together, and although they washed each other's bodies tenderly, they resisted the urge to end up back in bed, knowing they each had some serious decisions to make.

They walked down to the River Torrens and followed the path that would eventually lead to their lunch at the convention centre. They held hands as they walked. It was more of a stroll, really.

'Jennifer, what would you like to do?'

'For lunch or my life?' she asked, smiling, but before he could reply she said, 'It would be the same answer anyway. I want to spend it with you.'

Greg's heart rate increased. That was exactly what he wanted to hear her say.

'That's what I want too, my darling,' he said as he stopped to kiss her.

'Get a room!' a young lad yelled as he and his mate rode past on their push bikes.

They both burst out laughing.

They started strolling again.

'Would you live with me here in Adelaide?' Greg asked.

'Anywhere except the US. We would not be safe there,' Jennifer said without realising that was going to begin a lot of explaining.

'What do you mean?' Greg asked.

'Greg, my husband is a powerful man over there, dangerously powerful. When I call to tell him that I've fallen in love with an Australian and won't be coming home, he will be angry. Extremely angry.'

'I see. What is the best way to handle that then?'

'I don't think there is one. We will just have to set off the bomb, and hopefully we survive the explosion,' Jennifer said.

Greg stopped, pulled her to him, and whispered in her ear, 'Whatever it takes.'

'Sarge, we found the truck parked near the Avis depot at the Adelaide Airport,' Rebecca said.

'So they drove to Adelaide and flew home to wherever from there. They are long gone then,' Jones said.

'Maybe not, sir. I had a call from John Smith. He wants to meet me tomorrow in the mall.'

'So, he is still here then?'

'It does appear that way, sir. I could hear a pool, music, and lots of people in the background on the phone.'

'The Gap maybe?' Jones said.

'I sent a patrol down there straight away, and no one matched the description.'

'How do you want to handle it, Reed?'

'I figure I meet him, see what he has to say, and we nab him on his way out.'

'Okay, it's your baby, but keep me informed, all right?'

'Yes, sir.'

'And Reed, don't shoot anyone.'

'Yes, sir,' she said as she walked out.

'And don't get shot… again!' he yelled out.

'Yes, sir! Don't get shot! Got it!' she called back.

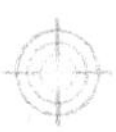

It was time for Ben to head up to his room and get ready for dinner. He showered and dressed and was already seated in the Dragon Court Restaurant when DeLuca arrived. Ben was happy for DeLuca to order, and of course he ordered far more than they could possibly eat. DeLuca asked about the details of the rescue, and Ben recounted every step, about finding the Mexicans and rescuing Donna, only to lose her again in a double-cross. He told him about the tunnel and the brave team of four that he recruited. How they had to drop a wounded police officer to the hospital to maybe save her life, which did slightly risk their escape. He told him all about the trip back to Adelaide in the little truck and that Steve, on one leg, had delivered Donna to his sister's door. DeLuca didn't interrupt until Ben had finished the story.

He then asked, 'The Mexicans, do you think they are still there?'

'I seriously doubt it. They know that we know where they were and what they did to Donna. I would be surprised if they aren't halfway back to North America. I am planning on telling the police that they were the other gang shooting that night, and where to find them, but I'm sure the place will be empty.'

'Will your man be okay—the one that was shot?' DeLuca asked.

'I believe so, but it is very hard to get a bullet wound looked at without creating a red alert with the cops.'

'How much did you pay your men, Ben?'

'$30K each, Mr DeLuca—err, Frank.'

'Double that, and make sure if there is any issue with the one that was shot, you let me know immediately and I'll get him the medical assistance needed, no questions.'

'Thank you, that is very generous,' Ben said.

They had now well and truly finished the meal and were swallowing the last of the wine.

DeLuca stood and nodded to the head waiter.

Outside the restaurant they shook hands, and DeLuca thanked him again.

'I hope you enjoy the rest of your night, Ben.'

'Thank you,' Ben said, looking at his watch; he was ready for bed.

Ben went up to his room, grabbed his toothbrush, and went out onto the balcony. He stood there cleaning his teeth as he watched the little fishing boats out at sea bobbing up and down in the gentle swell of the Arafura Sea. He was rinsing his mouth when he heard a soft knock on his door. He wiped his mouth and opened the door. A beautiful, tall lady with long blonde hair and a gorgeous smile was standing there. She was wearing a pure white wrap-around dress that contrasted beautifully to her tanned body. She was holding a small bottle of massage oil.

'Hello, Mr Woolford. My name is Cindy. Mr DeLuca said you may like a massage tonight.'

Ben stood there looking at her, still a little confused and unsure. Her eyes were filled with a delicious desire.

Eventually, he said, 'I think I probably do, Cindy,' as he stepped back and welcomed her inside.

Next morning when he awoke, Cindy was gone. He reached for the pillow where her beautiful head had slept and wrapped it around his face. He took in a huge breath, sucking in that delicious, sweet, perfumed smell that she'd left in her wake.

I really do need to do more of that, he thought as he swung his naked body out of bed and headed for the shower. It was 6:30 a.m., and his flight was at 8:00 a.m., so he needed to get moving. He was dressed and in a cab for the airport by 7:00 a.m. His rucksack was heavier now with the new clothes he had bought, and combined with the unexpected exercise through the night, his ribs were hurting again. The drone case was a stretch as carry-on luggage, but being business class, it wasn't questioned. The plane landed at 9:30 a.m. and Ben caught a taxi to the repair shop that had been repairing his Jeep.

By 10:00 a.m. he was in his shiny black Jeep and heading for the Todd mall.

He sat at the Red Dog Café with a coffee and decided to call his team to tell them of their little pay rise. He called Dan first, who insisted that he be called if there were any more jobs like that one. Ben assured him that he hoped not. Then Steve, who confirmed he had managed to get the antibiotics and that his leg was well on the mend. He told him that he was now walking around with only a small limp.

He called Greg, who was with Jennifer at their breakfast destination.

'Hello, Ben, nice to hear from you. Should I ask where you are?'

'In Alice, mate, just tying up some loose ends from our job. How about you? How's it going with Jennifer?' Ben asked.

Greg said, 'Mate, I made love to a beautiful angel last night.'

So did I, Ben thought to himself.

'Well, that must mean you are going to heaven,' Ben said. 'Now, Greg, about the money I owe you…'

'That's all cool, mate. Whatever is fine; it was a great adventure.'

'No, I met with Donna's father last night, and he has insisted that everyone is paid double, $60K for your part, so you will need to send me your bank details.'

'Wow, that's not bad for a limo-driving job, but double ten is not sixty.'

'Greg, you put your arse on the line as much as we all did. You deserve the same amount.'

'Well, I'm not going to argue with you!' Greg said.

Ben laughed. 'Better go, mate. Talk soon, and have fun, you two.'

Ben reached in and took out the satphone. There was a message from Skunk.

Hi Roo-man. In hiding, cops are probably looking for me.

Ben sent a message back.

Can we meet? I have a present for you.

A drone?

Yes, the drone, and one little favour as well.

Meet me in the back car park of the Hilton Double tree, ten minutes.

See you there.

Ten minutes later, Ben pulled up in the Jeep. Skunk appeared from nowhere, opened the door, and slid into the passenger seat.

'How's the nose, Peter?'

'Not too bad now. I'm guessing you got the girl out alright?'

'Yes, all safe; thank you for your help. I do understand why you did what you did.'

'I felt terrible, but Pig was going to kill me.'

'I get it. What happened to the Vipers?'

'I don't know really, but by the time I came out, there were none of them around. They were either all locked up or all got away. I do appreciate you giving me the drone,' Skunk said.

'I do need one last favour.'

'What's that?' Skunk asked.

'I am meeting with a cop who has promised to meet on her own, and I don't trust her. I want you to watch for any other cops that might be hiding in the shadows,' Ben said.

'Easy. When is it?'

Ben looked at his watch. 'In half an hour's time. You can launch from the other side of the river so you are safe.'

Ben gave him a radio and told him his plan in detail and exactly what to look for.

Ben set up at the Red Dog Café and watched Constable Rebecca Reed walk past on her way towards Sportie's Bar from the police station.

'Peter, do you have her?'

'Yes, I'm zoomed right in. It's her.'

'Nothing else?'

'Nothing yet,' Skunk said.

Ben could see Rebecca in the distance take a seat at one of the outside tables.

'Roo-man, I see a man on his own heading that way, could be

a cop.'

'Watch him, over.'

'There's another now, Roo-man.'

'Roger that.'

Ben called Rebecca on Ferret's satphone.

'Hi, Rebecca. I have changed the location. Can you head up the mall to the north, take the first turn left, and head west till I tell you to stop?'

'Why have you changed you mind, John?'

'I have learnt lately not to trust people.'

'Okay, but it's all good. I'm on my own.'

'Get going. I'll call back in a minute.'

Reed started off, her head searching for him. She turned the corner and headed west as instructed.

'Roo-man, three men running down the mall.'

'Yeah, I can see them. Thanks, mate. Pack it up; I'll meet you back at the Jeep.'

Ben just let her walk and didn't call her back. She would soon know he'd picked the set-up.

When Ben arrived back at the Jeep, Skunk had the drone all packed up and in the case.

'Peter, I just need the video card from the drone and it's all yours.'

Skunk popped open the case and removed the two one-terabyte cards from the drone.

'Everything is on these two cards,' Skunk said.

'Thank you, Peter, for all your help. I will keep in touch.'

Skunk held out his hand. 'I appreciate the drone. I promise I'll stay on the straight and narrow from now on.'

Ben shook his hand, and he disappeared through the foliage and was gone.

Ben called Rebecca.

'You didn't ring me back?' she said indignantly.

'Yeah, well the three cops running down the mall behind you discouraged me.'

'I don't know anything about that,' she said even less convincingly.

'Rebecca, you are young and keen to fast-track your way up the ranks, I get that, but sometimes you have to give a little before you can take. I'm not a baddy. I want them locked up as well. I was going to tell you everything I know, who the other gang was that killed the three bikies at Aileron and had the shoot-out at the clubrooms. I could give you video footage from our drone of the whole event, and the shoot-out at Amoonguna that you don't even know about. You stuffed it, Rebecca. I'm so disappointed, especially after I risked my bloody life to save your arse and risked our escape to take you to the bloody hospital.'

Ben could tell he was letting his anger get the best of him as he went on.

He hoped she felt terrible, that she was selfish, how her own self-promotion had been all she was interested in.

'I am really sorry,' she said softly. 'You are right; you did save my arse and I did that to you. I sincerely apologise.'

'Rebecca, if you tell me what happened to the Vipers, I will tell you who the other gang shooting the other night was.'

'We caught them all, except one. He tricked us, but we will get him.'

'Where are they all now?'

'They were all put on a plane to the Darwin Correctional

Centre, awaiting trial.'

'How long will they get, do you think?'

'With all the drugs, stolen property, and firearms, the sarge thinks they'll easily get fifteen to twenty.'

'Let's hope it's twenty, hey?'

'What can you tell me about the shoot-out at Amoonguna?' Reed asked, sounding calmer now.

'Mexican drug lord, top dog, Manuel Gonzales. Get him, and you shut them down as well.'

He told her his modified version of the story, in that the Vipers owed the Mexican cartel money and about eight had come over from Mexico to collect. Also, that they were the ones who killed the three bikies at Aileron and that he had photographed the whole event. He told her there may be two bodies buried out there as well. He suggested to her that they might be on their way out of the country as we speak, probably Sydney, as their vehicles were NSW registered. He told her to get on to the AFP and try and catch them as they try to leave.

'I appreciate all of that, especially with what I did to you.'

'Now I want a favour, Rebecca.'

'If I can,' she said sheepishly.

'I want you to take the heat off that missing Viper. He's a good lad and helped me get this stuff for you. He flew the drone for us, a good operator. He wants to go clean; he's no threat to society.'

'I will do what I can, but the sarge wants him pretty bad.'

'Do what you can for me. I will be in touch as I find out more information.'

'Can I have the pictures you have of the shoot-out?' Rebecca asked.

'I might just keep them for now in case I need another favour.

I will call back in a week.'

'John, John, one more question.'

'Yes?'

'Who was the girl?'

'An innocent bystander who the Mexicans kidnapped and raped. I was contracted to rescue her.'

Ben hung up and called DeLuca.

'Ben, what can you tell me?'

'Frank, the Vipers are in the Darwin Correction Centre, every one of them. Cops expect them to get fifteen to twenty depending on their roles. AFP will be after the cartel and will try and nab them as they attempt to leave the country.'

'That is very good news.'

'Yes, I guess it is,' Ben said back without emotion. 'Frank, I would like you to do something for me.'

'Anything, you just name it.'

'You are going to make a lot of money now, especially if the Mexicans go down as well.'

'Yes,' DeLuca said.

'Wouldn't it be nice if you became part of the solution to the problem, rather than the cause, and donate a few funds to a rehabilitation program, you know, the ones that want out?'

The phone was silent for a few seconds, and Ben thought he might just have overstepped the mark.

'You are right, Ben. I *will* do that. Let me know what happens with the Mexicans, and if they go down, I will make that donation, very healthy. Thank you. Oh yeah, I hoped you enjoyed dinner last night?'

'Yes, I did. Thank you, Frank, the dessert was especially tasty,' Ben said, smiling as he ended the call.

Still smiling, he started the Jeep and headed for Adelaide.

CHAPTER EIGHTEEN

IBBY, have you heard from Mrs Madison? Her phone has been off for three days.'

'No, sir, not since I helped her load cases into your driver's car, I assumed for a holiday.'

Keith Madison called the driver.

'Yes, Mr Madison, I took her and Libby to the airport on Tuesday as well. They were trying to find a man from Australia.'

'Is that right, is it?' Keith ended the call.

'Libby… Libby, get here now!' Keith screamed.

Libby stepped slowly down the stairs, and Keith moved to stand close in front of her as she reached the bottom step.

'Tell me, what you know, Libby. Where the fuck is she?'

'I don't know, sir. I am just the maid; she doesn't tell me these things.'

Keith took a small step back and slapped her hard across the face. It sent her sprawling across the white marble floor.

'The driver said you and her went to the airport looking for a man!'

Libby made no attempt to get off the floor, she just covered her face as the tears filled her hands.

'Tell me, you stupid lying bitch!' he yelled.

Libby turned her head towards him. She knew the CCTV cameras would show what happened anyway.

'A man came to the door asking for her… I sent him away as she was still in bed. I told her that someone had been here looking for her… and then we tried to find him. I don't know any more.'

Keith walked away, leaving Libby still sobbing uncontrollably on the floor. He made a call.

'Jerry, my fucking wife has gone to Australia. It looks like she is probably fucking some prick down there. I want you to track her down and find out who the fuck she is with.' He slammed shut his phone and went into his office and downloaded the security footage from the front-door camera. He found the part where Greg was waiting at the door, he even looked up at the camera at one stage. Keith studied him. He looked familiar.

'The man from the fucking cruise. That's him, the one that caught her when she fainted.' He remembered now, that he'd whispered something in her ear as she was coming to.

'How the fuck did he find us?' Keith said aloud.

Jerry called the Madison's travel agency and asked for the woman who handled the Madison account.

'Linda, this is Jerry Stokes from the Madison Corporation.'

'Hello, Jerry,' she said politely. 'How can I help you?'

'Linda, Mr Madison is concerned, as Mrs Madison took a trip to Australia a couple of days ago and he hasn't been able to contact her. Are you able to tell me exactly where she went? He just wants to make sure she is all right.'

'Jerry, I can't really give out that information,' Linda said politely.

'Linda, our next step is to call the police, and then they will call you. Telling me now could save us all a lot of time and possibly her life, especially if she is in trouble.'

Jerry waited, as Linda paused for some time.

'Adelaide, South Australia,' she said quietly. 'I can't tell you any more. I am sorry.'

'That's all I need. Thank you,' Jerry said, hanging up.

Jennifer listened to the phone ring, hoping Keith wouldn't pick up, until he did.

'Where the fuck are you? I told you specifically that you must be back here for the cattlemen's annual general meeting.'

'Keith, I won't be coming back. I have met someone, and we are in love.'

'You fucking whore, I know who it is! That fucking dick from the cruise, isn't it? I'll fucking kill you both, you get that?'

'But, Keith, you need to understand—'

'No, Jennifer,' Keith said now in a calm, scary voice. '*You* need to understand, my dear. If I don't have you, no one will.' Then he was gone.

Jennifer looked up at Greg with a terrified look on her face.

'I'm guessing it didn't go too well then?' Greg said.

'We may not survive that bomb, Greg,' she said slowly, trying to control the trembling fear in her voice.

Greg took her in his arms and said, 'Well, we will go down together then.'

Ben pulled into Coober Pedy for fuel and a bed. He found a room in an underground motel. He checked in and walked across the road to the pub for a meal. He had a spring in his step; it had been a big week, the job was a success, he had a bucket load of money in the bank, and he got laid last night. Life could not be better.

Then Ben's phone rang.

'Ben, it's Greg. Mate, you were right. Jennifer's husband is going to try and kill her.'

'Shit, are you sure?'

'He told her he would, and she said that he has had plenty of people killed before who got in his way.'

'She knows that?'

'Yes, she knows things that would destroy him. He will want to silence her.'

'Does he know where she is, who you are?'

'Yes, I believe so.'

'You will need to go into hiding, mate.'

'That's what I thought. We will go and stay on my boat at the marina for the time being.'

'Good idea,' Ben said. 'I will be back tomorrow, so let's catch up.'

'Okay, cheers. Enjoy your night,' Greg said.

Ben looked at his watch, did the calculation, and made a call.

'Thomas, Ben Woolford again. Are you awake?'

'Am now, Ben. What's up?'

'Mate, you know those cattle people I got you to find for me there in Dallas?'

'Keith Madison?'

'Yeah, long story but he has threatened to kill someone here, a friend. Can you put an ear to the ground for me?' Ben asked.

'I have a friend of a friend that works for him. Let me see what I can find out.'

'Cheers, mate,' Ben said, hanging up.

It wasn't long before Ben received the call back from Thomas.

'Madison's henchman, Jerry Stokes, left on a flight for Australia last night.'

Shit, it's serious then, Ben thought. 'Really appreciate your help, Thomas.'

Ben called Greg. 'We need to talk ASAP.'

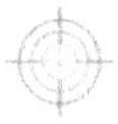

Rebecca walked into Sergeant Jones's office and closed the door behind her. He looked up; she had never done that before. She had his full attention.

'Sarge, the meeting with John Smith was a disaster. I blew it, he was on to me. Despite that, he called me and told me everything.'

Jones sat motionless as Reed told him the exact details that Ben had told her.

"Well, I guess that explains a few things,' Jones said once she had finished.

'Sarge, there is one more thing; he asked for a favour.'

'What does he want?'

'He would like us to take the pressure off Peter Watkins, or whoever he is. He said he is a good lad and helped save the girl.'

Jones sat there looking at her.

'Okay, but if that little prick even gets so much as a parking ticket, he will be on his way to Darwin with his mates.'

'I appreciate that, Sarge,' Rebecca said in relief.

CHAPTER NINETEEN

B EN, now acting as the bodyguard for Greg and Jennifer, kept an eye out for trouble as Greg motored the cruiser out of the marina, the same as he had done for the last three days at 10:00 a.m., again heading for the open ocean.

Today, Ben noticed a dark grey fishing boat fitted with two big two-hundred-horsepower Johnson outboards. *That's a lot of horsepower to go fishing with,* he thought. Jennifer sat at the rear table, the sea breeze playing havoc with her thick long hair. It was about thirty minutes into the trip when Greg pulled back the throttles and the big forty-eight-foot Riviera came to a slow, drifting halt. He dropped the anchor while Ben topped up Jennifer's champagne. Ben looked over at the fishing boat, which had also stopped off on their starboard side, all but a fair distance away.

Greg took a seat next to Jennifer while Ben went downstairs.

Ben took out his camera from his rucksack and screwed on the Jintu telephoto lens. He slowly opened a rear port-hole window, lifted the camera, and searched for the mysterious fishing boat in the lens.

Jerry had spent a few days tracking Jennifer and Greg down. With the assistance of a local thug who would do absolutely anything for money, he soon had an address and a full profile, with details of all of Greg's assets—including his berth and the Riviera at the marina. Jerry had been watching them now for three days. He quickly learnt that they were living on the boat and had the same routine each day. It was almost too easy to be true.

He'd ordered a very particular rifle to be made available, and it was in his hands within twenty-four hours of his arrival. Nothing was too hard when money was no issue.

Jerry had already assembled the weapon at the marina while he waited for Greg to get the Riviera underway. He planned to perform the execution out at sea. With no one else around, it should be quite a simple job. The sea was smooth, as it quite often was this time of year. He placed the bipod legs of the sniper rifle on the gunnel of the fishing boat. Through the scope he could see Greg and Jennifer clearly. The large, clear plastic side curtains that sheltered the table from the wind would blur any vision of him to them. Jennifer's head filled the scope. A flicker of sorrow pinged at him in that moment. He had liked her. She'd been the most beautiful and kindest of Keith's trophy wives.

He squeezed the trigger.

As Ben focused on the fishing boat, it took a second to realise he was looking down the barrel of a rifle. Ben yelled out, 'Gun!' as he simultaneously photographed the shooter and the puff of smoke from the barrel of the rifle. He then dropped the camera onto the leather seat he was kneeling on. Ben ran back up the four steps to the helm. He could see Greg holding Jennifer, who was now lying motionless in a pool of blood. He started the first engine, and as soon as it fired, he thrust the lever forward. Greg, who had hit the deck at the sound of Ben's call, had scrambled to Jennifer in a flash. He bolted into action, carefully laying the motionless Jennifer flat on the floor, averting his sight from her shirt, which was now completely covered in blood. He yelled to Ben, 'Tight circles and get the anchor up! She's hit bad. There's a doctor's surgery opposite the marina. We need to get there fast.'

With only one engine running, it would make it easier to spin the large cruiser. As soon as he heard the anchor clunk into place, Ben advanced both engines to full power. They were quickly to thirty-five knots, which was as fast as the twenty-tonne boat would go. They headed back to the marina, the two big turbo-charged diesels screaming. Ben could see up ahead, the two big sprays from those powerful Johnson outboards of the dark grey fishing boat.

Ben roared into the marina's four-knot zone at over thirty knots. He could see the fishing boat had already been abandoned and bumped casually into the pylon at the far end of the refuelling wharf.

Ben pulled the throttles into reverse to pull the big cruiser up, and the Riviera shuddered as it hit the mooring heavily. Greg already had the lifeless Jennifer in his arms as he scrambled ashore and raced for the gate, her arms now dangling like a rag doll as he ran. Ben threw a rope loosely around a pylon and tied a quick knot and chased after Greg and Jennifer. At the gate Ben took Jennifer from Greg, who was now exhausted. Greg pointed to the doctor's surgery that was in the shopping centre across the road from the marina. Greg stopped traffic as Ben ran, carrying Jennifer across the busy road. When they reached the other side, Greg took her again, and Ben ran ahead to open the door of the surgery. Ben saw in the corner of his eye a silver Camry pull up on the other side of the road. The driver was holding a long-lens camera.

Jerry had seen the blood splatter across her chest as Jennifer slowly collapsed to the floor. He yelled 'Go' to the boat-driving thug, as he started disassembling the rifle.

Jerry took out his phone and made an overseas call.

Keith answered, 'Yes?'

'Completed, awaiting confirmation.' And he hung up.

It was only minutes before a police car pulled up at the surgery. A uniformed officer and what looked like a detective in a suit jumped out and went inside the surgery. Jerry clicked away on the camera as Greg and Ben stepped out of the surgery. Greg squatted against the wall, his head in his hands, his friend doing his best to console him.

Keith Madison's phone rang again for the second time that evening.

'Mr Madison, it's Detective Sergeant Peterson from the South Australian Police Department. Are you in the United States, sir?'

'Yes, I'm in Dallas, Texas.'

'Mr Madison, I have some bad news. Are you okay to talk?'

'It's not about my wife, is it? She is over there.'

'Unfortunately, I think it is, sir.'

'My God, what has happened?' Keith said, trying to sound as concerned as possible.

'The doctor is with her now and has confirmed that someone we believe to be your wife has passed away, Mr Madison.'

'What happened?' he insisted.

'We don't have any details at this stage. Circumstances are suspicious, and we will be making a full investigation, I promise you that, sir. Do you feel you are in a position to confirm for us that it is your wife that we have here? We can change this to a video call.'

'Yes,' Keith said with a slight quiver in his voice. He wasn't that sure at how he would feel seeing her dead.

The detective switched to FaceTime, and Keith could then see a doctor in a white coat with a stethoscope around his neck, a police officer with a note pad, and a body lying on a bed.

'Are you ready, Mr Madison?'

'Yes.'

The detective moved the phone to show Jennifer's face, the first thing he noticed was that her face was white, and expressionless. He could see the blood splatter all over her shirt and down her neck.

'Yes, that's my Jennifer,' he said, almost feeling as sad as he sounded.

'I am very sorry for your loss, Mr Madison.' The detective turned the phone back from FaceTime.

After a pause, he continued, 'As you would appreciate, we will need to keep your wife's body here until the coroner has completed his findings and officially releases it. I hope you understand, sir.'

'Yes, I understand. Thank you, Detective,' Keith said and hung up.

Jerry kept his camera clicking as a black coroner's van pulled up and backed in towards the surgery's front door. Two attendants jumped out wearing grey overalls and opened the back doors. They pulled out a gurney and wheeled it inside.

Jerry clicked off more photos as the gurney returned, now with a body covered in a white sheet, which was placed into the back of the van. He put the camera away and started the Camry. He headed for the airport; he needed to be on the next flight out of Adelaide. He would leave the hired thug to return the car and rifle. He would be back in Dallas by tomorrow morning.

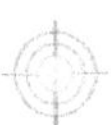

At first, Keith Madison had been worried about how the up-and-coming Annual General Meeting might look without his beautiful wife at his side. He was soon comforted by the realization that he would be the sad widower and could cash in on the sympathy vote. *The poor man, his beautiful wife gunned down in Australia while on holiday,* was what the voting members would be thinking—even his opponents. Jerry had sent him a picture of the gurney being loaded into a black coroner's van, her wavy brown hair just visible under the white sheet. It was bittersweet for Keith. She was a nice girl, and he did like her.

CHAPTER TWENTY

REBECCA Reed was busy trying to arrange a search party for two missing Japanese tourists who had disappeared somewhere between Alice Springs and Tennant Creek three days ago, when Ben called her again.

'Rebecca, John Smith. I hope you are well? Hey, I was wondering how it went with the Mexicans?'

'Oh, hi, John. We got 'em, all six of them. The two buried bodies were two of them as well.'

'I have since found out that they were the two that raped the girl. Manuel Gonzales shot them in front of her,' Ben said.

'Fair justice, I say. So, she witnessed that then?' Rebecca asked.

'Yes, but I doubt she would want to testify. How did you go with my little favour?'

'Sarge agreed, but I can tell you, he only needs to jaywalk, and he's on his way to Darwin with his mates.'

'That's great news, thank you,' Ben said.

'Rebecca, remember I have the photos of the Mexicans gunning down the bikies at Aileron when you want them.'

'We will definitely need them to help the prosecutor,' she said.

'I also have all the drone footage of the two rescues of the girl that Peter took.'

'*Two* rescues?' Reed asked.

'It's a long story, maybe over a drink one day.'

'I do owe you one, John Smith.'

'Yes, you do, Rebecca Reed.'

'Hey, you said Peter can fly a drone. Does he actually have one?' Reed asked.

'Yes, a very expensive one.'

'I can only guess where he got that from. Anyway, do you think he would help the police find some missing tourists lost out in the sticks? It would really help the boss turn that blind eye.'

'Let me see; I will call you back.'

Skunk's phone rang. 'Hello?'

'Peter, Roo-man. The cops have agreed to go easy on you, but you must stay out of trouble, all right?'

'Really? They said that?' Skunk asked.

'They have asked for a favour though; there's no free rides, mate.'

'I'm not saying shit against the Vipers. That would be suicide!' Skunk said.

'No, nothing like that. They have two lost people and would

like you to help find them with the drone.'

'How can we trust them? You didn't, and you were right not to.'

'I know, but I have since given them all the info on the Mexicans, and I'm pretty sure we are in credit now, so I think we can trust them. I still have the pictures of the shoot-out at Aileron which they need to convict the cartel, and I will keep that as security.'

'Okay, I'm interested. That could be my ticket out of this mess, I guess.'

Working for the cops, what a change of direction, he thought.

'Okay, are you happy for me to give them your number, or do you want to call them?'

'I'll call them. Who should I ask for?'

'Constable Rebecca Reed,' Ben said. 'Good luck, mate.'

'Hey, Roo-man. Thanks, I really appreciate what you have done for me.'

'Good luck, mate,' Ben said, hanging up the call.

Skunk turned his phone ID off and called the Alice Springs police station.

'Constable Reed speaking.'

'Constable Reed, this is Peter Watkins. The Roo-man asked me to call you, as he thought I might be able to help with some lost people.'

'Roo-man? Is that John Smith?'

'Who knows what his real name is,' Skunk said.

'Well, Peter, what's your real name?'

'Peter is real,' he said.

'Well, Mr Peter Is Real, we will need your proper name at some stage so we can pay you.'

'Pay me? Roo-man didn't say anything about that.'

'You will be hired as a contractor and will be paid on a day-by-day arrangement.'

'No offence, Rebecca, but how do I know I can trust you?'

'That's a fair question. John Smith, or Roo-man as you call him, gave us all the info on the abduction and the shoot-outs in return for you being, shall we say, overlooked. My sergeant has agreed, but only as long as you are so squeaky clean that you glow in the dark.'

'He did that for me?'

'Yes, Peter, that's all he wanted in return.'

'Wow, okay, what do we do from here?' Skunk asked.

'You and the drone come into the station, and an officer will take you out to check the hilly areas that the helicopter can't get to. Peter, you will need to start today, as these people have been missing now for three days.'

'Okay. I will be there in half an hour.'

'And, Peter… you *can* trust me.'

When Skunk arrived at the police station, he was nervous. This could go one of two ways. One really good and the other really bad. He opened the door and walked towards the counter. Reed looked over at him, with his right arm in plaster, a swollen nose, and what remained of two black eyes, and smiled. She walked through the security door and towards him, holding out her hand to shake his. Which was just a squeeze due to his right arm being in plaster. His anxiety was peaking.

'Come through. This is Constable Will Jackson. He will be the one taking you out there.'

Jackson looked judgingly at Skunk and said, 'Let's go; time is critical.'

Skunk sucked in a deep breath and let it out slowly with a sigh. 'Phew.'

They hit the road.

It was his first time in the *front* seat of a police car.

'Will—hey, sorry, can I call you Will?' Skunk asked.

'Sure, mate.'

'I only have three batteries, fully charged, and they only last about forty minutes each.'

'How can we make them last all day?' Jackson asked.

'We will need a two-thousand-watt inverter and then we'll be able to charge the spares from the police car battery.'

'Reed, do you read me?' Jackson said over the police radio.

'Come in, Jacko, over.'

'Bec, can you please organise a two-thousand-watt inverter for tomorrow please? Over.'

'Roger that, Will, over.'

Jackson looked at Skunk as they drove north along the highway. 'How much will that cost?' he asked him.

'A thousand bucks,' Skunk said.

'Shit, I didn't expect that. The sarge will freak. Anyway, Peter, the helicopter has searched the plains, their car was found on this road by the chopper this morning, out of fuel. We need to search these hills. The chopper makes too much dust, and not only can they not see anything, if they were up there, the down draft might blow them off the hill.'

Jackson pulled over, and they both hopped out. He spread a map out over the bonnet and told Skunk the area he wanted to work in today.

'What's the range, Peter?'

'Nearly ten kilometres,' Skunk said.

'Great,' Jackson said.

Skunk quickly assembled the drone and clicked in the first of the charged batteries. He placed the drone on a nice flat surface and asked Jackson to stand back. The drone took off like a rocket and headed towards the ranges. Skunk worked the drone back and forth, getting higher as he went until he reached the top. He would then work along the next section and so on. It wasn't long before the three batteries were flat, and they had to return to Alice Springs. Skunk felt he had somehow failed; he was so desperate to find the tourists and prove himself a value to the police. This could really turn into a real job for him. Having the police as his first customer would look pretty good on his CV. Skunk and Jackson didn't talk much on the dirt road, but once they turned onto the bitumen, Skunk looked over to Jackson and said, 'Officer Reed's pretty cute.'

Jackson looked at him and smiled, 'Yes she is, Peter.'

Next morning Skunk was waiting at the locked police station door when Sergeant Jones arrived.

'Have you come to turn yourself in, lad?' Jones said.

Skunk jolted with a little panic. 'Err… no, sir. I am helping Will and Rebecca find the missing tourists.'

'Just kidding, Peter. You are a very lucky young man. Your friends are going to be having quite a holiday up there in Darwin.'

'I know, sir, and I really do appreciate the amazing opportunity you have given me.'

'Thank me by showing me that I made the right decision. Good luck today, and I hope you find our tourists,' Jones said as he unlocked the door and walked off into the station. Jackson was the next to arrive.

'Did you see we have an inverter, Peter? It's only a thousand watt-er, but it's all they had in Alice.'

'That will be fine. It's just with the two thousand we could charge two batteries at once,' Skunk said.

'The mechanic wired it up with clamps so we can just grab it and go. He did say to leave the engine running while it's on though,' Jackson said.

Jackson and Skunk worked most of the day, crossing off areas searched and changing batteries every forty minutes.

'I've got 'em! Well, one anyway,' Skunk yelled. 'Three quarters of the way up the hill on that ridge.'

'Looks like they tried to climb over it and got stuck,' Jackson said, staring at Skunk's monitor. 'Zoom in close, Pete,' Jackson said.

The casualness of his name made him feel ten feet tall and a part of the team.

'God, he doesn't look so good,' Jackson said.

'Let's give him some water,' Skunk said.

'How the hell can we do that? I'm not climbing up there!' Jackson said, standing upright.

'Grab your bottle of water, some tape, and a pen and paper.'

Skunk brought the drone back, changed the battery, and taped the bottle to the battery housing of the drone. He took the pen and paper and wrote, 'Where is the girl? Take the water, then hold the drone high above your head.'

Skunk wasn't actually sure if the drone could lift the water, but if it didn't, he would just keep tipping water out till it was light enough to fly. It took off slowly but kept a fair rate of climb as it headed into the dense mountainside. It was difficult to manoeuvre, and it landed heavily on the ledge where the male Japanese tourist sat. He grasped desperately for the water and drank it all in one gulp. Skunk and Jackson watched through the monitor from the drone's camera.

'Did he read the note?' Jackson said.

'I can't tell, but he isn't lifting the drone as I asked,' Skunk said, concentrating.

The Japanese man picked up the drone and looked into the camera lens. He held up the note, and they both realised quickly he couldn't read English.

Skunk moved the camera up and down to show that he understood.

The man put the drone down gently and moved away. Skunk lifted it slightly and flew it out and back to base.

'Peter, we don't have much light left, and the police radio doesn't work all the way out here. We will need to go and come back in the morning with the SES, and they can abseil down to him.'

'Do we have any food or more water for him?' Skunk asked.

'No, nothing,' Will said, looking through the police car.

'Grab the high-vis vest, Will,' Skunk said.

The light was disappearing as Jackson folded up the vest and grabbed the tape. Skunk took another sheet of paper and drew a picture of a stick figure holding the drone above his head.

He set the drone off again, a little easier, as the vest didn't weigh nearly as much as the bottle of water. He landed it, again at the far end of the ledge. The man ran to it, unwrapped the tape, and looked at the picture. This time he did lift the drone above his head, and Skunk lifted it away with ease. Skunk packed up the drone. He felt so bad leaving him on the hill for another night. It would be cold; it was quite often freezing in Alice Springs at night. The police fluoro vest might just add a tiny bit of warmth, but more importantly it would make him easier to find tomorrow. Skunk and Jackson logged the position and jumped back into the police car and headed back towards the highway.

'You are a bloody legend, Peter. We still need to find the girl though,' Jackson said to him.

'Thanks and yes—we do,' Skunk said, feeling pretty good about himself.

Once they were on the highway, the police radio came into range, and Jackson immediately called in the news.

They could hear the cheering in the background as Reed replied.

Once they arrived back at the police station, Skunk grabbed the drone case and said to Jackson, 'I guess you won't need me anymore tonight,' Skunk said, starting his walk back home.

'Where are you going?' Jackson said.

'I'll just walk home. It's just a couple of kilometres. I don't have a car, and I can't ride my Harley with my broken arm.'

'Bullshit, mate. You are the man of the moment! Come inside and then I will drive you to your doorstep.'

My doorstep, Skunk thought. *God, they'll know where I live as well!* He really had started to second-guess himself. He'd spent his life dodging the cops, being careful and sneaky, but now, he was one of them. He was one of the good guys, and he could finally relax. It was a good feeling.

'All right then. 'Preciate it, thank you, Will.'

When the two of them walked into the station, they got a standing ovation, and Jackson went on to tell them how Skunk had flown water and a vest to the stranded tourist with his drone, and they all laughed about the notes. Skunk had never been appreciated like this ever. His father was an overpowering mongrel; he was Pig's brother after all. The Vipers treated him like shit, even left him behind in the clubhouse while everyone else escaped. *Well*, he thought, *we know how that turned out!* No, this admiration felt good, bloody good, and he wanted more of it.

Sergeant Jones even gave him a pat on the back.

'Will you need me tomorrow for the rescue?' Skunk asked.

'Probably not. We have the exact coordinates now thanks to you, and the man should be able to show us where the girl is. Who knows, they may have had a fight and she is sitting in Darwin drinking cocktails,' Sergeant Jones said.

Jackson spoke up, 'Sir, I do feel Peter would be a real asset to have standing by, as he's the only one that can actually get to him at the moment.'

'Okay, sure, I don't disagree,' Jones said, now walking back to his office to finish up for the night.

'We should get an interpreter there as well, and bring a spare walkie-talkie. I can fly it up to him,' Skunk said, now excited that he was still on the job.

Jackson looked at Reed. 'Impressive,' she said.

'Okay, you legend, let's get you home,' Jackson said.

They started to walk off when Reed called out. 'Hey, Peter Is Real, can you fill out these forms please so we can pay you?'

He walked back to her, took the forms and smiled back. 'Thank you, Rebecca, for everything.'

Now they would know his name, where he lived, and even his tax file number, and it didn't matter. Skunk decided he would no longer be Skunk, but Peter, the law-abiding citizen. He would ditch his colours and any reference to the Vipers, especially now that he was the only surviving member.

Next morning, he was again on the steps of the police station when Sergeant Jones arrived. He smiled at him more warmly this time.

'Well done yesterday, son,' Jones said as he unlocked the door and walked in.

Jones held the security door open for him and nodded for him to come on through. Peter jumped forward and caught the closing door with his good hand.

'Help yourself to a coffee, mate. Jackson won't be far away.'

Peter had just had his first sip when Jackson appeared in the kitchen doorway.

'Peter, we are meeting the emergency service there at 8:00 a.m., so we'd better get going.'

'I'm ready, Will.'

They were still along the highway when Jackson asked, 'Peter, how did you break your arm?'

Peter didn't know what to say, what he knew, or what might happen if he told the truth.

'I crashed my Harley,' he said.

'I saw it in your driveway last night. It was gleaming; you must have fixed it quickly.'

Peter didn't answer. He was wondering, *Is it a lie if you just don't answer?'*

Jackson looked over to him and asked again, 'What really happened, off the record, just you and me?'

Peter looked him. 'Just you and me, no matter what I say?'

Jackson looked at Peter.

'Did anyone die?' Jackson asked.

'Yes,' Peter said.

'Shit, Okay, I don't wanna know,' Jackson said as he turned from the bitumen onto the dirt road.

When they arrived, the SES were already there, and a Japanese interpreter was sitting in her car.

Jackson and Peter walked over to the SES chief.

'How are you going to get him, Steve?' Jackson asked. 'Oh, and this is Peter, the legend that found him.'

'Hi, Peter, I heard what you did, very clever.'

'I would have liked to have got the chopper to lower one of my men in there with a harness, but apparently the one we have been using is getting a bullet hole fixed today, and it's grounded.'

'Yeah, I may know something about that,' Jackson said.

'Why don't we get a radio to him, so we can talk to him?' Peter said.

'Is that easy?' Steve asked.

'Pretty easy,' Peter replied.

'I have a light one in the truck; the Motorolas' are quite heavy. I'll just grab it.'

Peter assembled the drone and taped the radio to it.

'Ready to launch. Stand back please.'

The drone took off and headed over to the ridge on the mountain. Peter called out to Jackson.

'Will, he's gone, he isn't on that ridge anymore.'

'Has he fallen off?' Steve asked.

'I can't see him anywhere below,' Peter said. 'Steve, is the radio turned on?'

'Yes.'

'Can we get the interpreter on a radio calling out for him to wave the vest please?' Peter asked.

'Good idea,' Steve said, who jogged over to get the interpreter.

Peter flew in close to the mountain while the instruction was called over the radio in Japanese.

'Found him,' Peter called. 'He's climbed up further and now looks injured. He's holding his leg.' The three of them gathered around the little monitor.

'Why the hell did he do that? Damn it! Just makes our job

harder now,' Steve said.

'And now I have nowhere to land the drone; that ledge was perfect,' Peter said.

'I will get my boys on their way,' Steve said.

'Shall we get the interpreter to tell him the SES are on their way and to stay put?' Peter asked.

'Let's do that, and you can bring the drone back,' Jackson said.

It took three hours for the SES to climb the mountain face to reach him.

'We have him, Chief,' eventually squawked over the radio.

'Jackson, get the interpreter quickly,' Steve said.

She jumped from her car and ran to Steve.

'Can you ask him where the girl is, please, Judy?'

Judy spoke Japanese into the radio, and a reply came back.

'A man with a gun in a white truck took her,' Judy said quickly.

Jackson jumped to attention.

More Japanese came over the radio, and Judy said, 'He was hiding in the mountains from him.'

'A real hero then,' Jackson said.

Jackson turned to Peter, but he was already getting the drone prepped.

'I'll go up really high and see if I can see any white trucks,' Peter said.

'You read my mind, mate.'

It was nearly dark by the time they had the stranded man down and back to their base on the flats. After thanking them profusely with bows and nods, he told them his name was Chikasi. He ate and drank while, with the help of Judy's interpreter skills, Jackson asked more about the abduction, to get a detailed account. Chikasi told them they'd stopped, filled the car with fuel, and were driving down this road, when he noticed a vehicle following a long way behind. Then their car just stopped. It had somehow run out of fuel again. The white truck pulled up and a man walked over. He then pulled out a gun, tied up the girl, and took her with him.

'Which way did he go with her?' Jackson asked as he pointed to the map.

'He continued down this road,' Judy said.

'What did he look like? Can he describe the vehicle?' Jackson asked.

'Tall, grey hair and beard, about fifty years old. Truck was white, said FOR on the back.'

Jackson took down his details and suggested they head back to Alice, as it was completely dark now. With their exhausted tourist in the back seat, they headed off down the dirt road back towards the highway.

'Can we stop at their car, Will, as we go past?' Peter asked.

'Sure, but why?'

'I'm sure our mate here might want to get some of his gear, and I want to look at something.'

The rusty white eighties-model Nissan Patrol appeared ahead in the headlights. They pulled over.

'Got a torch?' Peter asked.

'Sure,' Jackson said, handing him a long-handled police torch.

Peter went around to the back of the car and lay on the ground, shining the torch up at the fuel tank.

'Someone has put a small slit in the side of the fuel tank with a screwdriver or chisel, I would say. Would have drained a full tank to an eighth in half an hour. It would have left enough in it so that they would see the gauge low and have enough to get to the petrol station.'

'Well, look at you, Mr. Detective!' Jackson said.

Chikasi did recover some personal items from the Patrol, and then they continued on. The man refused going to the hospital, as he was feeling fine now that he had had some food and water and his injury was identified as just a sprained ankle. Jackson had phoned ahead to arrange a place for him to stay and managed to explain that he had to stay in town, and that the police would formally interview him tomorrow, and start their search for his girlfriend.

'Hopefully you guys will be able to use me again?' Peter said, breaking the silence.

'I'm absolutely sure we will. I can see so many uses for that drone and a good pilot like you. Just about everything we use a chopper for now, like car chases, search and rescue; it has many added benefits for sure,' Jackson said.

Jackson dropped Peter home. 'Come in tomorrow, bring in your forms, and we can have a chat with the sarge about more work.'

'Will do, thanks,' Peter said.

Jackson was busting to know the broken-arm story.

CHAPTER TWENTY-ONE

THE black coroner's van pulled up slowly into the garage of Greg Sheppard's townhouse. The two coroners jumped out, opened the rear doors, and slid out the gurney that was occupied by Jennifer Madison's body. Greg and Ben arrived shortly after, along with the doctor, the nurse, the police officer, the detective, the cameraman, Kaz, the make-up artist, and Lachlan from wardrobe.

Jennifer alighted the gurney as spritely as anyone would, anyone who had just come back from the dead. She was dying to have a shower; the fake movie blood had soaked right through to her three-hundred-dollar Bordelle bra. Kaz removed the blood squirter and remote-controlled pump that was taped to the inside of her shirt.

Greg ushered everyone inside, where they changed out of their police uniforms, doctors' coats, coroner overalls and handed them back to Lachie. He was happy that the blood-soaked clothes were Jennifer's and not from the studio's costume department.

'Ben, what time did the coroner want his van back?' Greg asked.

'Another hour, mate.' Greg cracked a bottle of champagne and thanked the actors individually as they sipped the cold, bubbly French liquid. He reminded them that the shoot and all its details were strictly confidential.

As all performers did, they stood around complimenting each other and saying how they would have done it better if they had another chance. Greg assured them that in a month or so they would be invited to see a screening of the mini movie.

Jennifer was soon back from her shower, wearing fresh clothes and a wide smile. Her fellow actors congratulating her on her outstanding lead-role performance.

Kaz, Lachie, and the actors were soon starting to leave, and the three of them stood looking at each other as the last actor closed the door behind them. They held up what was left of their champagne, and Greg said, 'Well, we did it. I think we bloody well pulled it off.'

They stood in silence for a moment, exhausted, until Ben said, 'Now for part two. Hey, Greg, we do need to go and tie the Riviera up properly. It's still at the back of the refuelling berth; I only threw one rope around the pole at the mooring,' Ben said.

'It's okay. I called Graeme at the marina, and he has secured it for us.'

'Good thinking,' Ben said, appreciating his foresight.

'Okay, Ben, let's drop the coroner's van back, the tow truck should already have the cop car by now, and we can put the Riv back in its berth. Let's leave that bulletproof screen till tomorrow.'

Greg couldn't have been happier; it went extremely well. The actors knew it was a one take only, do-or-die performance. There was no room for any mistakes, especially during the FaceTime with Keith. If Jennifer had moved in the slightest, it would have been blown. Ben's cue of 'Gun' was for Jennifer to squeeze the fake-blood-filled pump. The polycarbonate bulletproof screen that was measured perfectly to fit behind the flimsy clear plastic windows of the boat was the hardest to do in the time they had. However, an offer of a few extra dollars and the hint that it was for a big action movie that was coming up enabled it to be fitted in record time. Greg had driven the boat to lure the assassin to the starboard side, the protected side. If Jerry had gone the other way, they would've just had to turn the boat around.

The doctor was happy for them to hire his surgery for the day for the 'film,' simply working from his other practice in North Adelaide. The coroner's van was an old one and now just used as a spare. Greg had hired it before for another film shoot. The police car was also a fake, simply a rental car with stickers and blue-and-red overhead lights from a movie-vehicle wrangler mate he used. Someone from another country, like Jerry, would have no way of knowing it wasn't the real deal. But as Ben had said, that was only part one.

The next day Ben came over early, and he, Greg, and Jennifer sat around Greg's table making notes of everything she knew about her husband's business dealings, people whom he had arranged to be 'taken care of,' and apparently, those that had conveniently disappeared. She told them how he acted like a billionaire, but it was mostly a smokescreen. He had plenty of money but it was everybody else's. The house in Dallas and the ranch in Wichita Falls were inherited from his parents when they died. Sure, they were worth millions, but the rest of his 'fortune' was comprised of defrauded money from the banks or blackmailing other cattlemen. She told them how he would pay off police, councillors, and politicians to do favours for his fellow cattle ranchers, only to come back at them demanding the favour be returned. Sometimes by bringing thousands of head of cattle from interstate to his property on the day before a bank would arrive, where he would claim that they were his, to secure a massive loan or overdraft. The man was a fake, a cheat, a criminal, and now a proven murderer.

Greg and Ben looked at each other before Greg spoke. 'Would you have any idea if the properties secure any of the debt, or are you a co-borrower? We don't want him thrown in jail while you are left with all the debt.'

'No, the properties are not security, he made sure of that. He only ever used security he never owned, like borrowed cattle.'

'Okay,' Ben said, 'I'll contact a friend in the US and see if he can put us in touch with an interested party. I assume the FBI would be very keen to hear this story. We should be able to bury that Jerry Stokes as well. Now Jennifer, for the time being you are dead and need to act that way. You can't leave this place, as who knows, he may still have someone watching. And you too, Greg. He may want your scalp still, so keep your heads down.'

Ben continued, 'I'm off to Alice Springs tomorrow to deliver the evidence from last week and wrap up that little event.'

Ben looked at Greg as they both threw knowing smiles, each appreciating it was anything but a little event.

Frank DeLuca saw Ben's number as his phone rang and he answered it on the second ring.

'Ben, how are you doing? Any news for me?'

'Yes, Frank, all of the Mexicans have been caught and the AFP have them on multiple charges, including murder one. I don't think they will be a problem to you for a very long time to come.'

'Oh, Ben, that is very good news. My daughter will be able to come home now.'

'Frank, I do hope you honour our agreement,' Ben said.

'That and more, my friend, that and more.'

Frank DeLuca hung up the phone, knowing his life would be different from now on. He'd already decided that once the current shipment was sold, he was out. His only child had paid a horrendous price because of his illegal business, and the greed that went with it, and he had to live with that. He would spend the rest of his life making it up to her.

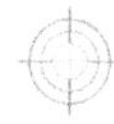

Ben arrived in Alice Springs late the next night. It was a fifteen-hour drive to do it in one day, but he had some good music and plenty to think about. He checked into the same hotel where just over a week ago, four fully armed men had stayed, who were about to raid a Mexican cartel's stronghold. But that was then, and this was now. No guns, drug lords, or bikies, just mum-and-dad travellers. He could rest easy tonight.

He did sleep well and woke with a fresh focus. His first call was to Peter, to check how he was going with the police job. Peter told him all the details, a lot he didn't need to know, but Ben was proud of him and inwardly happy that he hadn't wasted his time trying to help this lad. Ben asked him if and what he may have told the cops, just so their stories were the same. Peter assured him that they hadn't asked, and he hadn't told them. Ben hung up with a promise to see him before he headed back home. Next was to call Reed.

'Alice Springs Police, Constable Reed speaking.'

'You owe me a drink, Rebecca,' the person on the phone said to her.

With only the slightest delay, she said, 'And you owe me some evidence.'

'How about tonight? What time you finish?'

'Six o'clock.'

'How about we meet at Sportie's, seven o'clock. Just don't bring any friends this time.'

Rebecca did her best to sound serious, but the flirtatious smile in her voice gave her away.

'No friends. Got it. Will I need a bulletproof vest?'

'I really hope not.' He chuckled.

Rebecca's next call was about a campervan that had been parked in the car park at Standley Chasm for nearly a week, a popular spot for visitors to Alice Springs to see. There was no accommodation there, so a vehicle left in the car park overnight was very unusual. She asked for the registration number, and after a quick check she found that it was registered to a Marie Lovatt, a backpacker from Italy. Sergeant Jones suggested she head out and have a look, while he and Jackson interview the Japanese man, Chikasi, who they had pulled from the hillside.

Reed arrived at Standley Chasm about an hour later. The car was locked, with no one inside. Reed asked the attendants if they had saved any security-camera recordings of the car park on the day that she thought the van may have arrived. The manager located the footage and left it for Reed to look through while she went back to serving visitors. Rebecca eventually found where the van pulled in, parked, and the dark-haired teenager hopped out. Another vehicle drove in as the girl turned to face the camera, blocking the view of her face. The girl walked off towards the chasm and out of the camera's view. Rebecca turned to the manager. 'Excuse me, has anyone had a look to see if she is still out there somewhere?'

'Yes, we have had a pretty good look, but if she wandered a long way off track, she could be anywhere. You might need a helicopter.'

Or a drone, Rebecca thought.

'Can I please take the recorded footage?' Rebecca asked.

'Sure, it only stays there about a week, and then it just records over itself.'

She jumped back into the police car and headed back to town. On the way she called Jackson and asked if he could get a hold of Peter to come and have a look for her with the drone. Jackson said he was coming in any way to talk to the sarge about some more work. Rebecca assured him there was already more work.

Peter was at the station when Rebecca returned. As she walked in the front door, she saw him and said, 'I think we might have another job for you, Peter.'

'Okay, very keen to help,' Peter said.

'Come with me. I will show you what we have.' Rebecca put

the CD into her computer and played the recording. They watched it, and she played it again, letting it play through until after the girl was long out of frame.

'Hold on. Stop it there,' Peter called out. 'Go back. What's that truck?'

Rebecca replayed it, and stopped it on Peter's command. 'There—see? That white F-250; the Japanese man said a white truck took his girlfriend.'

'Really? He might still be here with the boss.' Rebecca jumped up and almost ran to Sergeant Jones's office with her laptop. The door was closed; she knocked and slowly opened the door. Jones, Jackson, Chikasi, and the interpreter were in discussion.

'Excuse me, sir, can I show our Japanese gentleman a picture of a white truck?'

Jones nodded and watched to see what she was doing.

Rebecca held the screen with the frozen video of the white F-250 in front of their witness. As soon as he saw it, he yelled something in Japanese and pointed to it.

'That's the truck,' Judy the interpreter said. 'The one that took Akira.'

'Show me,' Jones insisted, and Rebecca spun the computer towards him. He could see a man, with long grey hair and beard that fitted the description perfectly that he had just been told.

'Reed, can you zoom in on the driver?' Jones asked.

'A little, but it gets pretty blurry,' she said.

She compromised and showed the now distraught Chikasi.

He nodded, touching the screen.

'Yes, that is him,' Judy said.

Sergeant Jones looked up, slowly removing his glasses. 'We've a serious problem here, constables. We need to find this man quickly.

Reed, go through that recording and see if you see the vehicle leave and if so, who is in the car, better still a rego number. Action stations, people! We need to find him before anyone else disappears.'

When Rebecca walked into the bar, she wasn't really sure what John Smith looked like. She had an image in her mind, but she knew how that could sometimes go.

A tall man with a big smile walked up to her with his hand out. She shook his hand; it felt like a blind date.

'Nice to meet you, John,' she said.

'And you again, Rebecca.'

'You can call me Bec,' she said.

'And you can call me Ben.'

'What about Roo-man? I heard that was another of your aliases,' she said, taking a seat in the corner booth.

'Yeah, well, I was given that by some very unfriendly acquaintances. Drink?' Ben asked.

'A beer would be great, thanks.'

'Sure.'

He returned with two beers and sat down next to her.

'I can't help looking over my shoulder,' he said to her.

'I'm off duty; you're safe. I don't think the sarge would let me drink beer on the job,' she said, taking a sip. 'So, what can you tell me?' Rebecca asked.

Ben told her how he was a private investigator from Adelaide and how he'd been contracted to find a girl who'd run away from home, or so he was originally told. He told her how the locals had told him about the secret compound at Aileron, and how the bikies caught him, his breakout with his Leatherman, and all the detail with the bikies and Mexicans.

'So you're a bit of a MacGyver then! But I don't understand, why didn't you come to us for help in the first place?' Rebecca asked, finishing another beer.

'That part I can't tell you, Bec,' he said a little seriously.

'Okay, I understand… Hey, my buy' she said.

The hours slipped by. Ben found Rebecca to be one of those people who couldn't talk without touching you once she had a few beers under her belt. She spent a lot of time talking with her hand on his forearm or shoulder. Ben told her about his childhood and a little about his time in Afghanistan. She was captivated as he described the missions and how he and his team had rescued an American reporter that had been taken hostage by the Taliban. He loved how she hung on his every word, and he could tell she was imagining herself there as part of his team, sneaking through abandoned towns, ready for a rifle to appear from a window and start shooting at you.

They stopped talking for a moment, and she looked him in the eye. She lifted her hand from his arm and touched his cheek with her fingertips. She leaned forward and kissed him, quick but firm. She pulled back and looked again into his eyes. She moved forward and kissed him for longer this time. When she pulled away, she said softly, 'Your place or mine? I want to thank you for saving my life.'

Ben smiled back. 'Okay, how about mine?' he said, finishing his beer. He stood and helped her from the booth. She wobbled slightly as she started for the door, and he put his arm around her waist. He held her tight all the way to the cab that was parked outside the bar at the taxi rank.

This time when Ben woke up, his lover was still there. She was facing away from him. Her naked back and stunning red hair filled his vision. She was fast asleep; her soft deep breaths confirmed it. She should be tired, as they had made love for hours. He lay there, just looking at her as her body gently rocked as she took each breath. He'd often imagined being able to custom build the perfect woman for himself, and Rebecca fitted most of the criteria. He loved her fearless gutsy attitude, though that did almost get her killed. She was naturally pretty, smart, fit, a lively conversationalist, had a great figure, and she carried a gun! What more could a man want in a woman?

He looked at his watch; it was seven thirty. Surely, she had a job to get to. He slid up behind her, and the warmth of her body on his felt wonderful. She moaned as she started to wake.

'Do you need to get to work, beautiful?' he asked.

She jumped. 'What time is it?'

'Seven thirty.'

'Shit, I'm supposed to start at seven!'

Rebecca jumped out of bed and quickly dressed, and so did Ben.

'I will run you home, Bec. My car is here.'

'That would be great.'

Her hair was everywhere as they walked out the door.

They piled into his black Jeep, and she gave him directions to her house. When he stopped out the front, she opened the car door, leaned back, and kissed him and said, 'Don't you dare leave town without seeing me again,' as she turned and ran inside.

He drove off as the door closed behind her, and he felt a warmth, a closeness he had never felt before. He stopped at a coffee shop and went in to order his morning brew. The vision of her in his bed when he'd woken up sent a delicious pulse through him.

My God, he thought, *this must be what love feels like.*

As the day went on, it got worse for him. He was getting desperate to see her. She was all he could think about. He did still have the photos of the massacre that she needed, and the drone footage, so he would have to see her again. It was after lunch when he decided to call the station; the stress of her lateness should have receded subsided by now.

She answered the police-station phone.

'Are you the only person who answers the phone at that station?' Ben asked.

Recognising his voice she said, 'Hello lover boy, it goes to my desk first then works its way around the office till someone answers it.'

'Okay, fair enough, hey Bec, I'm really sorry I made you late for work.'

'My God, it was worth it, Ben. I am finding it a little hard to walk though. It's been a while, and never anything like that.'

'Sorry, about that,' Ben said, unable to wipe the grin from his face.

'Actually, I don't think the sarge even noticed, probably thought I did a job or something on my way in.'

'Well you were working on a suspect for most of the night.'

'Yes, and it was exhausting!' she said.

'Hey, I do still need to give you that evidence,' Ben said.

'How about dinner tonight?' Rebecca said.

'I would love nothing more,' Ben said. 'Here's my phone number. Send me a time, and I will pick you up. And Bec, I *really* enjoyed last night.'

'So did I... I better go; see you then,' Rebecca said softly.

Ben's heart was racing; it was like a virus had invaded his body and now superheated blood flowed through his veins. It had taken over his mind so that the sharp, observant killer had turned into a zombie—no, a puppy, whose whole existence evolved around its brand-new owner.

My God, he thought. *If I could make a drug that made you feel like this, I would be a very rich man.*

Rebecca paused for a second as she hung up the phone. She replayed in her mind the gentle way he had penetrated her body. Hell, she could still feel where he'd been, but it was more than that. Could it be a little part of him had penetrated her heart as well? She shook her head, then she felt her hair tie slip. She removed it and pulled together her hair, then slid the tie off her wrist and over the handful of bright red curls. Just then, a concerned-looking man marched in quickly through the police-station doors. Rebecca's smile vanished, having sensed he needed her immediate attention.

'Can I help you, sir?'

The man blurted, 'My name is Paul Williams. My daughter Vanessa is missing.'

A burning panic rose through her. This was quickly becoming a nightmare.

'One minute, sir. I will get my sergeant.'

She rushed to Jones's office. His door was partially open. She burst in.

'Sarge, we may have another one. I have a distressed father out here.'

'Shit!' Jones said with a silent yell, as his head almost headbutted the desk. 'Okay, bring him through, Reed.'

Senior Sergeant Jones took down all the details of the man's missing daughter and promised him he would do everything in his power to get her back safely. As soon as the man left, he picked up the phone and called the Northern Territory police headquarters in Darwin.

'Police headquarters,' a young woman answered.

'Peter Andrews in Major Crime please,' Jones said quicker than he needed, a sense of urgency starting to swell inside him.

'Andrews,' the man said as he answered.

'Pete, Tim Jones here in Alice. How are you, mate?'

'Great, and you, Tim?'

'Been better, mate. I have a big problem down here, Pete. I have at least three young girls that have gone missing in about the same number of days. I'm going to need some help—and fast. I think we should have media involved as well. We should let everyone know what's going on. I have a picture of the suspect car and identikit pic of the perp.'

'Shit, let me go and see the inspector, and I will get straight back to you.'

Jones walked out to the front-desk area and called out sharply, 'Reed, get all the traffic-camera footage you can, and get every single person you can rally up to go through it. I want that F-250 found, and fast!'

'Shall I call Peter to help, sir?'

'Yes, great idea, he knows the truck.'

Rebecca called Peter, who agreed to meet her at the traffic-management centre in the mall in thirty minutes. She gathered up Jackson and two Aboriginal community rangers to help, and headed for the mall.

Ben needed a distraction, as the thought of her was consuming him.

He called Thomas in Dallas, as it would be about eight o'clock at night there.

'Ben, I just heard the Madison woman was killed over there. So he got her then?'

'Yes, nothing I could do, a real shame.'

Ben hated lying to his mate, but he had no choice. If it was found out that she was still alive, he doubted he could save her again.

'Tom, I need a couple more favours.'

'Sure, mate, if I can,' Thomas said.

'I need to know if Jerry Stokes is back there yet.'

'He is,' Thomas said without hesitation.

'Good,' Ben said, knowing that meant Greg was probably off the hit list.

'Second, I need a good man in the FBI that doesn't mind stepping on toes.'

'How big are the toes, Ben?'

'Big, Tom. Crooked cops, pollies, and more,' Ben said.

'Phew! Okay, let me see what I can find out and get back to you.'

'I appreciate that, Tom.' And Ben hung up.

Once he had slipped the phone back into his pocket, he realised he hadn't thought about Bec for the last ten minutes. He pictured the smile of the tipsy redhead that flirted with him at the bar last night, and the warmth of adrenaline that only true infatuation could produce swelled through him again.

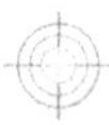

Jones's desk phone rang.

'Tim Jones,' he answered.

'Tim, Pete Andrews. Can you send me all the images you have of the vehicle and the perp? I will have police media get it all over the networks by day's end, and we will get a couple of detectives down there tomorrow.'

'Thanks, Pete, please keep me posted.'

Rebecca and her team spent hours going through the footage, with only one sighting of the truck heading north on Stuart Highway, though the number plates were not recognisable.

She called it a day and headed home to get ready for dinner with Ben.

Ben was there on the dot to pick her up. He was excited; he had been counting the hours down. He still couldn't believe she'd had the effect on him that she did. *But that's how it goes, isn't it?* he thought.

He knocked on the door, and she called out for him to come in. He turned the handle and stepped in, closing the door behind him. Seeing her house would tell him a lot about her. He wondered, *Was she a messy out-of-a-suitcase type, shoot-from-the-hip type, do-the-minimum-to-get-by type? Or was she anally tidy, everything in its place, and nothing she didn't need?* She was certainly the latter. The small house was spotless and clean. The only non-essential was a picture of who he imagined to be her mother and father on the mantel piece. He took a look at it; she took after her father, all right. She appeared from a bedroom door wearing a summer dress with vertical coloured stripes that tapered out from the waist; it made her look taller. He noted that she seemed not as excited to see him as he was to see her.

'Are you still keen to go?' he said, just a little concerned.

'Of course, it's just been a hard day at work. I'll tell you all about it at dinner, as it's going to be all over the TV tonight anyway.'

'Okay, well, you look lovely, Bec.'

She smiled and walked up to him and kissed him. 'Thank you, Ben.'

Ben had booked a table at the Chinese restaurant in the next street from her house. They walked there, holding hands like teenagers. After ordering a bottle of wine and two dishes that they would share, Ben asked, 'So what's going on at work, Bec?'

'We had Peter help us find a missing tourist, which turned out to be the boyfriend of a girl who was abducted at gunpoint after their car was sabotaged. Then we received a report of an abandoned campervan of a female backpacker at Standley Chasm. Then this morning, a father reported his daughter was missing.'

'That's not good. Any leads?' Ben said.

'Yes, a white F-250 Ford truck. The driver has long grey hair and a beard.'

'Can I help in any way?'

'Not really, we have two detectives coming down from Darwin tomorrow. They will probably take over the case from us.'

They finished dinner and walked back to her house. Ben took her in his arms and kissed her, which soon led to them undressing each other and finding her bed. They made love of course, but it wasn't like the night before. Tonight, it was soft, gentle, and just what she needed. If Ben had any doubts about whether he had fallen for this woman, he certainly didn't now. Just before his ultimate moment, he told her that he loved her, and he truly meant it. He had never said those words to a woman before. He couldn't imagine his life without her now. He spent the next hour of the night just holding her as she slept. She was now his to hold, love, and cherish, and he didn't plan on giving her up easily.

Rebecca was the first awake. She had showered and was standing at the bathroom door in a towel with a toothbrush in her mouth, looking at the man in her bed that she had made love to again. Last night was tender and with feeling, and she remembered he'd told her that he loved her. She'd wanted to say it back, but she hadn't. She wasn't sure, as they were big words, not to be said flippantly in a moment of passion. She knew that he meant it, and she was starting to feel the same. She turned, rinsed her mouth, and dressed as he watched her. He looked at her adoringly as she put on her knickers, her bra, and her khaki-coloured police uniform. She sat on the bed, and he stroked her back as he watched her pull on her elastic-sided police-issue boots. She finally said, 'Do you mind just closing the door behind you when you leave?'

'Nah, I'll go now. I just wasn't going to miss that for the world.'

She smiled, rolling her eyes as his muscular, naked body jumped out of the bed and dressed in seconds.

They walked out of her little house together, and she locked the door behind her.

What now? Ben thought.

Rebecca was two steps ahead of him when she stopped and turned.

'Ben, last night, you told me you loved me. Did you mean that?'

Without any hesitation, he said, 'Yes, I did.'

She took his face in her hands and said, 'I love you too.'

'Does that mean I'll see you tonight?' Ben asked as she walked off towards her car.

'How about I cook dinner. That's of course if no one shoots me today!' she said as she stepped into her Subaru and drove off to the Alice Springs police station.

Ben strolled off to his car; he couldn't be happier. He could live here in Alice Springs, or maybe she might like to come to Adelaide. He imagined them having babies, and what an amazing mother she would make. By the time he reached his car, he had planned the rest of his life with his new love.

Ben went into the Todd mall for breakfast at the Red Dog Café. He sat outside. He could still smell her, and his mind raced to the visions of last night, her naked flesh on his as she kissed him and loved him. His breakfast arrived, and the vision faded away for another time.

He had almost finished when his phone rang. It was a US number.

'Thomas, good afternoon?' he guessed.

'Evening, but close, Ben. I have someone very keen to talk to you or whoever about your information.'

'That's great, Thomas.'

'Mean as! Apparently, he exposed a ring of crooked cops in DC a couple of years ago. He will talk to you, and if he feels there's a case, he's happy to fly to Australia and meet up,' Thomas said.

'Okay, that *is* keen. The best thing to do is for me to have a chat with him. Tell him what I know, and then he can talk to Greg for the finer details,' Ben replied.

'I just spoke to him; he's happy for you to call now if you want,' Thomas said.

'You are an absolute fucking legend, Tom. I really owe you, mate,' Ben said.

Thomas gave him the number. Ben waited till he was back in his car, so he had no background noise and more importantly no one listening.

Ben dialled the US number.

'Martin Smithson speaking.'

'Martin, Ben Woolford here in Australia. Thomas Graves gave me your number.'

'Yes, Ben, Tom called me, said you have something I might be interested in, I believe?'

'Yes, murder one, attempted murder, fraud, blackmail, bribes to cops, and so on.'

'I'm very interested, Ben.'

'Well I'm not who you need to talk to really, I'm just a PI that was involved, but the other party has all the juicy details.'

'So, you say you have proof of murder and attempted murder here in the US?'

'I have a photo of a bullet leaving the gun of a hitman who was sent from Texas to murder a US citizen here in Australia,' Ben said.

'Okay, you have my full attention,' Martin said.

'I will pass your number onto the people that know the exact time, places, and names, if that is okay, and you can go from there.'

'Sure thing, get them to call me tomorrow, 9:00 a.m., DC time.'

'I will, thank you, Martin.' With that, Ben hung up.

He then called Greg and told him the details.

CHAPTER TWENTY-TWO

I was busy at the front desk of the Alice Springs police station that morning, following the big announcement on TV last night.

Rebecca walked in to find at least eight different groups of people at the counter reporting white Ford trucks and men with grey hair and beards. Jackson did a double take, flashed a look of pure jealousy, and said in a muffled voice, 'Rebecca, is that a bloody love bite on your neck?'

Rebecca quickly covered her neck with her hand. She had forgotten Ben had done that.

'You better go and cover it up. The sarge will lose it if he sees it,' Jackson said, looking like he was desperately trying to hide any emotion.

With her hand on her neck, she said, 'What's going on?'

'We have sightings of every white Ford in Alice, I think,' he said, turning back to the front counter.

Slowly, every officer was dispatched to look at each of the white trucks that had been reported. The sarge was with the two detectives from Darwin, and a part-time lady named Trudy had been called in to man the phones. She was called in whenever it was busy. Trudy was a retired receptionist from Telstra and was perfect for them to call on at a minute's notice. Trudy called over to Rebecca to take another call from a sighting. There had been twenty or more today, all leading nowhere, but still they all needed to be checked out.

'Hello, Constable Reed speaking.'

'Hi, I know where the white truck is that you are looking for,' an older-sounding lady said in almost a whisper.

'Can I have your name please?' Rebecca said.

'No, I need to remain anonymous,' the caller said.

'Okay, that's fine. What can you tell me?' Rebecca asked.

'That truck belongs to a strange, scary man. I think he's Russian. He lives some hundred kilometres down a dirt road that's about a hundred kilometres north of Alice on the Stuart Highway.'

'Do you know the name of the road or the name of the person?'

'Nobody knows his name; he is evil, and he drives the truck you are looking for. The road sign has gone, but you can't miss it. It's the only road out there, and his property is the only one on that road,' the caller said, and with that, she was gone.

Rebecca looked at her watch. *That's a four-hour trip and will get me nicely out of the office for the rest of the day.* She touched her neck where Ben had left his mark of passion.

Rebecca grabbed her bag and said to Trudy, 'Tell the others when they get back, I'm just going to have a look at another white truck sighting out of town about a hundred kilometres north. I won't be back till about five.'

'Okay. Oh, and Bec,' Trudy said.

'Yes, Trudy?'

'Good night last night, hey?'

Rebecca grabbed her neck, blushing, and said, 'Yes, extremely good, thanks, Trudy.'

Rebecca jumped into the last police car left in the park. She checked the fuel gauge and set the odometer to zero and settled in for the drive. Her mind soon thought of Ben and how he made her feel. She knew very well he was from Adelaide and would probably be gone any day soon. She had to be careful to not fall too deeply for him before he disappeared and broke her heart. *Or was it already too late?*

She'd told him this morning that she loved him, and she meant it. He said he loved her too. She drove for the next hour thinking about him and how comfortable she felt with him. She knew that not many men would be her type, and she certainly didn't want to get involved with another cop. This man was tough. He had taken on a Mexican cartel, rescued a hostage, and had been a real soldier. He was handsome and fit, kind and gentle, and fitted every part of her perfectly. A smile formed on her face as she imagined just that.

The road to the left was at one hundred and two kilometres. She turned left and headed down the dirt road. It deteriorated quickly into a two-wheel track.

It was nearly an hour later when the odometer's trip meter ticked over two hundred kilometres, and what looked like an abandoned farmhouse appeared ahead in the distance. She played back in her mind what the caller had said and decided to park a little way out, walk to a disguised area, and just have a look from a distance. If he really was evil, she would need some backup. She pulled over, checked her gun and taser, and walked slowly in the shadows of the trees. She could see a lot of sheds of all shapes and sizes, one big enough to be a hangar. There was no sign of life, not even a dog barking or the odd chicken. The farmhouse looked like it had been abandoned for years. She decided to walk north to circumnavigate the farmhouse from a safe distance and then maybe come back with Jackson. There was something spooky about the place, and although she was armed with a fully loaded Glock pistol, she didn't feel brave enough to knock on any doors. She could see fresh-looking tyre tracks that led to a shed with an entrance facing the west. She continued to walk the large circle, keeping as inconspicuous and quiet as possible. As the entrance came into view, she could see the F-250, the blue Ford logo on the rear tailgate with the faded *D*. She immediately lay down, her khaki uniform blending in well to the surroundings. The situation had now changed significantly. If this was the kidnapper, and she was now pretty sure it was, he was most likely armed and dangerous. She took out her phone and zoomed in as best she could and clicked off two photos of the truck.

She said softly, 'I've got you now, you bastard.'

'No, my dear. I got you,' said a strong Russian accent. He pushed the deadly end of a double-barrelled shotgun hard into her back.

Rebecca dropped her forehead onto the sand. *Fuck! Why me all the time?* she thought.

The man reached down placing his knee in her back and removed her pistol from the holster. He rocked it back and forth to free it, a safety feature built into police holsters so it couldn't be taken easily from an officer during a scuffle. Rebecca wondered how he knew to do that.

'You make big mistake come here,' he said.

'I am just looking for a missing person,' she said as innocently as she could.

'I know exactly why you here. You stand up slowly and walk to barn.' He pointed with the rifle to what looked like horse stables.

It was now she again realised how silly she had been, as no one really knew where she was. Her HiLux didn't have a GPS tracker like the newer ones that she would normally have taken, but all the other cars were out looking for the truck that she had now found. As she walked towards the derelict homestead, she imagined how different her night tonight would now be compared to last night, when Ben had held her tenderly as she faded off, exhausted, to sleep. Then the realisation hit that maybe last night might have been her last night ever. She was truly scared now.

Ben decided that tonight, he would tell her how he felt and that he would like to discuss a longer-term arrangement. He wanted her to fall asleep in his arms every night, for her to be the one he adored, cared for, and loved, with all his heart.

He called the police station, realising he still didn't have her personal mobile number.

'Alice Springs police, Trudy speaking.'

'Hi, Trudy, can I speak to Rebecca please?'

'She is out on a job, sir. Can I give her a message?'

'No, that's okay. What time do you expect her back?'

'Any minute, sir.'

'Okay, thanks.'

A small wave of panic shook through him, and he soon dismissed it.

It was right on 6:00 p.m., her knock-off time, when he called again.

'Will Jackson speaking.'

'Could I please speak to Rebecca?' Ben said.

'Can I ask who this is please?' Jackson said.

'I'm a friend.'

The one who gave her that fucking love bite, Jackson thought.

'Can I please have your number, and I will have her call you back when she returns, sir?'

'Why, what's happened? Wasn't she due back an hour ago?' Ben said, knowing full well they wouldn't tell him anyway.

'Sir, we are just waiting for her to get back from a job now. I will have her call you when she returns.'

Ben gave Jackson his name and number, as his ability to analyse the full consequences of giving those details out was not possible at the moment.

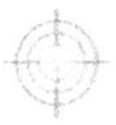

Rebecca found herself in a concrete-walled shed, now stripped of her phone, keys, taser, cuffs, and pistol. She tried desperately to listen for the other girls. If they were still alive, her chances of living another day would seem to be a little better. She heard her police HiLux being driven past, and a squeaky shed door close behind it. She sat in the dark corner of the shed and put her new love aside for a minute and thought about her first year as a police officer in Alice Springs. She had been shot at while in a helicopter, she tried to shoot a suspected bikie in the back, who she ended up sleeping with, she was shot during a siege and put in hospital, and now she was probably going to die at the hands of an Ivan Milat copycat. She picked up the scent of paint, then, did she hear a noise. *Was it the distant scream of a woman?*

Senior Sergeant Tim Jones sat at his desk with his whole team, who were making calls. It was now 7:00 p.m. and no word from Reed.

'Someone must know where she is!' he said in frustration.

'Sir, we have tried her phone, and the police radio. She was here when we all left to look at sightings of the white F-250.'

'We have maybe two hours of daylight at the most. Get Peter with the drone to look west and get the helicopter to head east. On to it, now!' he yelled.

Jackson immediately left to call Peter.

Jones had a thought and called Trudy, who had finished work long before there was any panic in the office.

'Trudy, Tim Jones. Sorry to bother you, but do you have any idea where Reed may have gone this afternoon?'

'No, sir, she went out about one o'clock, and she didn't tell me anything. Hang on, she did say something about going about a hundred kilometres north.'

'Nothing else?'

'No, that's all, sir.'

'If you think of anything else, please call me straight away. She hasn't come back.'

'Oh my God, I hope she is all right!' Trudy said.

'So do we, Trudy,' he said solemnly as he hung up.

Jones called Jackson on the police radio.

'Jackson, come in.'

'Go ahead, Sarge, over.'

'Change of plan. Go a hundred kilometres north up Stuart Highway. Search the west side of the highway with Peter's drone, and I will send the chopper to search the east. As fast as you can, over.'

Peter was still setting up the drone, when he saw the helicopter fly past at speed and peel off to the east. They had less than an hour before it was too dark.

Once the sun had gone he switched the camera to the thermal imaging option, but all he found were kangaroos and a handful of other smaller animals. Eventually they called it, packed up and headed back. The sarge was still at the station waiting for more news when the phone rang again.

'Sergeant Jones speaking.'

'Sergeant, has Rebecca been found yet?'

'Who am I speaking to?'

'My name is Ben, and I am… err, her boyfriend, I guess.'

'I see… Ben, all I can say now is that we are still looking for her. We have no reason to think she is in trouble, but we just don't know where she is. We've had a drone and a chopper out looking for her at her last known position. It just may be her car has broken down and she is out of radio range.'

The drone, Peter's drone, Ben thought.

'Okay, thank you, Sergeant. Please call me when you know something.'

Ben went and parked outside her house and waited, thinking.

At 10:00 p.m. he called Peter.

'Peter, Roo-man. No, actually, my name is Ben. What do you know about Rebecca being missing?'

'They have told me I can't talk to anyone about anything or I will never get any work with them again.'

'I don't want you to tell anyone, I want you to tell me so I can find her.'

'I'm sorry, Ben. The police work is really important to me now, and I don't want to jeopardise it.'

'Peter, now listen carefully, how much work do you think you will get when I come around there and smash the fucking drone over your fucking head?'

'Fuck, all right, all right, fuck, I didn't tell you, all right?' Peter said.

'Not a word, my friend.'

'She went out at about one o'clock to look at a possible sighting of the white F-250 with the *D* faded on the tailgate. We were looking around an area one hundred K's north up the Stuart.'

'Anything else, anything?'

'Looking for a man, long grey hair and beard. Three young women have gone missing this week, same truck and same man.'

'Anything else?'

'He took the first girl, Japanese, at gunpoint. Left her boyfriend stranded in the middle of nowhere.'

'What car was Bec driving?'

'One of the twin-cab police HiLuxes, one with the cage on the back, same as most cars they have.'

'Peter, if you find out any more, call me on Ferret's satphone. I desperately want to find her, and you know I am her best chance.'

'I know you are,' Peter said.

CHAPTER TWENTY-THREE

REG dialled the number of FBI inspector Martin Smithson.

'Smithson,' he answered.

'Mr Smithson, Greg Sheppard. A mutual friend said you may be interested in some information that will rock some boats over there.'

'Yes, Mr Sheppard. If half of what I have heard is true, I will jump on a plane and come and meet you. I'm sure this stuff is not for over the phone.'

'No, probably not. I have every detail, names, places, and times. Some heavy hitters,' Greg said.

'Okay, let me talk to my boss, and I will get back to you. I may bring a colleague from the CIA, as this is potentially an international situation as well.'

'Well, if you call attempted murder of a US citizen in another country an international situation, you had better bring him along.'

Ben wished he still had the STAR Force tactical gear that was now back in Adelaide, waiting to be returned to Mark the armourer. Although he did have his rifle that was secretly hidden under the back seat of his Jeep. He drove around to the back alley behind the police station and parked his Jeep up against the fence. He climbed onto the roof of the black Cherokee and placed two rubber-backed floor mats over the barbed wire that was spread in three strands above the iron. He spotted an empty pallet that would help his exit back over. He jumped over the fence, landing on his feet and rolling to distribute the landing force. He could see Bec's Subaru still parked in the yard. He checked the tyre brand on the three police HiLuxes. It was no surprise to see Bridgestone D697 Duelers fitted; he knew the tyre well. He took out his tape measure and measured the exact width of the tyre and then the distance between the two rear tyres, as the track was quite often different between the front and rear of a car. The rear tyres would run over the front tyre prints as the car drove forward, making the rear the measurement he needed.

He shone his torch into the car. He could see the dispatch screen and the police radio, but nothing else of interest. He put the pallet against the fence and easily climbed back over. He fitted the car mats back into the Jeep and wrote down the measurements that he had just memorised.

Ben stopped to fill his car to the brim with fuel and bought two large bottles of water. He hopped back in and looked at his odometer and mentally added one hundred kilometres to the number. As soon as he had left the city, he accelerated up to the legal one-hundred-and-thirty-kilometre speed limit. From about ninety kilometres out, he slowed to thirty kilometres per hour, shining his torch from side to side, while his double row lightbar lit up the road for nearly a kilometre ahead. At the and one-hundred-and-two-kilometre point, there was a dirt road to the left. He pulled up before it, jumped out, and walked up to the intersection. He used his torch to search for the Bridgestone tyre prints. He saw them straight away and followed them for a short distance on foot. He noted they were fresh, certainly from today. A quick measurement confirmed a perfect match to the police car at the station. He walked a little further, noting the tyre prints had stopped, did a three-point turn, and headed back to the highway. He studied where the car had stopped: two sets of footprints, and a lot of them. One set perfectly matched Bec's police boots that he watched her put on just that morning. He squatted down to study the second set; they were far too big to be Bec's. Then he could see a swept circle where the drone had taken off. He quickly realised that this was Peter, and Constable Jackson's car and prints. He walked on and found another set of Dueler tyre prints, all but a little older than the ones from Jackson's car. He also measured these prints, and they also matched perfectly to his measurements. After a check on the other side of the road, he saw that the car had not done a return trip. He ran back to his Jeep, took out some black tape, and covered the top and bottom of his headlights to greatly reduce the chance of him being seen a long way off. He always gave thanks for this old World War II trick. Next, he lifted the rear seat, retrieving the rifle and a packet of shells. He popped out the magazine and loaded five shells into it and clicked it back into the rifle.

He headed down the road, stopping constantly to check for the

Dueler tyre prints.

After slowly driving for some fifty kilometres, following the Bridgestone tracks, there was still only the one set of tracks, none returning and no situations where the tracks had been over run. Bec's police car was most likely the last vehicle to drive down this road.

Eventually, two hours later, he could see where she had pulled over to the side of the road. He stopped and got out. Here was the confirmation he needed. Her footprints, a lady's size, police-issue boots that walked away from the car. He also noted there were a set of large boots with a narrow heel, maybe RMs, walking towards the car and not away. One print had stepped on top of one of hers. The tyre prints showed that the car headed back onto the road and towards the homestead that he could now see ahead of him in the moonlight. He realised that Bec had stopped and headed north on foot and never come back, however someone else, a tall male by the size of the boot, must have come back and collected the police car. His girl was clearly in trouble, and a strange mixture of panic and anger pulsed through him.

Ben turned off the Jeep's lights and engine, grabbed the rifle, and proceeded to follow Bec's footprints through the bush. With his torch on the lowest brightness, he was able to follow her prints easily. He found where she had stopped, and from a scramble of footprints, deduced this was where the same man had snuck up behind her. His prints were the same as the ones that had moved her car. The sun hadn't risen but was starting to light the eastern sky. He needed to be quick, as he didn't need to be caught snooping around here in daylight. He followed the two sets of prints to an empty concrete barn with a large bolt-type lock. He looked into the cell. There were two water bottles, one full and one almost empty, and her police boot prints covered floor. He followed the single set of man's prints as they walked out; they were the last prints, and they were heavy. *He must have been carrying her.* Another rush of panic flooded over him. *Was she already dead, and he has gone to bury her body?* He felt a rise of panic pulse through him.

He followed the footprints to a shed where the police HiLux tyre tracks appeared again, reversing out of the shed and heading further west into the desert. He ran at pace back to his Jeep, started it, and drove quickly through the homestead and headed west, following the HiLux's tyre tracks. He knew now, he would just follow the road until he found her.

Some Time Earlier:

Rebecca heard him approach the cell door. She braced herself and called out in the strongest voice she could muster, 'You can't imprison a police officer. You will be caught and spend the rest of your life in jail, you hear me?'

'Would you like drink of water?' he asked calmly, his Russian accent somehow soothing as he opened a little hatch in the door.

She was parched. It must have been forty-five degrees in her cell during the day, but now she was cold, but still very thirsty.

She looked through the hatch to see two bottles of chilled water on a tray, condensation covering each of the bottles.

'Help yourself,' he said. She could almost taste the cold liquid on her parched palate as she reached through the hatch. Just as she grasped the bottle, the Russian grabbed her wrist and stabbed her with a needle; she could only watch as the yellow liquid emptied from the syringe into her forearm.

'What is that?' she yelled as he let go of her hand.

'Just to calm you before your trip,' he said, as the two water bottles landed at her feet through the hatch before it slammed closed.

She had only finished half of the first bottle before she needed to sit down. The room was starting to spin. Shards of colour flashed across her vision.

The door to her cell opened, and he walked up to her. Her mind was alert, although her vision blurred. She tried to talk, but her mind was now scrambling to form any words. He lifted her sixty-kilogram body over his shoulder like a butcher would carry a side of beef. He laid her, quite gently, in the rear cage of what she was to realise later was her police HiLux with the signage and chequers painted out with a white spray can, and the police lights torn off the roof. As she looked up from the floor, she could see three young women looking down at her. They helped her onto one of the small bench seats that ran along each side of the cage. She recognised where she was now; she had put many a drunk in the back of this vehicle.

The HiLux started, and they bumped along for what seemed like hours. Rebecca was nearly out of her drug-induced state when the driver stopped to pour two cans of fuel into the vehicle he took from the back seat of the cabin. Rebecca could see that the girls had a false sense of confidence with the fact a police officer was in there with them.

The dust was unbelievable, they'd all taken their shirts off and used them to filter the dust from their nose and mouths. She could see through the vent in the rear door that the sun was well and truly up now and that they had been travelling due west for most of the trip. *We'd have to be nearly in Western Australia by now*, she thought. The driver jumped back into the driver's seat and continued the trek west.

Sergeant Jones was at work early that morning, as he'd been called about one of the motion sensors in the rear car park, having picked up an intruder and recorded the footage. Jackson had also arrived early with Peter in tow, whom he picked up on his way into the station.

'Jackson, come in here,' Jones called out, and Peter followed.

'Look at this. A man dressed in black jumps the fence, and it looks like he is measuring the wheels on your police car. He then put a pallet against the fence and jumped back over. What do you make of that?' Jones said, looking at him.

'He has a tape measure, that makes no sense at all.'

Peter saw the recording over Jackson's shoulder and knew exactly who it was and what he was doing. He kept that to himself.

'Anyway, nothing is missing. Now we need to get Peter and the drone back out there this morning. This time, swap sides, you two do the east side and the chopper can do the west. Go further and deeper and cover as much ground as you can. We need to find that F-250 and that police car.'

'Sir, if I may,' said Peter, 'I feel we should concentrate on the road to the west, as that is the only significant thing at the hundred-kilometre mark.'

Jones thought about that for a second. 'Thanks, Peter, but let's go with my plan for now and start eliminating places.'

Peter knew Ben would now already be a day ahead of the police. He knew he would find her one way or another.

Rebecca felt the HiLux come to a final stop. She was completely sober now after the haze from the drug the Russian had given her. She looked out of the vent to see an airfield; the runway was in perfect condition, which she figured must be regularly used, and probably owned by a mining corporation. There were about six hangars that did, or could, house small aircraft, and she spotted a new windsock and what looked like a runway long enough to land a commercial jet. Then the reality of this situation jolted her. She was taken by a Russian, there were other young women, and an airfield big enough to land a jet. Her heart sank, as the scene from the movie *Taken* flashed through her mind, when the girls were drugged, sold, and used as prostitutes in Albania until they died of drug overdoses. She looked at the other girls, who were younger than her, and so innocent. She had to stop this somehow.

Two different men, both Russian as well, she suspected, opened the back of the cage and pointed automatic weapons at them. They ordered the women out, as they quickly refitted their shirts. All the women were happy to get out. They were covered in red dust, and just the lower parts of their faces where the shirts had been were slightly cleaner.

'Shower, now!' one of the men yelled, pointing his gun in the direction of a building that would be where passengers might wait for their flight. The two younger girls, Marie Lovatt and Vanessa Williams, were now crying, and Rebecca gave them a hug to reassure them that help would be on the way. She wished she could believe that. The two men walked them into what was the ladies' bathroom and pointed to the two shower cubicles with their guns.

'Shower!' one yelled.

The girls looked at Rebecca, who nodded. The two young ones undressed, and each stepped into the shower cubical; their sobs could be heard over the running water.

'I want to talk to your boss,' Rebecca demanded.

'Shut up, bitch!' one said, lifting his rifle as if to strike her.

She cowered instinctively, just as four towels were thrown on the floor by the other guard along with four white sari-type wrap-around dresses.

'Put on dresses and *only* dresses after shower,' the Russian yelled at Rebecca.

CHAPTER TWENTY-FOUR

MARCUS Chen had been working at the Pine Gap Joint Defence Facility just outside Alice Springs for nearly two years now. He was single and looked like your average Chinese ICT professional. A short, dark, thin, friendly man, completely focused behind his black-rimmed glasses. He was popular with his workmates, although he usually kept to himself. He was desperately trying to work his way up through the ranks. But something had changed for him lately: a new employee, who was asking a lot of questions. Which for most people wasn't a problem, but for Chen, it was a huge problem. Unbeknown to anyone, he'd been carefully stationed here by another authority. Devoted to his mother country, he'd managed to feed information back to the MSS—Ministry of State Security in China. He'd been actively sharing intel since first being posted there, under the guise of being a foreign 'friendly' with high-level skills, but he suspected that they were onto him now. He would need to keep his head down. Although some Australians worked there and it was called a joint defence facility, it was really an American satellite spy base, and the Americans wouldn't be as understanding as the Australians about a Chinese spy in their institution. He knew that being of Chinese heritage would make him a prime suspect, especially once someone picked the anomalies in his encryption codes. He'd noticed that today the security had increased around the centre, and he sensed an uneasy calm and odd sideways glances from his supervisor. Chen was now convinced that they were onto him.

He knew they would probably get him at the main gate as he left for the end of his day. Arresting him on site would cause a scene they wouldn't want or need. He wouldn't be taken away for questioning on suspicion of espionage or treason and dragged through the Australian courts for years until finally a deal was done with China for his release. No, the American way was that he would just disappear or have an unfortunate accident on his way home.

He looked at his watch. He had a couple of tasks to do that had been planned, ready for a time just like this.

It was now 4:00 p.m., the knock-off time for the day shift, which was 80 percent of the staff. Only the control room worked through the night, and they would be at their stations by now. He noticed that the security on the main gate was now complimented by two extra AFP police cars. His suspicions were accurate. He ran into the main satellite control room, closed and locked the door behind him. Not many people noticed, but as it was not his normal area, the shift supervisor watched him as Chen took out his phone and called the security desk.

'Security,' the guard answered.

'This is Marcus Chen. Listen carefully. I have hostages in the control room. I want the entire complex vacated in the next fifteen minutes or I start shooting people. For everyone I see this side of the perimeter fence, I will kill one person in here. Do you understand?'

It was only seconds later that the alarm sounded with an automated recording that called over the speaker, 'Evacuate, evacuate, evacuate.'

Everyone in the control room stood and started for the door. Chen pulled out a handgun and fired a shot into the ceiling, 'No! We all stay,' he called out. They were all rendered into shock and fear, motionless on the spot. 'Now, everybody please sit down,' he said calmly. He knew that it was unlikely that anyone would have a mobile phone or gun, as they were banned from the complex. He was confident his was the only one, although he'd smuggled his in quite easily.

Chen checked his watch; he'd activated his plan.

Exactly fifteen minutes later, he received a call back. 'Mr. Chen, this is Dave Sanders, head of security. To the best of our knowledge, the complex is completely vacated,' he said in a heavy American accent. 'Mr. Chen, it is very important that no one is hurt. What is it that you require for us to do to have a peaceful resolution to this situation?'

'I want a chopper, private hire, to be here at 8:00 a.m. tomorrow morning, or I will execute one person per hour,' Chen said in very calm voice.

'Okay, Mr. Chen, let me see what I can do. Is anyone injured; do you need medical assistance?' Sanders asked.

'No, we won't be needing medical assistance, just body bags if that chopper is not here.' Chen ended the call.

Chen had it all worked out. He would get into the chopper,

turning his gun immediately to the pilot's head. He'd instruct him for the transponder to be turned off, and then give the coordinates of the destination. He'd order the pilot fly at five hundred feet, to avoid radar. Chen would have an accomplice pick him up once on the ground. He would tie the pilot to the skid of the chopper, which would probably take him about an hour to free himself. By this time, he would be long gone and with his fake ID would fly out of Perth and back to Beijing. But he still had a lot of work to do before then. He locked his eighteen hostages in an adjacent storeroom and sat down at one of the computers.

Ben looked at his fuel gauge; he was now a long way past the point of no return. It had taken him three quarters of a tank to get here, so if he didn't find Bec or her kidnapper soon, he'd be walking, and he was now probably four hundred kilometres from the next town. He did have Ferret's satphone though, which gave him a little security, although the battery was getting very low. But at this stage he didn't want the police turning up with all guns blazing and getting his lady killed. That's if she wasn't already dead.

The first thing he saw was the windsock, and he skidded to a stop. He backed his car in behind some overgrown saltbush that would somewhat partially hide it. He felt for his Leatherman, clipped the satphone to his belt, and made sure it was turned to silent. He lifted the back seat, filled his pockets with the spare magazine and a packet of bullets and collected up his rifle. He placed the Jeep keys on the ground, in behind the right-hand rear wheel. He could see that the HiLux tyre prints had turned right as it hit the clearing.

He crept through the bush towards a small building, what looked to be a makeshift departure lounge. He ducked without looking, as a small business jet flew past low above him, at maybe less than a thousand feet. As it went over, he looked at the tail of an unmarked G5 Gulfstream, whose wheels were coming down and at least one stage of flap was deployed. It was definitely landing. He wondered, *Were these goodies or baddies?* But he already knew the answer. A picture of what was going on here was quickly developing in his head. The good news was that the girls were most likely still alive. He had to make sure they didn't get on that plane, or they would be gone, probably for good.

Just then another jet flew overhead, a Citation II, turning onto a downwind leg of a right-hand circuit. The G5 had touched down and was taxiing towards the bitumen apron. The Citation was on final now and would be parked next to the Gulfstream soon enough. Ben's head was racing, desperate for the best way to keep everyone alive and get his girl back. He moved in closer and was able to sneak in behind one of the hangars. The main door of the G5 opened, and what looked like a bodyguard dressed in black stepped out. He quickly surveyed the surroundings and nodded for what must be an Arab sheik, dressed in a pure white robe and headpiece, to step out of the aircraft.

The Citation had also landed and was pulling up alongside the G5, the jet engines drowning out any other noise. Ben had now worked out exactly what was going on here. The girls were going to be sold, and the first bidders had just arrived. The door of the Citation opened as well, no security-guard scan for this bloke. A tall Middle Eastern man stepped out with confidence, his security skulking behind him. The jet engines slowly wound down, bringing peace and quiet to the airfield. The two new arrivals walked up to a tall grey-haired man with a matching beard, who appeared from inside the terminal, and they all shook hands.

For a start, Ben needed to calculate how many there were in total. It appeared to be one businessman and two security men per plane, plus two pilots each, who would be no threat to him. If he started a ruckus early enough, they would all run to their planes and be wheels up as fast as they could, before any purchasing of the women had started. If the sales had been completed, the women would be dragged aboard as well. How many were on the ground though? Ben watched intently through his riflescope as he waited for a plan to form in his head.

Two men armed with semi-auto rifles pushed the first of the girls out of the small lounge building. Their black beards and olive skin suggested they may be Middle Eastern. Then a second girl appeared, then a third, who looked Asian, and then the fourth out was Rebecca, who was significantly resisting being pushed around. A wave of emotion surged through him, that combination of love and anger. The sight of his lover had softened his resolve, but combined with the anger of her being manhandled, the swirl of emotions he felt were confusing. He desperately wanted to waste that man. He knew once he fired his first shot it would all change in a big hurry. This was a time for unemotional, calculated decisions.

The four girls were all dressed the same in white saris. The man with the grey beard walked up to the first girl, and with a simple action, pulled the sari from her, leaving her completely naked in front of her audience of men. The man yelled a command at her as she tried to cover herself. He reached for the second and did the same, rendering both girls completely naked and crying with fright and indignity. Rebecca turned and confronted the man who tried to disrobe her. He slapped her hard across the face, sending her flying across the rough bitumen. She lay half naked on the ground, as her sari had partially unravelled.

Rebecca felt a small spray of warm blood splatter her as a gunshot echoed out through the air. The guard yelled and wailed as he stared in shock at the fact that part of his hand was missing. The girls screamed, and everyone hit the ground. Guns were waving everywhere; no one had any clue as to where the shot had come from. The two businessmen quickly stood and ran back to their planes, heads down and protected by their trailing security. The sheik had sent one of his men back to grab the Japanese girl, who was desperately trying to get her sari wrapped back around her, while the others who could speak English heeded Rebecca's instruction to stay on the ground, naked or not.

The sheik's guard grabbed the Japanese girl by her arm and took only two steps before another shot rang out. The guard fell to the ground, gripping his left leg. He screamed in pain as blood oozed through his fingers. He limped towards the plane, and Akira ran back to Rebecca. The four girls all huddled together on the tarmac, in a tight group. The engines of both planes were now spooling up, and with the doors still closing, the planes both taxied away at pace. The Citation was the first back onto the runway and at full throttle roared off with the wind at its tail. That was not ideal; it meant a lot faster ground speed and a lot more runway required before it could lift off, but that was a lesser concern to the pilot than having to fly through a volley of bullets. The G5 was a larger aircraft and didn't have that option. It did roar off to the far end of the runway though. The Citation had only just lifted off, but it used every available metre of runway. The Gulfstream's pilots would have seen that, confirming that taking off downwind was not an option for them; they would have hit the trees at the end of the runway. They stopped at the far end of the runway, turned into the wind, and held their position, hopefully out of rifle range. They sat there with the engines running, ready for the first opportunity to leave.

The four girls had remained huddled together in trembling fear and shock. Only Rebecca looked up, trying desperately to take in the situation. One of the kidnappers shot off a round of automatic gunfire as another ran out and grabbed Marie and Vanessa, one in each arm, dragging them into the departure lounge building. The skin of their bare feet tore on the abrasive bitumen as they tried desperately to keep up. Jolted into action, Rebecca grabbed Akira and ran to the back of the building. As she peeked around the corner, her eyes fixed instantly on the man crouched to the side of the next hangar. It was her man, her lover. He was the one who'd come to save her life, again. She ran as fast as she could, almost dragging the naked Japanese girl with her. They ran and tucked themselves down in behind Ben. Rebecca touched a hand to his back. Keeping close watch on the building, Ben reached his left hand behind him to touch her bare leg. She was right there, safe and alive. Rebecca saw a wave of relief start to rise through him, but she knew he couldn't indulge that feeling, not yet. Ben forced his concentration back to his rifle and the other two girls. Without warning, a window smashed, and a shower of bullets rattled the tin above his head. They had found where they were hiding.

Ben turned and said to her, 'Take the girl, see if you can find something to wear, and if you can, find out what is in these sheds.

Start at the other end away from here. Go!' Rebecca noticed Ben's satphone vibrating as she sped away, and hoped it would be the cavalry. Ben answered it as another string of automatic fire tore through the iron above his head.

CHAPTER TWENTY-FIVE

GREG opened his door to the FBI and CIA agents.

'Martin Smithson and Frank Willis,' the tallest of the two men said in a strong American accent.

'Come in, gentlemen. This is Jennifer Madison, deceased.'

The two men looked at her quizzically.

'Yes, her husband had her killed, or at least he believes he did. We have it all on film.'

'I can't wait to see that,' Martin Smithson said.

'Take a seat, gentleman. We have a lot to go through.'

Greg and Jennifer poured out pages of places, names, and crimes that her husband had committed over the years. She explained that Jerry Stokes was the thug who would sort people out, some that may have just needed coercing, and on at least three occasions they had actually disappeared. Politicians, police, and councillors were either on his blackmail or bribery list; they would fall into the trap of owing him a favour, and he would force them to do him illegal favours in return. They explained about how he defrauded the bank with security that he didn't actually own, including other ranchers' livestock and property.

They recorded the whole interview and took down notes. Greg had supplied copies of everything that they had.

He had edited the footage that was taken from the five GoPro cameras of the assassination attempt, and handed them a copy.

'Would you like to see it?' Greg asked.

'Oh, you bet,' the two Americans almost said at the same time.

Greg knew they would. He hit Play on his laptop computer.

The two men sat in silence for the ten-minute duration.

As the screen went black, they both looked at Jennifer.

Finally, Frank said, 'That is just the most amazing thing I have ever seen, real Hollywood stuff.'

'And some damn great acting,' Martin said.

'It was all planned by Greg and a friend, and it was the only option we had. My husband would not have stopped till I was dead. He knew that I was privileged to so many details of his criminal activities.'

'May I ask, how did you know it would be that actual day and have all the actors and everything ready?' Frank asked.

Greg looked at Jennifer and answered, 'We knew it would be that week sometime, as we knew he was on his way here. So, we set ourselves a routine of going out in the cruiser at 10:00 a.m. every day, knowing he'd assume that that would be the best time to hit us. The actors, surgery, and vehicles were on standby. Then, we found out from a friend of a friend who works for the Madison Corporation that Jerry was booked on a flight that night back to Dallas, so it had to be that day, and it was.'

'Very clever,' Frank said. 'Maybe we can find you a position at the FBI; it's not every day that the victim can provide a video of their own murder.'

'Ma'am, may I ask, could any of this incriminate you? You do realise that the FBI will be thorough, and we look at absolutely everything. My boss will be hunting for every scalp. There isn't any document or deal that you have signed or could be linked to that might implicate you as an accessory?' Martin asked.

'I was not involved in any way to the business. I only know what I know from overheard conversations or from papers I glimpsed at. Keith kept me only as a trophy—definitely not for business.'

'As I thought. That's good,' Martin replied.

With that, Martin stood up, and Frank followed.

Martin looked squarely at Greg and Jennifer, standing directly in front of them. 'Well, it will take a while to assemble all of the evidence to make up the case for all the specific charges, but I think Frank here will be able to get it together pretty quickly. Most likely, we hope to have them both locked up within two weeks on the attempted murder charge for starters, then we will hit them with the rest of this. Ma'am, he will be spending the rest of his life either in court or jail. You can count on that.'

'Thank you. I would like to ask a favour, if I may?' Jennifer added. 'Could you please let me know beforehand exactly when and where you are going to arrest him?'

'Not our normal procedure, but I guess we can do that, ma'am,' Frank said.

'And, gentleman, he must not find out that she is still alive,' Greg said.

'Of course not. Jennifer won't need to face court either, as normally a wife wouldn't testify against her husband.'

They all shook hands at the doorway before the agents paced swiftly back to their silver hire car and drove off with a cursory wave.

Greg put his arm around her as they walked back inside his apartment.

'Well, Jennifer, my love, we have that ball rolling now, and that bomb we had to duck from has just bounced its way back to Texas.'

'Yes, I guess it did. I know he tried to kill me and all, but he is my husband. He was always nice to me,' Jennifer said.

Greg looked at her. 'You're not regretting what has happened?'

'No,' she said as she hugged him.

In a more serious tone, she paused and said, 'Greg, I asked them to tell me when they will arrest him for a reason.'

'So you can feel a little safer?'

'No, I really want to be there when they cuff him. I want him to see me, very much alive. I want him to know that he didn't outsmart me and that his so-called "dumb little trophy wife" outsmarted him.'

'Wow, I guess I can understand that. Actually, I would like to see his face when he sees you as well,' Greg said.

'I guess everything will be yours when he's incarcerated with a life sentence?'

'No, nothing. It will be the same as it was for his two previous wives. The two properties are to stay in the family, and I had to sign a marriage contract, or a prenuptial agreement if you like. The deal cost me a couple million dollars. I brought that money to the marriage, and it just disappeared into some hole.'

'Well that's not fair. You should at least be able to get that back,' Greg said.

'If he is locked up, everything would be frozen and turned over to his sister and then to her children.'

Greg thought about this for a while. They both took a seat on the couch, the television was on, and the latest news was telling its story.

Greg was a problem-solver, and Jennifer's two-million-dollar problem was something he wanted to solve. It was only minutes before a smile started to form on his face.

'Jennifer, have you ever read Jeffrey Archer?'

'No,' she said.

'He wrote a book back in the seventies, his first I think, based on a true story called, *Not a Penny More, Not a Penny Less*. It was about four people who were cheated by a millionaire scammer, and they all got their money back by finding ways to trick and outsmart him. I'll call Ben and run my little idea by him. I bet he's just sitting around drinking beer under a palm tree in Alice Springs anyway.'

He dialled the satphone.

'Peter, is that you?' Ben answered, hurriedly.

'No, it's Greg. So, how's the resting go— Shit! Is that gunfire?'

'Yeah, Greg, wanna give me a hand?'

'What the hell are you doing?'

'Well, I met this girl, and two days later….'

'Shit, anything I can do?'

'Nah, not from Adelaide you can't.'

'Mate, call me when you're free, hey,' Greg said, ending the call and looking at Jennifer who had heard the gunshots.

'What movie is he on?' she said innocently.

'Something about a woman, apparently,' he said, looking a little concerned.

In a more serious tone, he turned to look closely at Jennifer and asked, 'Now, what can you tell me about your husband's dealings? What does he have a weakness for, something he is passionate about that would lower his guard and suspicion?'

'He's greedy and loves buying and selling paintings. They are quite often a tool of trade for him. If it's a bargain, he will find the money and buy it, however, they come and go. He takes advantage of people desperate for money, so he will offer someone less than half of what the painting is worth, then sell it when they default, and they usually do, and he profits handsomely. He knows his stuff though; he has an expert art dealer that will inspect the art and deliver it to his door. He sometimes even uses third-party dealers— so it doesn't even seem like he is involved—just an innocent buyer of fine art.'

'Mmm, there is a plan forming in my head. We might need to go to Texas sooner than we thought.'

Ben clipped the satphone back on his belt with the low-battery light flashing. He looked back to see that the two girls were trying to open the door at the far end of the hangar.

Ben called out, 'I am not the police; I just want the girls, and you can go. You don't mean anything to me. I just want the girls.'

'You shot my fucken hand off, you fuck!' one of them yelled.

'You slapped my girlfriend!' Ben yelled back.

The man with the grey hair called back, 'So, you not police?'

'No, I just want the girls and you can go. I won't chase you. I won't shoot at you. Your buyers are gone. Save yourselves, just leave the two girls, and I will put my gun down.'

It was quiet for a moment as the Russians considered the offer.

'Put gun down and step out where I can see you,' the Russian in charge yelled.

Ben lent his rifle against the iron on the shed; it was out of sight to them. He took a step to his left with his hands up, knowing that if he saw a gun barrel appear in the window, he could dive back to cover and his loaded rifle. The two girls, still naked, appeared on the veranda, no longer as concerned about their privacy as their lives.

'We will walk to car. If anyone moves, we will cut girls in half, you got that?'

'Yes, I will not move. You are free to go,' Ben called back.

The three men stepped out of the departure building and walked swiftly backwards towards the painted-out police HiLux, their rifles pointing directly at the girls. As soon as the three men were in the car, Ben yelled to the girls to run to him. They ran as fast as they could with their injured feet on the gravel ground. They reached him and tucked in behind his back. The police HiLux started, and the car roared off and quickly out of sight. Rebecca and Akira were now back, and the four girls all hugged each other.

'Bec, take the girls and get them dressed.'

Ben heard the HiLux stop.

'Wait,' he called.

He heard about five seconds of automatic gunfire, and then the HiLux roared off again into the distance.

'You have got to be fucking kidding!' Ben yelled.

'What?' Rebecca said.

'My bloody Jeep. They just filled it with holes again! I just had it fixed. Go, Bec, get the girls dressed and let's see what we can find in these sheds, because it's a bloody long walk from here. The satphone is nearly flat, and no one knows we're here.'

Ben had completely forgotten about the G5 Gulfstream that

had been idling at the far end of the runway nearly two kilometres away until it roared past him at full power in a steep climbing turn.

Ben reached for the satphone and tried to ring Peter, but his phone was off.

Ben walked into the departure lounge as the girls were getting the last of their clothing on.

'Bec, what is the number for the police station?'

Rebecca called it out as Ben dialled.

'Alice Springs police, Trudy speaking.'

'Trudy, can you tell the sergeant that the kidnappers are heading back to the homestead, which is one hundred kilometres west of the Stuart Highway… Trudy, are you there?'

Ben looked at the phone. The battery was dead, and he had no way of knowing how much Trudy had heard. He knew the Jeep would be out of action; they would have made sure of that. He did the sums: he had a full tank of fuel when he left Alice, it did seven hundred kilometres to a tank, it was two hundred to the homestead, and it had a little under a quarter of a tank left. They were probably three hundred kilometres west of the homestead, too far to consider walking in this heat.

'Bec, what did you find in the sheds?' Ben asked.

'Not much. There is a little plane in the first one.'

'What type, could you tell?'

'Skyhawk, or something like that.'

'Cessna 172, perfect. I wonder if we might be able to get that going?'

Ben walked down to the hangar and slid back the door with the four women in tow. The Cessna was covered in dust; it obviously hadn't been operational for a long time. He opened the door of the plane, and of course, there were no keys in it.

'Ladies, I need you to search for the keys. They will be here somewhere.'

'What makes you think that, Ben?' Rebecca asked.

'Think about it. You drive probably two or three hundred kilometres to fly your plane and realise you left the key in your room at the mine site. It will be here somewhere, trust me.'

It didn't take long before one of the girls found the keys hidden on a nail under the desk in the little office.

Ben turned the propellor. The engine was free, which was a very good sign.

He turned the key, and of course, the battery was completely flat. He checked the fuel situation with a stick, and both tanks had less than a quarter of a tank. He checked the fuel drums in the hangar, and they were all empty. He asked the girls to check the other hangars for any fuel.

'We will need to get the remaining fuel out of the Jeep. See if you can find a hose, and grab a drum or two, please, Bec.'

'There was a garden hose at the back of that lounge building.'

Ben took out his Leatherman, flicked out the still-blunt blade, and handed it to her.

'Cut off about two metres, can you?'

'Ben, can I ask you something?'

'Sure.'

'You told those scumbags that I was your girlfriend. That sounded nice.'

'More than just a girlfriend, babe, but I had people shooting at me,' he said with a smile. She smiled back, turned, and ran off to get the hose.

There was a vending machine in the lounge, and Ben instructed the girls to stand back and carefully smash the glass to get what they could from it without cutting themselves.

Ben took an empty twenty-litre container and the hose and walked to the Jeep. He approached, shaking his head; he could see that they had shot out both front tyres, the headlights, and the radiator. He siphoned what he could from his fuel tank, which was only about fifteen litres. He carried it back and poured it into the Cessna's starboard tank.

With the help of the girls, they pushed the plane out of the hangar, and a cloud of dust blew off as it left the shade into the light desert breeze and bright daylight.

Ben knew that the four-cylinder Lycoming engine would have magneto ignition and mechanical fuel injection so it wouldn't need a charged battery to start it, as long as he could turn it over fast enough by spinning the propeller.

'Bec, jump into the right-hand seat. Now, you see the pedals on the floor, the tops are the brakes and the bottom steers it. I am going to try and start the engine by cranking the prop; it is very important that you hold the brakes on tight, okay? I don't trust that handbrake.'

'Yes, push the tops of the pedals, got it,' she said, looking down at her feet.

Ben turned the ignition switch to both magnetos and the mixture lever to full rich. He gave it a little throttle and jumped back out. He checked the direction of the engine rotation, which he determined easily by looking at the pitch of the propeller. He then started hand-cranking the engine. It took quite some time, and he had quite a sweat happening before a cylinder fired—a *chug, chug,* then died. He cranked it again, and it chugged for a little longer on one cylinder. Eventually it kept going on its own, picking up a cylinder as it went. Finally, a cloud of blue smoke filled the air as all four cylinders fired. The smoke was to be expected from an engine that hadn't been started in so long.

'Okay, ladies, I'll get the plane into the air and see if I can make contact with anyone. If I can get through to the Alice Springs control tower, I will report your location and the police will come and collect you, but I will need to keep flying towards Alice till I can make contact.'

'You aren't leaving us here on our own, are you?' Maria said.

'What if they come back?' Vanessa said.

'I will leave my rifle with Bec. To be honest, I don't think you will see them again,' Ben stated.

'No! We're coming with you,' Maria said.

'We only have four seats,' Ben said.

'We can fit,' Vanessa said in desperation.

'Ladies, if the plane— No, *when* the plane runs out of fuel, we will have to land it somewhere out there,' Ben said, pointing to the endless scrub.

Rebecca hadn't commented; she was torn between the options.

'We don't care if we crash. We just want to stay with you,' Vanessa said despairingly.

Ben looked at Rebecca. 'What do you think?' he asked.

'Do you think you can land it?'

'Most likely, but it probably won't be pretty,' Ben said.

Rebecca shrugged, her need to leave this place overruling her common sense.

'All right, ladies. Bec, grab my rifle, and you three, grab all the food and water you can carry, because when the engine dies and if we haven't made contact with anyone, we could be stranded with a long walk ahead of us,' Ben instructed.

They each collected armfuls of chips, chocolate bars, and

bottles of water from the smashed vending machine. The five of them then piled into the four-seater aircraft. Five people would have normally put the plane overweight, but because they didn't have a lot of fuel and no baggage, he figured the weight and balance should be fine. The three girls were tight in the two rear seats.

Ben estimated that they had about an hour and a half of fuel; they wouldn't make it to Alice Springs. He slipped the dusty David Clark headset that was hanging over the steering column on his head and turned on the two radios. He decided to take off downwind to save time and fuel. After all, if the Citation could do it, the little Cessna 172 would do it easily. Ben turned onto the runway, quickly checked full movement of the control surfaces, and pushed the throttle to full. The engine coughed and spluttered, but it increased speed at a nice rate. At sixty-five knots, he pulled the stick back, and the nose of the 172 lifted towards the sky with plenty of runway to spare. The engine was running better, but it still wasn't perfect. He eased the throttle back and established a nice gentle rate of climb; the Jeep fuel was nowhere near the one-hundred-octane low-lead fuel it needed, but it was a lot better than nothing. He turned east, the two-wheel track back to the homestead in the distance to his left. He wanted to get to at least three thousand feet, as the higher he was, the more options he would have to find somewhere to land when the engine died, but also, he wanted to not waste fuel trying to climb any higher. The aircraft was fitted with an HF radio, which was no surprise in an outback aircraft. HF radios were the worst quality but could reach by far the greatest distance. The waves bounce off the ionosphere rather than line of sight like VHF or UHF. He put out a call, but no one responded. He wondered if the radio worked at all.

He trimmed the plane at three thousand feet, turned on the

transponder, and squawked the emergency code of 'Seven, seven, zero, zero.'

It was about an hour when a call came through on the HF radio from Alice Springs airport.

'Aircraft squawking an emergency, this is Alice Springs tower, do you read?'

Ben called through his call sign, Whisky Lima Yankee, which was the aircraft's registration, and reported his location, height, persons on board, and intentions. He declared a mercy flight and explained the engine was running rough and they didn't have enough fuel to make any known airfield.

The helicopter pilot that was working with the police heard the call from the Cessna.

The police had found the F-250 at the homestead and were busy searching the property. The helicopter had been scanning the little track to the west, but it seemed to go on forever, and he didn't have endless fuel and so turned back to the homestead. The chopper landed, and the pilot ran to Sergeant Jones. 'Sarge, we might have them; there's a Cessna 172 in trouble, a mercy flight with low fuel, five passengers, it might be them.'

'Who's the pilot?' Jones asked.

'I don't know, but they are heading this way. If you want, you can talk to them on the radio in the chopper.'

'Let's go,' Jones said.

'Whisky Lima Yankee, this is Juliet Foxtrot Yankee, I have Police Sergeant Jones to speak with you, over.'

'Whisky Lima Yankee, go ahead.'

'Can you confirm you have the four missing women? Over.'

'Yes, Sergeant, they are all safe and on board, but more importantly you should be seeing three heavily armed Russian kidnappers heading east towards the highway. There is a homestead a hundred kilometres west in from the highway.'

'We are here now,' Jones said.

'Sir, you might be able to ambush them. They're in Reed's police car and should be there any minute.'

'Will do, thanks for the intel,' Jones said in amazement and relief.

Just then the engine started to splutter. Ben quickly switched the fuel tap from both tanks to starboard, but it was too late, as the engine had now stopped. There was an eerie silence as they all looked at each other. The stationary alloy Hartzell propeller filled the windscreen.

Ben quickly pulled up the nose and converted what extra speed he had into altitude. He trimmed the Cessna for seventy knots and desperately looked for somewhere to put it down. There were no easy options, which was not what he had thought would be the case when he left the airfield. It was now that he wondered whether he should have left the women behind and flown the plane by himself to get help, but it was too late to worry about that now. He could see what looked like a claypan some five miles to the south. He turned the Cessna to the right and headed for that, doubting that he could actually make it, but there just weren't any other easy options.

'Mayday, Mayday, Mayday,' Ben said over the radio. 'Whisky Lima Yankee, two hundred miles north-west of Alice Springs, five pax on board, engine failure, passing through two thousand five hundred feet.'

The tower came back over the radio, 'Whisky Lima Yankee, acknowledged. When free, what are your intentions?'

'We are going to try and make a claypan to the south, over.'

'Roger that, Whisky Lima Yankee, we have you on radar. Search and rescue are on their way. Good luck.'

CHAPTER TWENTY-SIX

GREG and Jennifer left the next day for Texas. Jennifer visited the hairdresser at the Kingsford Smith airport in Sydney between the connecting flights to cut, shape, straighten, and dye her hair blonde. They knew they had two weeks maximum to find a way to get Jennifer's money back from her husband before it was frozen by the authorities.

With the time difference between the US and Australia, they actually landed in Dallas an hour after they had left Sydney. They quickly left the airport and caught a taxi, trying to keep as low a profile as possible. They checked into a hotel in downtown Dallas, where Jennifer would spend the next two weeks out of sight. Greg's first trip would be to the Dallas Museum of Art.

Greg walked into the big square grey building, trying to act with more confidence than he felt. He asked an attendant if he could speak to the director of the museum about a donation. The director enthusiastically appeared within seconds and introduced himself.

'Mark Slade, director of the museum,' he said, holding out his hand to Greg. 'How can I help you, sir?'

'Greg Sheppard, can we go somewhere where we can talk, Mr Slade?'

The director ushered Greg into his office and offered him a seat.

'Mr Slade, I am working with the FBI and CIA to bring a group of criminals to justice.'

'So you are FBI?' Slade asked.

'No, but let's just say I am a contractor for now.'

'I don't understand,' Slade said.

'Mr Slade, we are setting up a sting, and we need a piece of artwork to use for the operation.'

'I see; that's very unusual, Mr Sheppard.'

'Sir, we do plan to donate a heathy sum to the museum for your assistance in this.'

'How healthy?'

'One hundred thousand dollars.'

Greg watched Mark Slade's eyes, noting the figure was enough to get his attention.

Although one hundred thousand was not a huge sum in the scheme of things, it would make it appear that the director was still actively sourcing donations.

'What assistance would you need?' Slade asked sceptically.

'We would need a painting for twenty-four hours,' Greg explained.

'Sir, we cannot loan or rent out priceless artwork. It just

isn't possible.'

'Mr Slade, wouldn't one hundred thousand dollars be a benefit to the museum?'

'Of course it would, sir. Donations are what keep us going.'

Greg assured him that he would pay a cash bond that would exceed the value of the painting, and on its return, they would have a written agreement that the gallery would return the funds to him less one hundred thousand dollars.

'Mr Sheppard, as attractive as that sounds, it's just impossible. I would lose my job if it got out that I loaned out a painting, even to the FBI.'

Greg thought for a minute as he looked at the pain in the directors face; he could see he needed that money.

'Mr Slade, when can a painting leave the museum?'

'Only for an exhibition really, and then that takes months of planning, and the security detail is intense.'

'What about for a repair or cleaning?'

'That is normally done in-house, but for a major repair, it might be outsourced.'

'So, what would that look like if it had to leave the museum for a repair?'

'It would be accompanied by an armed security guard that would never let the piece out of his sight, and it would be transported by a purpose-built vehicle.'

'What if you employ my company to clean a particular piece of art, and I pay for the security guard from a company that you trust. I will cover all the professional transport costs as well?' Greg said.

'How would I be assured that the painting would not be damaged?'

'We would have three million reasons to look after that painting,

Mr Slade.'

'Mr Woolford, can you tell me what you are proposing to do with the painting?'

Greg explained his plan, and while possibly slightly exaggerating the FBI and CIA's involvement, he outlined it with accurate detail. He could see the director's interest in the plan and that he was considering how he could make it work.

'What painting are you considering, Mr Woolford?'

'It needs to be one that can be copied easily, something like the cubist style of Picasso.'

'Sir, the Picasso paintings we have are worth far more than two million dollars, would a Picasso engraving be suitable? Then I could possibly find a way to assist you?'

'That might work,' Greg said.

'I am not agreeing to anything, but let's go and have a look and see what you like, shall we?' Slade said.

Greg looked at the amazing Picasso collection. The style, with its obscure, abstract lines, would make it a lot easier to replicate, also making it less obvious for anyone to know if it wasn't perfect at first glance.

Greg decided on the Picasso, *The Lovers: Geneviève Looking for Me ll* a lady, naked with an abstract face. It was worth about two and a half million dollars and fitted the bill perfectly. Mark Slade clearly felt that a three-million-dollar security for the item was fair, but he was nonetheless still hesitant.

'Mr Sheppard, please give me a day to think about it.' He shook Greg's hand.

'Thank you, Mr Slade, please let me know as soon as you can.'

With Slade's permission, Greg took photos of the artwork from every angle, close-ups of the texture, frame, and Picasso's signature.

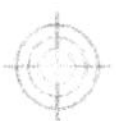

The museum director went back to his office and closed his door. He fell back into the chair behind his desk. He deliberated. He needed that money. This was an opportunity to help lots of people, most especially help keep the museum afloat and, subsequently, keep his position. He knew he could create a paper trail that verified this was a legal transaction—so it would prevent him going to jail if it all went wrong. He made the call to Greg and nervously agreed to the deal.

Next on Greg's list was to find an artist who could replicate the Picasso. After a few discreet calls to a number of galleries, dealers, and artists, he'd uncovered two people, both of whom were highly recommended and were available to start work straight away. Greg and Jennifer carefully checked out samples of each of their work and promptly received quotes. Each artist was looking for around five thousand dollars to produce the replica, in around seven days.

Greg decided to get them both to recreate the Picasso, as it would double his chances of getting a good copy. It had to be pristine. To further assist, Greg organised to have the Picasso image printed onto a similar-looking canvas so the artists would have a perfect outline to copy and had these dispatched.

Next was the frame. That turned out to be the hardest to source. He found a company that said they could do it, but would involve them going into the museum themselves. Greg made sure Slade would arrange their visit, so as not to arouse suspicion and enable a close inspection.

Next was to get a small truck that he could modify into a professional-looking art delivery van. He ended up hiring one and soon found an engineer that would make the improvements he needed in the time he had. The last piece of his intricate plan was to find the three million US dollars to secure the painting. Rather than going through the complication of a short-term bank loan, he had an idea.

Ben found that the wind wasn't favourable and the chance of him making the only clearing in the area was looking worse. He was looking for any options to try and get what might turn out to be the few extra feet to get them over the scattered bushes that surrounded the claypan. They were down to five hundred feet now. Unfortunately, the flaps on a Cessna are electrically operated, and although the battery was now charged from the hour cruise, they were still quite slow to deploy. The big wing of the Cessna had a stall speed of around thirty-seven knots, or even better given there was no fuel weight. Two hundred feet now. Ben turned to the girls in the back and instructed the lightest one, who was probably the Japanese girl, Akira, to sit on someone's lap and put the seat belt around them both.

Ben said to Rebecca, 'When I say, push this lever all the way down.' He pointed to the flap lever that was positioned in the middle of the dashboard. The flaps would increase lift and lower the stall speed, but it would significantly add drag, and that would slow the plane as well: it was a fine line. One hundred feet. Rebecca had her forefinger nervously on the flap lever. Ben lifted the nose slightly, and the speed started to fall away. Fifty feet. With the ten-knot headwind, the plane hardly felt like it was moving. The stall warning sounded, an ear-piecing scream to warn the pilot his aeroplane was about to become a brick. Twenty Feet. They were heading right for a bush that was actually a small tree now that they could see it better. If he hit the trees, it would pull the engine into the ground and flip the small plane onto its back. The stall warning continued to scream as Ben saw the speed dip below thirty-five knots. The controls had become light, and a shudder was felt through the plane as the airflow was breaking up over the ailerons.

'Now,' Ben said, and Rebecca pushed the flap lever down, selecting full flap. The back of the plane lifted as if being hit by a gust of wind. Ben hit the starter, and the engine fired on the last few drops of fuel in the tank. He hit full throttle, and it ran for about two seconds before it died again, but that was just enough to delay the descent and for them to only clip the top of the tree with the undercarriage. They were only ten feet off the ground when the left wing stalled. A quick push of the right rudder pedal kept the plane level as it dropped heavily to the ground from probably six feet. It bounced a few times before settling onto the dry, dusty claypan. The relief was felt throughout the plane.

Ben wiped the bead of sweat from his brow and said, 'Well, ladies, welcome to Claypan Central Airport. Please remain seated until the seat-belt light goes out.' Rebecca looked at him with a smile and relief. 'The airport is sending people to get us. Enjoy the snacks, ladies.'

Ben opened his door and helped the three girls out of the rear seat. They introduced themselves and hugged him. They probably couldn't imagine how different their lives would have been if Ben hadn't turned up when he did. Ben and Reed gathered the girls around and explained that, while they would be safe from here, the police would want to question them when they got back to Alice Springs. He watched as Bec gathered the girls together and asked each for a little favour. Akira, the Japanese girl, took a little longer to understand, but she got it in the end. They'd all willingly accepted, without hesitation.

Peter had the drone up high. There was no way the approaching vehicle could see it.

'Here they come,' he called out, and the police took their positions.

The white HiLux drove slowly into the homestead, with the three Russians on high alert. The car stopped by the back door of the farmhouse. The three men exited the vehicle slowly with guns raised.

'Police, drop your weapons! You are surrounded!' someone yelled from behind a shed.

There was a moment where this could have gone either way. But when Jackson appeared from behind them through the back door of the house, his gun at their backs, it helped them make the most sensible decision.

Jackson badly wanted to blow away the men who kidnapped the woman he loved.

They placed their guns down and put their hands up. Jackson

cuffed them quickly as Detective Inspector Scott approached the grey-haired leader of the group.

'Where are the girls?' he demanded.

'I don't know what you talk about,' the Russian replied.

'I want to know what you did with the girls, you fucking piece of shit. Where are they?'

'You can see, no girls here.'

'What happened to your hand?' the detective asked one of the other men, noticing the bloodstained cloth that was wrapped around what was left of his right hand.

'Nothing. Scratched it.'

'Big scratch,' the detective said.

Jones could see the Cessna parked at the edge of the claypan. The chopper circled and landed into the wind. Sergeant Jones jumped out and walked over to Reed.

'You have a lot of explaining to do, my dear,' he said like a relieved parent who knew there would need to be a scolding for putting him through this much worry.

Jones turned to the man at her side 'And who are you?' he said, offering his hand.

'Ben Woolford, sir, Bec's boyfriend.........I guess.'

Jones looked at him and back at her, now realising that he was the one who had jumped the back fence of the police station last night.

'Sir, she promised me dinner, and I don't like being stood up, so I went looking for her,' he added.

'I see,' Jones said, not really knowing how to respond to that.

'We can't fit you all in the chopper. We will take the three girls and come back and get you two,' Jones said.

'It's okay, Sergeant, search and rescue are on their way. We can go back to Alice with them,' Ben said.

Jones agreed and then escorted the three ladies into the chopper.

'Reed, I want you in my office at zero seven hundred tomorrow actually, *both* of you!' Jones yelled from the door of the chopper as the pilot started to increase the revs and lift the collective control.

As the chopper lifted away, it circled the Cessna before heading south, and Jones looked down to see Rebecca kissing the hero that had saved her life again, her right leg bent up behind her and her left on tippy toes as she stretched to reach his lips. He smiled as he remembered his own days of young love. She was like the daughter he never had, and like all fathers, no one would ever really be good enough for her. *But hell, this bloke might just come close,* he thought as he looked away from the lovebirds and in the direction of travel.

Ben stood in the shade of the Cessna's wing with Rebecca's head on his chest. Neither of them had slept for about thirty-six hours, and they were tired. Rebecca had almost dozed off when the distant sound of the SAR chopper was heard coming from the south-east. Ben quickly removed his rifle from the back seat of the aircraft and placed it in the rear cargo compartment; he didn't need SAR seeing it.

The chopper landed, and two men dressed in bright orange coveralls walked towards them wearing smiles.

'Great to see you are okay. This is how we like to see a Mayday call end. Wasn't there five of you?'

Ben explained that the police had taken the other three. Ben hated leaving his rifle behind, but carrying it into an international airport might just get him arrested. They hopped aboard the Bell 206 JetRanger and were very thankful for the lift back to the Alice Springs.

Next morning promptly at seven o'clock, Rebecca and Ben walked into Sergeant Jones's office.

'Close the door and sit down please,' Jones said.

'Tell me everything that happened, Reed, *exactly* what happened, every detail, off the record, before the suits get here,' Jones asked.

She told him all about how she went to check an anonymous call of a sighting of the car and was caught. Then everything that happened from there, including the attempted sale of the four women to international buyers who flew into the airport in their private jets. She explained how Ben negotiated with the Russians to let the girls go, and how they had no way to contact anyone until the plane was halfway back to Alice and the HF radio would work.

'Okay, I need you both to write out statements, leave out anything to do with you shooting anyone or guns of any kind on your part, or they will be throwing you in jail, Ben.'

'Roger that, Sarge.'

'Then, Reed, you will be on a two weeks stress leave, and I suggest you both find somewhere else other than Alice Springs to assist in your recovery.'

They looked at each other and smiled.

'Ben, completely off the record, you saved the lives of these four women, one being this one here'—gesturing towards Reed—'whom you have actually now saved twice. You helped put a criminal bikie gang in jail and gave us a Mexican drug lord on a plate. I can't thank you enough. We owe you, and the country owes you, hell, the world probably owes you.' He paused, before saying with a cautious tone, 'But officially, we do not condone vigilantes taking the law into their own hands, and there will be some people here soon'—Jones looked at his watch— 'where that type of action will not be tolerated, and they'll be looking for a scalp. But meanwhile, is there anything I can do for you?'

'There is one thing, actually, two. My Jeep is all shot up at that airfield on the WA border. I would love that to be picked up and taken to the local panel beater in town; he knows the car well.'

'We will need to go out there anyway, so yes, we can bring that back. What else?'

'My rifle is in the Cessna's rear cargo compartment, I had to hide it from the SAR team, and I would love that back too.'

'I will send Jackson out there to get it. Okay, get those statements done and get the hell out of town.'

'Sarge, the key for the Jeep is on the ground inside the right rear wheel.'

'Okay, I'll sort it.'

CHAPTER TWENTY-SEVEN

IT was getting dark in Dallas when Ben called Greg.

'So, Greg, tell me what you've got cooking over there?' He paused as he realised. 'Hey, you don't have Jennifer there, do you?'

'You mean the straight-haired blonde lady with the dark sunglasses? Yes, she is keeping a very low profile though. Now, I have found out that once her husband is incarcerated, all the family property will go to his sister, and all assets will be seized by the banks and the IRS, so Jennifer will get nothing. She brought two million bucks to the marriage that her husband had made vanish somewhere. I want to get that money back for her, but we need to do it before he is arrested in the next week or two.'

'Go on,' Ben said.

'I have a plan and a lot of it is already in place, but one thing I do need is three million US dollars for a few days, and I thought our friend in Darwin might do a short-term loan.'

Greg went on to tell Ben about the rest of the plan in finer detail.

Ben could see that a lot of things would need to fall perfectly into place, but he liked it.

'That's very clever, Greg. Let me call DeLuca and see if we can get the funds for you. I'll call you back.'

Ten minutes later, Greg's phone rang.

'How did we go?' Greg asked.

'He went on about us being family, and I think the fact his daughter arrived home today had him in the best frame of mind. So yes, he's happy to lend it to us, interest free.'

'That's great. I guess we did help make him a very rich man,' Greg said.

'We sure did,' Ben said.

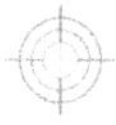

Senior Sergeant Tim Jones could hear the two sets of footsteps getting closer to his closed door. There was a quick knock, and the door opened. The two detectives entered without waiting for an invitation.

'Tim, I would like to know what the fuck is going on here. Who the fuck is this Ben Woolford with a disqualified pilot's licence flying that Cessna, who appeared to be three steps ahead of us the whole time?' Inspector Russell Scott demanded.

'That was Reed's boyfriend. Apparently, she promised to cook him dinner, and when she didn't turn up, he went looking for her.'

Scott stared at him, about to explode. He took in a deep breath and as calmly as possible said, 'Yes, I have heard that fucking story. I want to question him myself. He could have been in on it, then found he was on the losing side and jumped ship.'

Not the first time that's happened around here, Jones thought, he then frowned. 'He's her boyfriend, all right. I saw them from the chopper; you can't make that shit up. We have their statements and those of the three girls, and they all say the same thing: they would all be in fuck knows where now, if it wasn't for him.'

'Yeah, I read the fucking statements. So, explain this to me then, this bloke's girlfriend is late for dinner, and so he goes looking for her and finds her in three hours, where the Northern Territory police force have been searching for them for three days. He cruises in with his little black Jeep, convinces two planeloads of foreign gangsters and three Russian people smugglers armed with fully automatic rifles that they are naughty boys? Then gets them to hand over their four hostages unharmed, before he miraculously just flies off into the fucking sunset with the girls in a plane—that just happened to be there ready to go, that he also doesn't have a licence for, armed only with his bare hands?'

'Actually, he had a Leatherman,' Jones said.

'Oh yeah, a fucking Leatherman, right! You've got to be fucking kidding! Next, you'll be telling me he has a red-and-blue Lycra suit with a big *S* on it. Someone is fucking lying, Jones—so what are you not telling us?' Scott said, leaning forward over Jones's timber desk, his knuckles white as he tightly clasped the edge. 'If I find out that Superman has fired one shot, just one shot, I'll have him locked up so fast his cape will be caught in the cell door.'

'Gentlemen, let it go. We got the girls back, no one's dead, and we caught all the baddies,' Jones said.

'This is bullshit, Jones. I can't go back to Darwin with a report that says we couldn't find the girls in time, but it didn't matter because Superman turned up with his Leatherman and saved the day! I want to talk to Reed and Woolford now. I bet he has gunshot residue all over him!' Scott said.

'You can't, Reed is now on stress leave, Woolford has been cleared of any charges, and I believe they are now both headed interstate.'

'I *will* get to the bottom of this, Jones. I will!'

The two detectives left, far more frustrated than they were when they arrived.

Sergeant Jones picked up his desk phone.

'Jackson, get to that Cessna as fast as you can and get the rifle out of the cargo hold, and don't let anyone see you.'

'Yes, Sarge,' he replied.

Inspector Scott saw Jackson put the phone down and look at them as he grabbed his cap and rushed out the door. The two detectives looked at each other.

Ben went back to his motel room and packed his gear, although he really didn't have much. The next few months, or even years, could be so different for him. The only thing he did know was that Rebecca had to be with him. He checked out of the motel that had certainly seen some action in the last couple of weeks. He would stay at Rebecca's tonight, and tomorrow they would catch a flight to Adelaide and start a much-needed break.

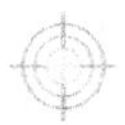

The two detectives flew out to the little airport that was just over the border in Western Australia. The WA police were going to meet them there, as it was technically in their state, but they really didn't want to know about it. Scott could see the many bullet holes that filled the corner of the hangar where Ben had taken cover, and he could see Ben's footprints and those of the bare feet of at least two of the girls. He noted there were no shells on the ground; he hadn't fired back, or he'd carefully picked up his shells.

They surveyed the walls of the departure lounge, and there were no signs of shots being fired in that direction either. It didn't make sense. They just needed to find one bit of evidence of him firing a shot and they had him, one slug, one shell that matched the gun that must also be around somewhere. Then they could put the vigilante away and also have Jones's badge for covering up his involvement. They had one man with half his hand missing as a witness, but he was still insisting it was just a scratch.

They searched the Jeep. It had had the shit blasted out of it: the headlights, grille, radiator, and tyres were all destroyed. No sign of weapons; it just made no sense. They didn't look under the back seat where he had a specially made mount for the rifle and packets of bullets. The WA police soon arrived by plane, landing on the perfectly maintained runway.

The police from the two states all greeted each other and were taking notes and photos. The silk saris still lay where they had been torn from the bodies of the women.

'Who owns this place?' Inspector Scott asked one of the WA police.

'It is an old airfield that was built by a mining company that shut down three years ago. The Cessna is unregistered and was owned by one of the managers who worked there, but he's since died, so I guess no one knew it was still here.'

'The runway is in pretty good condition for one that hasn't been used in three years,' Scott said.

'The farmer that owns the land said that the payments still come in each month for him to maintain it, so he does, and besides, the flying doctor has used it on occasion. He said he has no idea who comes here but hears a few planes come and go. He's never bothered to ask; they were paying good money to have it.'

'Do we know where the two jets came from?' Scott asked.

'No, basically, we assume they came in with transponders off and probably at five hundred feet from New Guinea to avoid any radar.'

'I see,' Scott said.

'What about the three Russians you have in Alice?' the WA police officer asked.

'We have enough on them to put them away forever. They aren't talking, but I suggest any unsolved cases of missing women you've had in the last year or so could well be victims of these scum,' Scott said.

They all spent another hour taking photos, notes, and evidence before they shook hands, jumped back into their respective planes, and left.

Later that afternoon, the two detectives walked into the Alice Springs police station. 'Jackson!' Inspector Scott called out, looking from side to side, checking to see who might be listening as the two detectives walked up to the counter.

'Yes, sir,' he replied, walking over to him.

'Jackson, this is your first year out of the academy for you and Reed, right?'

'Yes, sir.'

'You fancy her a bit, don't you, son?'

'We are good friends, sir.'

'Come on. I've seen you with her. You can't take your eyes off her, or that tight arse of hers. You'd like a bit of that, hey?'

Jackson looked down at the counter and picked up a pen, which answered the question.

'You must be pretty pissed about her running off with this Woolford fella, hey?'

'It's none of my business, sir,' Jackson said with evident pain.

'Why not help us lock him up? He's been shooting up this town like the rules don't apply to him, and then he runs off with your girl. He's probably screwing her right now, you know that, right?'

Jackson's head flew up at him, anger instantly burning through him as the vision flashed through his mind. The detective was using a pretty basic interrogation technique he'd used many times when trying to get a criminal to sing.

'What can I help you with, Detective?' Jackson said, almost gritting his teeth. 'I have a lot of work to do now with Reed away.'

'I want to know where the fuck you went this morning as soon as Sergeant Jones got off the phone to you.'

'The sarge sent me out to the Cessna to make sure it was secure, sir,' Jackson said.

'Bullshit, what did you get out of it?'

'Um… Nothing, sir,' Jackson said unconvincingly.

'William Jackson, you know that if you lie to a detective inspector, your career is over, finished.'

Jackson's head shot up again, his eyes darting from one

detective to the other. The second detective just smiled and nodded in agreement.

'I collected a rifle from the plane while I was there as well,' Jackson said, looking back at the pen he was rolling between his fingers. He knew that he may have just got his boss in a lot of trouble.

'Exactly what sort of rifle was it, Jackson?'

'Tikka bolt action, sir,'

'Is that right? Where is it now?'

'The sarge has it.'

'I see. Okay, thank you, Will. You can get back to work.'

Jackson sat back at his desk, his head in his hands, feeling his life falling apart by the minute.

He had been playing the long game with Bec. Maybe too long. He had it all planned: he would consolidate their friendship here in Alice Springs, her feelings slowly turning towards him till that one day he would have her alone in his arms and he would show her how much he loved her. But now she had run off with this fucking Rambo, giving *him* that beautiful body that he had fantasised about from the first day he had ever seen her, just because he was the one that dragged her out of harm's way that night at the bikie compound.

It should have been me; I'd started to run to her on that night, and I would've been her saviour and the receiver of her ultimate gift. But just my fucking luck—the sergeant stopped me, and now my woman is with someone else.

The two detectives had left to go and look at the Viper Motorcycle Gang clubrooms. Scott turned to the junior detective and said, 'See what you can find out about this Ben Woolford. He must be ex-military or something.'

It wasn't long before Detective Scott had a full account of Sergeant Ben Woolford's service history, and it all made sense now. *This guy's record is impressive. He's done some tough tours,* Scott thought as he continued to read through the records. Three tours to Iraq and Afghanistan, Platoon's Designated Marksman, led an extraction team into the Taliban headquarters for which he received the Medal of Honour.

Scott's need to bust Ben Woolford had softened significantly, when his phone rang.

'Scott speaking.'

'Russell, are you still in Alice and free to talk?' He quickly recognised the police commissioner's voice.

'Yes, sir.'

'Russell, I have just had a call from the American embassy in Canberra. There's an incident at the Pine Gap facility, and the Americans want it dealt with, efficiently and quietly. Are you interested in having a look at it before we send in the calvary?'

'Yes, of course, sir. What are the details?'

'A Chinese national holding about twenty US citizens hostage and making demands. Neither ASIO or the AFP know anything about this yet. The US foreign secretary called me personally to ask if we deal with it, should I say, the American way, if you know what I mean.'

'Yes, sir, I know exactly what you mean.'

'Let me know if you can't or if it's too dangerous, and I will send the TRG in there. I'll give you twenty-four hours.'

'You won't believe it, sir, but I might just have the person for the job,' Scott said.

'I'll email you all I know, you have twenty-four hours, Russ.

Nice and quiet, remember. I will call you this time tomorrow. Oh yeah, and Russ…'

'Yes, sir,' Scott said with his mind already racing.

'Pull this off and it will go a long way to that promotion you are after.'

'Yes, sir, thank you. I will do my best.'

Wannabe Deputy Commissioner Russell Scott immediately called the Alice Springs police station as soon as he'd hung up from the commissioner, and Trudy answered.

'Trudy, is Sergeant Jones there?'

'Yes, sir, but he is in his office. He's in a meeting with Constable Jackson at the moment.'

'Shit, okay, can you please ask him to not go anywhere? I need to speak to him urgently, and I am on my way.'

'Yes, sir, I will tell him now,' Trudy said.

Jackson was in his boss's office explaining everything about his 'conversation' with Detective Scott, and how he'd threatened him with losing his job if he didn't tell him why he'd gone out to the Cessna. Jones told him not to worry and that he won't be losing his job either way. Sergeant Jones was pretty pissed at Scott and was still fuming when Trudy tapped on his door.

'Excuse me, Sergeant, but Detective Scott just called and asked me to tell you he is on his way to speak with you urgently.'

'Thank you, Trudy,' Jones said. He was getting angrier by the second. Scott did outrank him significantly, but this was his station and his staff, and even the commissioner couldn't just come in there and intimidate his team.

CHAPTER TWENTY-EIGHT

WITHIN twenty minutes, Detective Scott knocked on Sergeant Jones's office door and stepped in without waiting for a response. He grabbed a chair that was pushed back against the wall and casually pulled it over towards the desk and sat down.

Jones stood and attacked him straight away.

'What's the bloody idea of accosting my constable? And I am sick of your obsession with nailing Woolford! He did in *one* day what you couldn't do in three! If it wasn't for him, those four young women would be gone, never to be seen again!' Jones said, frustrated by Scott's expressionless acceptance of his statement.

Scott knew he had to let Jones get it out. Once Jones had stopped to take a breath, he said,

'Sorry, Tim. You are completely right. The four girls would be gone if it wasn't for him. Consider it all behind us. The reports will go through exactly as you have presented them.'

'What?' Jones said in disbelief. He felt the heat and fury he had built up inside in preparation for the ensuing clash with Scott suddenly drop to a low simmer without the appropriate pressure relief. 'What's happened?' Jones asked, a lot calmer.

'Tim, we have a major issue at the Pine Gap facility. The Americans were worried that there was a leak from the complex and sent someone in two weeks ago to snoop around from the inside.'

'What's it to do with us? That's the AFP's problem, surely?' Jones said, the fire now completely extinguished from his voice.

'Technically, it would be. But it gets worse. The snoop found out who it was. Turned out that one of the employees who'd been there for nearly two years was in reality a Chinese spy. He'd worked out his cover had been blown, and he's now taken a bunch of staff hostage, mostly Americans. The Yanks want it solved as quickly and quietly as possible, and of course with as little collateral damage as we can manage.'

'We don't have the resources here for that,' Jones said.

'I haven't told you the worst bit,' Scott said, reading from the email on his phone. 'The Chinese spy is a Marcus Chen; he wants a private helicopter to pick him up from the complex tomorrow morning at eight or he will start executing a hostage per hour. There could be a couple of Australians amongst them. We don't know yet.'

'Why tomorrow, why not straight away?' Jones asked.

'I figure he has some work to do there, steal some more shit, who knows, but it at least gives us some time.'

'You haven't come here to ask for backup—have you? I feel you have a plan that you are going to tell me about,' Jones said.

'I have checked the airlines, and I see Reed and Woolford don't fly out till tomorrow. Tell me if I'm wrong, but I'm guessing that hole in the Russian's hand wasn't from his Leatherman?' Scott said.

Jones knew what Scott was alluding to.

'I checked the mag in the gun. He only fired two shots, and I guess he used them well,' Jones said.

Jones stood and walked over to his gun safe, spun the combination dial back and forth three times in each direction. He turned the handle, and the heavy door opened. He removed the black rifle and handed it to Scott.

'Phew, nice. You know Reed's little boyfriend is not your average boy scout, Tim?' Scott said, looking at him.

Jones looked at Scott and asked, 'Military?'

'SAS Sergeant, Medal of Honour.'

'I guess that all makes sense. I'll call her.'

Jones picked up his phone.

'Reed, I know I sent you on a break, but can you and Woolford come back into the station straight away? We have an incident— rather urgent one.'

'Sure, Sarge. We will be there in ten minutes,' Rebecca said, ending the call.

Ben was looking at her with a serious look of interest.

'What's up, babe? Are we in trouble?' he said.

'The sarge wants us both in the station straight away.'

'Should I be worried?' Ben asked, already feeling vulnerable that they now probably knew exactly who he was.

'I don't think so. He's on our side, don't you think?'

They arrived at the police station about ten minutes later and walked straight to Sergeant Jones's office. Will Jackson watched the pair walk in; they were both casually dressed and walked with purpose. Rebecca gave Jackson a little smile, but his eyes were on Ben. Ben looked over to him and offered a casual smile. He recognised the man who had questioned him at the rollover. Jackson had no control of his expression, and it was a mixture of hate, jealousy, and resentment. In the passage that led to Jones's office, Ben whispered in Rebecca's ear, 'What's going on between you and your mate back there?'

'I think he fancies me, but he doesn't have a hope in hell, for lots of reasons,' she said, looking over her shoulder towards Ben with a smile.

Rebecca knocked on the door and slowly opened it.

'Come in and grab a seat. You both know Inspector Detective Russell Scott here from Darwin CIB?'

They all shook hands and sat around the sergeant's desk.

Scott took the lead. 'Ben, I've done a bit of research on you, and I believe you were a sniper in Afghanistan?'

'I was a designated marksman with my battalion, sir, not a sniper as such, just a good shot,' Ben said. 'But I'm retired now, just a PI from Adelaide.'

'Well, mate, we have a problem and we need someone with your skills to help save about twenty people that are being held hostage.'

'I see,' said Ben. 'How can I help?'

'We need to take him out,' Scott said.

Ben sat up and said, 'I'm retired, sir. It would be illegal for me to do that.'

'You don't need to worry about that, Ben.'

'Where's the problem?' Ben asked.

'At Pine Gap.'

'I know of the place, sir,' Ben said.

'Before I tell you any more, would you be interested in helping us?' Scott asked.

'Of course, but why aren't you flying in your tactical team to flush him out?' Ben said.

'Two main reasons. The Yanks want it sorted quietly with minimal collateral damage. The people working there would take years to replace, and the Chinese would know that, so they may just try and kill them all anyway. They also don't want the media telling the world that a Chinese spy infiltrated their surveillance complex and has been feeding out intel for fuck knows how long to China. Second, the TRG team will come marching in waving their dicks around, make a huge fuss, and bullets flying everywhere. You remember the Lindt Café siege, right?' Scott said.

Jones continued, 'He has threatened to kill a person every hour from tomorrow morning at 8:00 a.m. if we don't comply with his demands.'

'I see,' Ben said, looking at his watch and over at Scott and then to Rebecca.

'Okay, so we don't have much time. Tell me what you know,' Ben said, leaning forward from the slouched position he was sitting in.

Scott went on to tell him about the demands and everything else he knew.

'Sergeant, were you able to retrieve my parcel?' Ben asked.

'Yes, and the ammo; it's here in my gun safe.'

'I will need to have a good look at the site. Can we get Peter here with the drone?' Ben said.

'He's already on his way,' Jones replied.

Scott unfolded a map and laid it out on Jones's desk. 'This is where I imagine we could land the chopper, so you will need to be set up in this area here,' Scott said, running his finger around a mountain range near the southern side of the complex. Ben checked the distance roughly by the scale on the bottom corner of the map.

'It's about a kilometre and a half. That's a big ask if he is surrounded by hostages,' Ben said.

'And he probably will be, Ben,' Jones said.

'There are so many factors in taking such a long shot: the wind, Coriolis effect, and spin drift, for a start. I would've had someone do these calculations for me on such an important hit.'

Rebecca sat back in amazement as Ben went through the intricate details of a long-distance sniper shot.

Ben continued, 'I will need to go out and find a similar place and set up my scope for that distance, then we'll need to think of a way to separate him from the hostages, and time it precisely, even if for only a second. I won't do it if it means risking an innocent life.'

There was a knock on the door, and Peter stepped in. Everyone acknowledged him, and he stood next to Rebecca.

'Do you have a helicopter and pilot prepared to do this?' Ben asked.

'Yes, I think so. That should be confirmed shortly,' Jones said.

Ben turned to Peter. 'Peter, I think, you, Bec, and I should head out there now. Let's get the drone up, have a look, and then let's do some target practice. Sarge, we will need radios good enough for the distance.'

'Our digital Motorolas are more than good for five kilometres, line of sight,' Jones said.

Ben stood and faced Scott. 'One more thing. If it all turns to shit, will I be thrown under the bus?'

'You were never here, Ben.' The detective shook his hand and said, 'Thank you also for saving the women. I don't know how you did it, you embarrassed us, but one hell of a job, mate.'

'I had a bit of incentive, Detective,' he said as he put his arm around Rebecca.

Scott smiled and said, 'I guess you did. She must be a good cook!'

Sergeant Jones gave Ben his rifle back and suggested he not walk out the front door carrying it. Bec left to get her car and drove it around the back to the staff car park.

Rebecca, Ben, and Peter headed out on Larapinta Drive in her Subaru. It was only a twenty-minute drive before the warning signs to 'Turn Around. Joint Defence Facility Official Entry Only' appeared. They drove on till the front gate was in sight. Rebecca parked well off the road. Peter had the drone up within minutes, and Ben studied the landscape. He needed to find a spot that he could get to by car or on foot, because dropping him off by chopper wouldn't be an option.

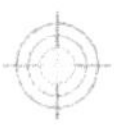

Detective Scott called Marcus Chen.

'Mr Chen, the helicopter has been arranged as you requested. Are all of the hostages safe?'

'Yes, but not from tomorrow.'

'Mr Chen, we have planned for the chopper to be there at 8:00 a.m., he will land on the southern side of the main office building.'

'No, that is too open. I want him to land between the radomes and the main building,' Chen said.

'But that is too dangerous for the pilot,' Scott insisted, seeing his plan go out the window. 'I will need to talk to the pilot. And I will want to see every man and woman standing outside the building before I will let the chopper land. If one is missing, I will then let the army go in there and get you.'

'If you do that, everyone dies. They are all safe for now. If the helicopter is not on the ground by 8:00 a.m., I will start shooting them as I have told you,' Chen said.

'We are doing the best we can here, Mr Chen. Just don't hurt anyone, and you will have your chopper,' Jones said.

Reed's phone rang. Scott explained that Chen had requested the chopper to land where the radomes sheltered his path from the building.

'Peter, let's get that drone up and see what we have to deal with,' Ben said.

Ben watched the monitor for quite a while as Peter scanned the area from about a thousand feet up. He compared the topographic map he had laid out on the bonnet of Rebecca's Subaru. Peter had almost flattened all three batteries by the time Ben had come up with a plan.

'Okay, let's pack this up,' Ben said.

The three of them arrived at Sergeant Jones's office as the sun started to set on the hot Alice Springs day. Ben knocked on the door, and Jones was very keen to hear what he thought. Jones had quickly sent Scott a message, and he arrived within five minutes. Ben already had the map laid out again on Jones's desk.

'I can only see one way of doing this,' Ben said, holding everyone's attention. 'I will need to go in at night and set up on the flat ground that surrounds the complex, where I can get a clean shot between the radomes. Do we know if there are surveillance cameras outside the perimeter?' Ben asked.

'Only along the fence line,' Scott said, pointing to little red dots that he had placed on the map earlier.

'Do we have a plan if I miss him or can't get the shot in?'

'The safety of the people is what is most important, so we would have to let him go,' Jones said.

'Is there any chance that he may have set explosives to detonate once he leaves and kills everyone anyway?' Ben said.

'I didn't think of that,' Scott said.

'Do we have any contact with anyone on the inside?' Ben said, looking at Jones and Scott.

'No, we don't,' Scott said. 'Mobile phones are banned on site.'

Ben stood there staring at the map, deep in thought.

'Right, first thing, I need some camo gear, pants, jacket, a net, spare radio, with earpiece and batteries. Can we get that tonight?'

'I will send Jackson out to get the ammo and gun shop opened up for us. He has all that stuff; get whatever you need,' Jones said.

'Thank you. I will sneak in, in the cover of darkness. Let's just hope he isn't watching the perimeter cameras all night long. Once I am in place, he won't notice me. I will look like the many bushes that surround the area. I don't want to shoot through the mesh fence; I can't be relying on luck.'

Ben continued, 'The way I see it, we only get one shot at this, so to speak. It will reduce my distance to four hundred metres, improving our chances of a positive hit substantially. I will need Peter up high, feeding me info. I only have the width of that laneway before he is out of my sight, and he will know that. If he runs, it will be twice as hard. We will need to get those people away from the building as soon as we can, just in case he has set a timer—or most likely a remote-control detonator on him.'

Peter suggested, 'Why don't we put a radio on the drone? I can drop the drone like a brick, and we can tell them to run, the same as we did with the Japanese tourist.'

Ben looked at Scott and Jones, both offering affirmative nods.

'Might just work. I can't think of a better plan,' Ben said.

Ben and Rebecca met Jackson at the door of the gun shop. He had no idea what was going on, only that he was told to get the shop opened up.

Ben didn't waste any time to find what he needed. He selected khaki pants, shirt, and a jacket; he knew the night would be cold. A bipod to mount to the front of the Tikka, and a mesh netting to drape over himself once he was in position. He thanked the shop owner, and Jackson, who only casually acknowledged it. Ben asked Rebecca to take him out on the highway so he could let off a few shots and adjust the scope to the new distance. Ben instructed her to stop at a roadside marker and then drive on for exactly four hundred metres. He jumped out with his rifle and asked her to drive back to the original marker and shine her lights onto the marker from the other side of the road. He lay down on the warm bitumen. The highway was quiet at this time of night, as the kangaroos would be busy looking for a car to jump in front of. He flicked out the bipod and pushed the stock against his shoulder. The little reflector was large in his scope. He pulled back the bolt, and the spring-loaded shell clicked up in front of it. He let it slide back to load the .308

shell into the breech. He took aim and squeezed the trigger; he saw the dust fly up about a 100 millimetres to the right of the reflector. He easily recalled the minutes of angle formula, adjusted the scope four clicks to the left, and lined up the post again. He squeezed the trigger once more and saw the reflector fly off through the air. He was happy with that. Rebecca could see him stand in the moonlight, and turned the car around to pick him up. He placed the rifle onto the back seat and jumped into the passenger seat next to her.

'That looked good,' she said, looking at him for confirmation.

'Yeah, near enough. I hope I can do this, Bec. If those people die because of something I haven't thought of, it's going to be a hard pill to swallow.'

'You are the best option they have, Ben,' she said.

'This is a very American way of doing things, Bec.'

'What do you mean?'

'Sending in a civilian to do the dirty work, and when it turns to shit, everyone runs for cover, leaving you holding the baby, only to spend the rest of your life in jail or on the run,' Ben said.

Ben called Peter. 'Mate, get those batteries on charge and bring that invertor so we are not left high and dry. You will be my eyes. Bec will be with you to help. We will pick you up at zero three thirty. See you then, Alpha 5.'

They all managed some sleep before the alarm went off at 3:00 a.m. Ben was already awake anyway and caught the alarm on the second buzz. Sleeping next to Rebecca was the greatest pleasure he had ever experienced, but this morning he wasn't able to fully appreciate it. His mind was somewhere else. They still had their flights to Adelaide booked for twelve thirty, but he really doubted they would make the plane. Rebecca didn't wake from the alarm, so he woke her with small kisses on her neck and cheek. She turned towards him with a smile that said, 'Please don't stop.'

'We have to go, babe. We have a big job ahead of us,' Ben said.

Rebecca soon sprang out of bed, and they both quickly dressed. Ben gently put the rifle into the back of the Subaru. As they pulled up at Peter's little flat, he was out the front waiting. He loaded the alloy drone box onto the back seat and slid in next to it. He was still closing the door as Ben started to drive off to the rendezvous point.

Jones, Scott, and an ambulance were waiting at John Flynn's Grave Historical Reserve.

'Chen will be expecting us to try something,' Jones said as he handed out radios to everyone. 'Ten kilometres out, we turn off our lights and drive the rest as best we can in the dark,' he added.

'Ben, you and Reed go in as far as you need, but be careful not to be seen,' Scott said.

'Roger that,' Ben replied.

Peter, Rebecca, and Ben pulled up in the same spot they did when they came for the last look. Ben slung the rifle over his shoulder, and Rebecca placed the netting into his rucksack. Ben reached out to shake Peter's hand as he was unpacking the drone. Ben shook his hand and said, 'Let's do it again, buddy.'

'Yes, sir, Alpha 1,' he replied.

Ben kissed Rebecca with a kiss that was probably longer than it needed to be, before he turned and quickly disappeared into the dark. It was about an hour later and close to 5:00 a.m. when Ben called to say that he was in position. He had attached the rifle bipod and had the netting fully covering him. Only three inches of the barrel poked out through the net. Using his recently sharpened Leatherman, he cut a small hole for the scope to have an unobstructed view. He practiced the movement of the rifle to simulate the target walking and then running. The bullet would only take half a second to get there, so he tried to imagine him walking through the driveway. He would need to shoot three feet in front of him. If the guy was running, it would just have to be a guess, as he would have no idea about how fast his target might run.

Ben pressed the talk button on the Motorola. 'Scott, how old is this Chen fella?'

'Thirty-four,' Scott came back instantly.

That didn't help, Ben thought.

'Alpha 5, come in,' Ben said with a tone of seriousness.

'Go ahead,' Peter came back.

'Peter, I will need to know every bit of information you can give me, like if he is walking, jogging, or running. Does he have hostages, and where are they in relation to him and me? I will need a countdown as to when he will appear in the driveway. As soon as you hear the shot—get straight to the people on the wall and tell them to run like hell! Better still, tell them to follow the drone, and direct them to the clearing in the north.'

'Will do, Alpha 1, over,' Peter replied.

It was silent for another thirty minutes as the sun started to rise in the east. The Pine Gap complex was surrounded by the west MacDonnell Ranges, and it would all be over one way or another before the sun actually lit up Ben's position.

It was now seven thirty, and Ben loaded the rifle. He had a five-shot magazine, however he was really hoping that one shot would be all he needed. At seven forty-five, Jones reported, 'Chopper is in the air. Good luck, Ben.'

'Thank you, everyone. Now, unless there is an abort situation, Peter is the only one I want to hear from,' Ben said. 'Talk to me, Alpha 5, when you see something. Switch to voice-activation mode so I can hear you as you see it; the radio is yours.'

Ben could hear the chopper a few miles out. It was seven fifty-five. Ben saw the drone go up behind him, and it was soon out of sight.

For the last few minutes, Ben could hear Peter's heavy breathing in the mic.

'Door of main building opening,' Peter said. 'First of the hostages are coming out, hands tied behind their backs, and he is leaning them against the wall, western side of the doorway.' Ben saw the helicopter disappear behind the radomes as it landed. It was eight o'clock.

'Fourteen hostages only, outside on the wall,' Peter called.

Ben could see the huge dust storm that the chopper was creating; leaves and dust covered the area.

'Four more hostages with Chen in between them, walking very slowly towards the chopper,' Peter said.

Ben adjusted himself, his finger relaxed but tight on the trigger, the crosshairs one metre from the wall that he would appear around.

'Approaching the driveway in three, two, one,' Peter said softly.

The five people filled the scope as they shuffled across the driveway. Chen was smart, having picked the four tallest men to shield him.

While parts of Chen's head appeared for brief moments as they crossed, Ben had no chance of getting off a safe shot.

As they disappeared out of sight behind the last radome, Ben called to Peter, 'Get the people out, now!'

Ben jumped up, flicked off the netting, and ran as fast as he could with his rifle along the fence line till the chopper came into view. He placed the rifle barrel on the wire fence and adjusted the scope for the extra hundred metres, which he guessed was now the distance. The five shuffled into view. Ben had his crosshairs on

Chen's left shoulder. The dust was playing havoc with the hostages, as they couldn't protect their eyes with their hands tied, they could only shut them. They had almost come to a stop, as they were nearly under the chopper's spinning rotor. Ben's finger was tight on the trigger; all he needed was that clear shot. Suddenly Chen, in sheer frustration, burst from the huddle of the hostages and ran the last five metres towards the helicopter passenger door.

Ben had thought many times about what it is like when you squeeze the trigger, knowing that you are about to end someone's life. You must forget that they are someone's son, brother, or father, and that the job you are doing is for the greater good. Clear your mind of any emotion or thoughts. Only your finger moves, and after the click, your part of the job is done. In about half a second, the bullet will do its job. You stay frozen as you see the target go down, no emotion. It's just a horrible, disgusting job. You pack up and move on, no celebration or high fives, just mission accomplished.

Chen never reached the chopper, the projectile entered his ribcage just under his left arm, and he collapsed to the dusty ground. The helicopter pilot lifted off straight away as he had been instructed, and within seconds was away and outside the complex grounds. Ben, without moving his eye from the scope, slowly lifted the bolt, ejected the spent cartridge, and loaded the next shell into the breach. His finger softly found the trigger again. The four men that were used as shields had run off, away from Chen. Peter had called them through the radio on the drone to join the others as quickly as they could. Ben kept the crosshairs on Chen's head.

He saw Chen's hand move slowly for his pocket. He fired again, saw the bullet hit, and he knew Chen wouldn't move again.

'Scott,' Ben called over the radio, 'be careful. He reached for something in his left pocket, it could be a detonator.'

'Roger that. Superb job, Ben,' Scott said.

Ben didn't reply.

Jones and Scott soon arrived at the scene with the ambulance in hot pursuit. The ambulance could see Chen wouldn't be needing their help and then rushed off to check the hostages. Scott and Jones stayed with Chen and carefully checked his pockets.

Ben walked back to his original location and slowly packed up his gear. He didn't feel good or bad. You can't feel good about killing someone no matter how bad they were. He simply wanted to get packed up and on that plane to Adelaide with Rebecca.

About forty-five minutes later, Ben appeared through the bush, and Rebecca ran to him. She didn't say anything, just gave him a long hug as he looked over her shoulder at Peter who was watching them. He had the drone already packed and was sitting on the back of the Subaru under the open hatch. Ben gave him a wink, and Peter gave a light smile back.

'Let's get out of here, Bec. We have a plane to catch,' Ben said, breaking the hug and putting his arm around her.

'Shall we tell the sarge before we go?' she asked.

'Nah, let's just go. Our job here is done. Let's drop Peter home and get to the airport; they will be out there for hours.'

CHAPTER TWENTY-NINE

REBECCA slept for most of the ninety-minute flight. Ben loved the feel of her asleep on his shoulder. He thought of how close he had been to losing her, to end up being abused as a sex slave or a drugged-up prostitute in some third-world country and most likely never to be seen again, along with the other three young ladies. He felt a warmth in knowing he had saved them all; he would never forget them, and he was sure he would always be their hero.

They landed in Adelaide and were waiting to catch a taxi to Ben's apartment when Rebecca's phone rang. She answered it without looking at the number.

'Reed, Jones. How is Adelaide going?'

'Just arrived, sir,' Reed said.

'Hey, can you tell Woolford he was right? The whole place was wired to blow. He will never be recognised for what he did because we can't tell anyone, but let's just say he has a few 'Get out of jail free' cards up his sleeve in the Northern Territory.'

'Thank you, Sarge. I will pass that on,' Rebecca said as she hung up.

They arrived at Ben's apartment, unpacked, and decided to have an early dinner and then try and get their sleep pattern back on track. With Ben's Jeep shot up and still probably in the Western Australian desert, they jumped on his Kawasaki and rode into town for a meal. They sat down at an outside table at his favourite Chinese restaurant. Ben took Rebecca's hand and said, 'I want to spend the next little while doing nothing, just relaxing and getting to know the real Rebecca Reed.'

It was then that Ben's phone rang.

He looked at Rebecca, who nodded for him to take it.

'Greg, how are you going, mate?'

'Good, mate. No one shooting at you today?'

'No, all work completed, and I'm just in Gouger Street, having some Chinese with Constable Reed.'

'What, the cop that got shot! How is that even possible?'

'It's a long story,' Ben said.

'Can't wait to hear that. Do you have one minute, Ben?'

'Hold on.' Ben looked at Rebecca and said, 'Can I be rude for sixty seconds, babe?'

'Of course,' she said, smiling.

'Go ahead, Greg, we have permission for a minute of rudeness.' Ben winked at Rebecca.

'Okay, are you up for another adventure?' Greg said. 'We are going to need a little help from a professional here in Dallas.'

'Can we find a job for Bec as well?' Ben said.

'In actual fact, I might just have the perfect job for her too.'

'Okay, count us in. I'll see what flights there are available, and we will be there as soon as we can. Anyway, our sixty seconds is up; I'll call you back tomorrow,' Ben said, hanging up the call.

He looked at Rebecca. 'Looks like we are going to Dallas, babe.'

Rebecca looked at him, shaking her head. 'Is this what our life together is going to be like?'

'No… well, babe, maybe yes, it probably is. But it certainly won't be boring.'

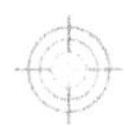

When Ben and Rebecca landed at DFW, it was the middle of the afternoon. They grabbed a cab and headed for the hotel where Greg and Jennifer were staying. Greg had arranged a room next to theirs.

Both Greg and Jennifer met them as they arrived in the foyer. There were handshakes, kisses, and hugs all around, and Greg handed Ben their room key. Ben could see why Greg had been so obsessed with this woman. Even with her dyed blonde hair, absence of make-up, and large dark sunglasses, her natural beauty was dazzling. They were like teenagers, holding hands and touching each other at every chance. He then realised he and Rebecca were much the same; he loved seeing it in them, and he loved feeling it himself. He felt a wave of warmth radiate through him. Greg was a client. He had done a couple little jobs for him, just normal PI stuff, but now they had become mates. Greg's bravery at the Mexican house was beyond the call of duty, and he quite possibly saved Steve's life.

For that, he would be forever grateful.

'We should get Jennifer out of sight. Your room is next to ours, so go and settle in and come over when you are ready, and we can run through the plan,' Greg said.

They caught the elevator to the sixth floor, and Greg pointed out their room.

'We will be there in a minute, Greg. If we are in the room for too long, we may end up being quite some time.' Everyone smiled. Rebecca went to hit him but stopped at the last second, an irrepressible grin on her face.

'They seem really nice,' Jennifer said as their door closed behind Greg.

'Yes, their relationship's very new. She's a cop in Alice Springs. I can't wait to hear that story,' Greg said to her.

It was only a minute or two later when Ben knocked on the door. They were welcomed in, and the four of them sat around a quite small laminate table.

'So, Greg, tell us what you have got us into here.'

Greg spent the next hour explaining to them all the details of his plan to get Jennifer's money back. Ben sat there as he listened to the plan. Rebecca couldn't believe the detail he had gone to. How he had every piece of the puzzle laid out. Nor could she believe that she was here in the US being a part of all this. She was torn between the excitement of it all and the realisation that she would be helping them to possibly break the law. *But, well, was it really breaking the law if you were tricking your husband to get back the money he'd taken from you? Especially given the fact that he had just arranged to have you murdered?*

When Greg had finished, Ben had a few questions that Greg answered. They ordered dinner in Greg's room and continued refining the plan as they ate.

Ben and Rebecca retired early and caught up on some much-needed sleep.

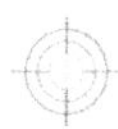

Greg was up before everyone else and did the rounds to check the progress on the truck modifications, the picture frames, and the duplicate engravings. Although they were mostly done, the way the two artists went about them was completely different. He was now very happy that he had made the decision to have two of them create the replica. The frames were finished, just getting the paint to look nearly a hundred years old was the challenge.

Ben met Greg at 10:00 a.m. to confirm the schedule for the day. First it was a visit to the museum to meet the director, to make sure the plan was still all good to go ahead, to book the security guard that Slade made conditional, and to prepare for the transfer of the money. Next was for Ben to make the call to Keith. Jennifer suggested calling him mid-morning, as that should catch him in the best mood.

'Mr Madison, my name is Benjamin Wall. I am from the UK, London,' Ben said in the most English sounding voice he could, knowing most Americans couldn't tell the difference between an English accent and an Australian one anyway.

'What can I do for you, Mr Wall?' Keith said with very little interest. But before Ben could answer, he said, 'How did you get my number anyway?'

'From an art dealer in Dallas, sir. Mr Madison, embarrassingly, I have found myself in need of a short loan, and I have the Picasso, *The Lovers, Genevieve looking for me ll*, that I purchased not long ago for three million US dollars.'

Keith sounded noticeably more interested now. 'Go on?'

'Yes, Mr Madison, I have been told that you have a keen eye for said investments,' Ben said.

'I may be interested. I thought that piece was in the museum here in Dallas?' Keith said.

'It was, my dear fellow. I acquired it recently and have a receipt with a buy-back guarantee for $2.9 million that I am happy to forward to you,' Ben said, happy with how his accent was sounding.

'So what are you proposing, Mr Wall?'

'Sir, I need $2.5 million for two weeks. I will give you the artwork as security with the buy-back agreement from the museum. Then in two weeks, I will repay the money plus the appropriate interest.'

Keith knew that most people defaulted on these types of loans. These Picassos didn't come along very often, and he could make a huge profit on the open market, but at worst he could sell it back to the museum for $2.9 million wholesale. It was still a quick buck whichever way he looked at it.

'I am interested, Mr Wall. I would need my expert to see the artwork first, of course.'

'Of course. I can have it available for you tomorrow, if that suits you?' Ben looked at Greg, who was shaking his head, miming the day after.

'Or maybe the day after might be better,' Ben said.

'Give me your number, and I will call you back, Mr Wall,' Keith said.

Ben gave him the number, and as the call ended, he threw Greg a wink and a grin.

The sting was underway.

Jennifer had arranged for the "Texas Art Security" signage for the truck to be printed and a shirt with the same logo for Rebecca to wear as the driver. The truck with the modifications to the cargo compartment had been completed.

Rebecca picked up the shirt and collected the truck signage from the printer. Greg met Ben at the engineer's and fitted the new logos over the top of the hire-company signage.

Next was to transfer the funds to the museum, and once they were clear, they would take the truck to the museum and collect the Picasso.

Greg had arranged for both of the ghost artists to finish their works of art together in a common studio, where he would bring the original for them to make any finishing touches.

The four of them met up back at the hotel. Jennifer, being the one hotel bound, became the coordinator.

The truck was ready; the funds were transferred and were now awaiting confirmation that they were cleared.

The shirt that Rebecca would wear as the driver of the truck fitted perfectly, and the embroidery looked great. Jennifer washed it twice so it didn't look brand new. The two artists were now waiting for the real Picasso to arrive, and the frames were ready and the paint nearly dry.

Later that afternoon, Ben's phone rang.

'Wall speaking.'

'Mr Wall, Keith Madison. My man can inspect the item tomorrow as you requested.'

'Thank you, Mr Madison. I would assume the Picasso will be covered by your insurance once it is in your possession?'

'That is correct,' Keith said. 'My lawyer will have all of the documentation ready for our arrangement.'

'So, up until that time, it is my responsibility, so I will have a professional art-transport company and a security guard collect the painting from me, and they will take it to your expert. After he has inspected it, he will then watch it be placed into the rear of the truck and, himself, lock the truck cargo area with two of his own combination locks. An armed security detail will follow the truck from behind in a separate vehicle. Once the truck leaves him, he will call you with the combinations and you can unlock the truck when it arrives, and then the security will officially be in your possession. At the time between when the truck arrives and you open the doors, you can send me the $2.5 million. How does that sound?' Ben said.

'Mr Wall, that all sounds fine, but I can only lend two million on that particular piece.'

'But Mr Madison, all due respect, it is worth three million dollars,' Ben said, sounding a little frustrated.

'I'm sorry, Mr Wall. That is my final offer.'

Ben gave a slight delay for effect, but they all knew he would make a counteroffer at the last minute.

'Okay then, I can make that work, but I *will* be coming back for it,' Ben said.

'Now the interest component, it would be 5 percent flat,' Keith said.

'You are a tough man, Mr Madison, but I have no choice. Do the conditions I have proposed suit you, sir?'

'Yes, if my man says it's a go,' Keith said.

Keith went on to tell him the address of the art valuer and the address of his mansion in Dallas for the truck to deliver it to.

Ben gave a thumbs up to everyone as he wrote down the details. The museum had called, and the funds were in the bank. Greg left immediately to collect the masterpiece.

He arrived at the dispatching area at the rear of the museum. He met the nervous museum director at the top of the loading-bay ramp, and they both watched the Picasso being loaded into the specially built frame. The rear doors were locked, and with the security guard in tow, the artwork was rushed around to the artists who were keen to finish off their work.

The two artists were initially mesmerized by the fact that they were standing in front of the original artwork of the Spanish genius, but they quickly got back to work retinting and scaling their own pieces.

'Gentlemen, we have twenty-four hours for them to be finished,' Greg said, closing the back of the truck. 'For your safety and that of the artwork, I will have the security guard here with you for the night. I will see you in the morning. Don't lose that Picasso,' he said, winking at the security guard as he walked out.

That night they discussed what could go wrong and how they might handle it. It all appeared to be going well. They again ordered room service, and they ate in Greg and Jennifer's room.

Rebecca asked, 'So, how did you two meet?'

Greg and Jennifer looked at each other with a smile before Jennifer said, 'I was at a pool bar on a cruise ship from Miami to Jamaica, when this man here came and stood next to me. Our eyes met, and he was all I could think about from that moment on. The next night I'd gone out for a drink with a lady that I met on the ship, who all of a sudden ran off with a man and left me on my own at the bar. Greg came over, and we talked, we walked, we kissed, and we made love. It was about as romantic as it gets! But what about you two?' Jennifer asked.

Ben decided to reply. 'Well, ours isn't quite so romantic. The first time she saw me, she tried to shoot me in the back. Then she was shot trying to stop a shoot-out with drug dealers, so I risked my life dragging her sorry arse out of the firing line until I was shot myself and went down as well. Then Greg here rushed her to hospital unable to breath, and next she tried to ambush and arrest me.'

'But he was too smart for me,' Rebecca said, cutting in.

'Then she decided to buy me a drink and take me home.'

Rebecca sat there with a big smile on her face. 'That's about it.'

Jennifer couldn't decide if they were telling the truth or if it was a joke, or just some strange Australian sense of humour.

Greg put her out of her misery.

'Jennifer, Rebecca is a cop in Alice Springs, and sometimes Ben's work clashes with the authorities.'

Jennifer was still confused but happy to just let it go for now.

Next morning was D-Day. Greg and Ben were up early and arrived at the painters' studio; he couldn't pick the better of the two. With the painters having the original to copy, they had done an amazing job. He congratulated them both on the work they did and paid them the five thousand dollars each that they were promised.

He explained to them that one would soon be on display in place of the original and the other would be hung in his own home in Australia. Greg ended up deciding on the one with the better frame for the sting. They collected the two fakes and the original Picasso and loaded them into the new Texas Art Security truck. The security guard ended his shift, and another followed as they drove back to the hotel and set the truck ready for the 'transaction.' The guard was instructed to stay with the truck at all times, not the painting, which did confuse him, but he of course would do as the museum director had asked.

It was soon time for the meeting with the art dealer to evaluate the authenticity of the Picasso. Rebecca dressed in the Texas Art Security uniform, jumped into the truck, and headed to the art gallery for the Picasso's inspection.

CHAPTER THIRTY

REBECCA pulled the little truck up at the Highland Park Gallery, closely followed by the museum's security guard. The security guard stayed with the truck, and Rebecca walked in, asking for Anthony Russo.

'Mr Russo, sir, I have a Picasso for you to inspect for a… Mr Keith Madison,' she said, reading the name from her delivery docket.

'Yes, let's have a look.'

Rebecca unlocked the back of the truck, and the specially made frame held the painting secure. It was carefully wrapped in a protective felt blanket. Russo carefully took the artwork from her, and she quickly closed the doors. The guard and Rebecca followed him into the gallery. 'Mr Russo, sir, I hope you don't mind, but we can't let it out of my sight.'

'Of course, my dear, follow me.'

He laid the package down gently and unwrapped it, pulling

back the blanket with great care. He took out a magnifying glass and started to look over the artwork. He made a few noises as he studied the signature, the grain of the canvas, the age of the paint, and then finally the frame.

'This is certainly an original by Pablo Picasso,' Russo said to no one really, as he wrapped the piece of art back in the protective cloth. He handed it back to Rebecca. 'Hold on a second. I will just put my certification sticker on the back to show I have inspected it,' Russo said, reaching for the wrapped parcel. Rebecca felt a wave of panic; this wasn't something they had thought about happening.

'Sir, is it easily removable? This is still owned by someone else,' Rebecca said.

'It can be removed easily, but once the adhesive is dry, it will only come off in pieces so it can't be transferred,' Russo said.

He unwrapped it and turned it over. He signed the small sticker and placed it on the canvas. He wrapped it again and handed it to Rebecca. He followed her out and watched her place it in the specially made frame in the truck. As she put the last strap around, she called out, 'Mr Russo, do you always put a security sticker on the back of a painting?'

'Yes. It all adds to its authenticity, ma'am; you would understand that,' he said.

Rebecca closed the rear doors of the truck, and Russo fitted his own two heavy combination locks.

'Okay, thank you, Mr Russo,' she said as she went to leave.

'Madam, would you mind if I came with you? Just to add to the security, and it would be good to catch up with Mr Madison again.' This was another eventuality they hadn't thought of.

'Mr Russo, that is quite unusual,' Rebecca said.

'I must insist. This way, Mr Madison and I can be fully assured that the transaction is legitimate.'

'Yes, sir, that's a sensible idea, but I won't be able to bring you back.'

'That's fine. I'll catch a cab.'

He ran to the gallery door and called out to someone who called back something in Italian. He then took out his phone, made a short call, and then jumped into the truck's cabin next to her. Rebecca then pulled out into the busy Dallas traffic. She was really coming to grips with the left-hand-drive vehicle now.

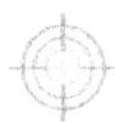

The Madison mansion was only fifteen minutes away from the gallery, and it wasn't long before the little truck pulled up in front of the house with the security guard in tow. The same house that Greg, only two weeks ago, had knocked on the door of asking for Jennifer. Russo jumped out and stood by the back of the truck as he called Keith to say they were out the front. Ben, dressed in a double-breasted black suit, walked up behind the truck in the guise of Benjamin Wall. He shook hands with Russo and then the Dallas Art Security driver with a look of 'What is he doing here?'

Keith Madison walked down the five steps from his big white front doors with another man, who wore a serious expression and held a leather-bound document folder.

He held his hand out to Ben. 'Keith Madison.'

'Benjamin Wall,' Ben said back. 'Now, Mr Madison, this is where the responsibility of the piece changes from me to you. Your good man here has inspected and confirmed the authenticity of the Picasso, and he has also accompanied it here. I would like to see the funds in my account before we unload the truck.'

Keith looked at Russo, who nodded in confirmation.

'Okay, ol' fella, we can do that.' The man that was standing behind Keith stepped forward, opening the document holder.

'Please check that the terms are what were agreed, and then could you and Mr Madison both sign the last two pages?'

Ben signed the two copies of the document and handed it back to the lawyer along with a copy of the agreement from the museum to pay $2.9 million for the return of the artwork.

Keith signed it as well and handed Ben a copy. The lawyer looked at Keith, who nodded, and the lawyer took out his phone.

'Can I have the bank account details please, sir,' the lawyer asked.

Ben produced a document that had the bank details printed on it. The lawyer typed in the details while they all stood around awkwardly.

'Two million has been transferred, Mr Madison,' the lawyer said.

Ben checked his phone, and there was a message saying the account had increased by two million dollars.

'Thank you, Mr Madison. I promise you *will* see me again in the next two weeks,' Ben said.

'Have a nice day, Mr Wall,' Keith said, not even looking at him.

Ben walked back to his car and drove off slowly as Anthony Russo undid the combination locks. Rebecca opened the rear doors of the truck and locked them back in the open position. She removed the locating straps and lifted the package gently out. Russo reached for it. He pulled back the blanket and checked that his sticker was still in place, and when it was, he rewrapped the blanket, and with a very insincere thank-you to Rebecca, followed Keith and the lawyer inside the house. Ben watched from down the street as Rebecca closed the back of the truck and drive off with the security guard following. He let out a sigh of relief. The sting was complete; the money was in the bank.

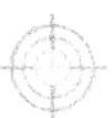

Anthony Russo unwrapped the picture and sat it against the wall, so that its potential new owner could stand back and appreciate it.

'Old Pablo had a strange style, didn't he?' Keith said as he admired it from two metres away. Russo was studying it from its side, maybe only a metre away, when a wave of uneasiness rocked through his body. He stepped forward and tilted it forward to check the sticker that he himself had put there only thirty minutes ago. He placed it back against the wall, and Keith said, looking a little concerned, 'Is everything okay, Russo?'

'Yes, yes, just making sure the security sticker was still secure.'

But he knew Keith could tell there was something more, and that the lawyer saw it as well.

Russo continued to stare at it. *Could he have been wrong when he checked it?* He now had no choice but to just hope Mr Wall reclaimed it in two weeks' time and this all went away. He had never been wrong before, he was absolutely positive when he inspected it, but in daylight, the ink looked fresh. He was feeling faint, and a bead of sweat ran down his cheek. He needed to get out of there.

'I will call a cab, Mr Madison. I had better get back to the gallery.'

'Nonsense, Russo, my driver will take you,' Keith said.

'Thank you, Mr Madison, I will wait outside,' he said almost in a panic. He then noticed a tiny bit of gold paint on his finger, the same colour as the frame. His heart sank; he may have just cost his best client two million dollars. *How could he have got it so wrong?*

The little truck pulled up at the back of the museum, and Ben parked his rental car next to it.

Rebecca walked to the rear of the truck and opened the big doors. First thing she saw was an original Pablo Picasso sitting in the painting restraint that Greg had had specially made. Then she saw Greg sitting next to it with a big smile on his face. The security guard did a double take as Greg jumped out and was soon met by a very relieved museum director.

'What about when he put that sticker on?' Rebecca said to Greg.

'I heard you say it nice and loud, and I had it off within seconds of him affixing it, so the adhesive had no time to set,' Greg said.

'And then he wanted to come with me!' Rebecca said.

'I think that was actually a good thing,' Ben said.

'I agree,' Greg said.

'How was it behind that false wall, Greg?' Ben asked.

'It was tight, only just enough room.'

Greg released the straps that secured the real Picasso and handed it to Mark Slade. The director placed it on a desk that sat just inside the loading dock. A man, who Greg assumed was the museum expert, quickly assessed it for originality and any damage. Greg waited nervously as he thoroughly examined every inch of the artwork.

Finally, he nodded to the relieved museum director, who asked Greg to follow him to his office.

Mark Slade transferred the $2.9 million back to Greg's account and held out his hand, thanking him for the donation.

'And Mr Sheppard?'

'Yes, Mr Slade?'

'Please don't ask me to do this again. I think it has taken ten years off my life,' the director said.

'Mr Slade, I doubt you will ever see me again, but thank you, and the FBI thanks you.' Greg couldn't wipe the smile from his face.

Greg walked out to the loading dock and dismissed the very confused security guard. He hugged Rebecca and gave Ben a very warm handshake.

'We bloody did it,' Greg said, the happiness bursting out of him. He called Jennifer. Ben and Rebecca turned away, as they could see the tears of joy in his eyes as they spoke.

Greg turned back to Ben and Rebecca and, still with damp eyes, said, 'Okay, before we celebrate, we still have a little work to do. Let's get the engineers to remove the wall and the painting frame from the truck while we get the stickers off the side and then we can return it to the hire company.'

Rebecca took Ben's hire car and headed back to the hotel. She was greeted by a very happy Jennifer in the foyer.

Rebecca, still not able to believe what had just happened, walked to the elevator with Jennifer's arm around her. 'Now we have some hair to dye,' Rebecca said.

CHAPTER THIRTY-ONE

KEITH Madison had put the Picasso in his safe and the whole deal behind him, as he needed to focus on the annual meeting for Southwestern Cattleman's Association and his re-election as president tonight. He would wear a black suit, of course, to mourn the death of his beautiful wife, who was gunned down so mercilessly in that dangerous country down under. He had used the ten thousand head of cattle that he had feeding in his empty paddocks to secure the money for the Picasso, but they would all be heading back to Oklahoma soon; the bank had approved the temporary extended overdraft. The free cattle feed also secured a vote for him from that farmer.

Keith's lawyer was still suspicious, as most lawyers are. So, he decided to go to the Dallas Museum of Art to ask some questions about the recent purchase of the Picasso and confirm that the buy-back arrangement that Ben Wall had given to Mr Madison was in fact a legal and valid document. Although he knew the sale would be confidential, he may learn something from someone.

He found an attendant and asked, 'Hello, I am interested in Picasso, in particular, *The Lovers, Genevieve looking for me ll.* that you had here.'

'Yes, sir, please come this way,' the attendant said.

'But wasn't it sold recently?' the lawyer asked as he followed the attendant down a passage.

'No, sir, I doubt the museum would ever sell artwork. It was gone for a day or two, I assumed to be cleaned, but you're lucky it's back now.'

The attendant stopped, standing in front of the identical piece that now sat in Keith Madison's safe. The lawyer stood there in shock with his mouth open as he took his phone out of his pocket. He turned to the attendant.

'Thank you, that will be all.' The attendant nodded, turned, and walked away.

'Yes, Michael?' Keith said, answering the phone.

'Mr Madison, sir, we have a problem.'

'What?' Keith said.

'I am in the Dallas Museum of Art looking at the Picasso, *The Lovers, Genevieve looking for me ll.*'

'What! It can't be.'

'The attendant here said it had just come back from being cleaned.'

'Fuck! Find out who the fuck that Wall character is—he's a dead man—and what fucking account that money went to.'

Keith slammed his fist down on his office desk and called Anthony Russo.

'Russo, you fuck, that fucking Picasso that's in my safe owing me two million is also sitting in the fucking Dallas Museum.'

There was a pause before Russo answered.

'I don't understand, sir. What I checked was the real deal, I am 100 percent sure.'

'Well one of them is a fake and you had better fucking hope it's the one in the museum.'

Keith hung up, wishing desperately it was the old days so he could slam the receiver down into its cradle. His phone rang almost straight away.

'Yes, Michael?'

'Mr Madison, I have the name of the account that the money was transferred to.'

'Who the fuck is it? I'll fucking kill him!'

'Mrs. Jennifer Madison, sir.'

'What?' Keith said slowly. He hung up the phone, not saying another word, and fell back into his seat. He had never been this out of control of a situation in his life. He was a shrewd, conniving businessman, a Plan A, B, and C for every eventuality, but this, this was something like a tornado he had no control of. He had spent his life cheating and deceiving people, always one step ahead of them, and no one had ever gotten the better of him, until now.

How could his dead wife just sting him for two million bucks? How can that be? His shaking hand dialled Jerry's number.

'Jerry,' Keith said calmly. 'Is there any chance my wife is still alive?'

'No way, Mr Madison. I fired the shot myself. I saw the blood spread across her chest as she fell and hit the floor. I saw the morgue take her body away, and you saw her on the gurney yourself, sir.'

'Well, she just did me for two million fucking dollars. Explain that to me?'

'What do you mean?' Jerry said.

'She just sold me a fucking fake Picasso for two million bucks.'

'Sir, I did everything except feel her pulse.'

'Well, explain it to me, because I am very confused here, Jerry. I sent you to do a job.'

'Sir, you have the re-election tonight. Focus on that, and I will find out what the hell's going on.'

FBI Special Agent Martin Smithson removed the headset from his head. 'We've fucking got him, both of those fucks. Get me the deputy director on the phone; I want these two arseholes behind bars tonight.'

The FBI had been listening to Keith Madison's phone calls since Smithson's return from Australia. He had heard the sting of the Picasso happen, which really humoured him. He also heard how Keith Maddison had moved ten thousand head of someone else's cattle to his property, to use as security for another overdraft extension. He was aware that tonight was the meeting for the Southwestern Cattleman's Association, and that Madison was likely to continue his corrupt presidency.

'Well, after tonight, life will be different for those two crooks,' Smithson said to the phone tap operator who had called him in.

Smithson explained the situation to the deputy director and played the recording of the last phone call. The director gave him full power to execute the arrest warrants for Keith Madison and Jerry Stokes at the Southwestern Cattleman's AGM tonight.

After hanging up from the deputy director, Smithson quickly made a call.

'Mrs Madison, it's Special Agent Martin Smithson.'

'Hello, Martin.'

'We are going in tonight to arrest your husband and Jerry Stokes for the attempted murder of Mrs Jennifer Madison. I can't tell you any more, and I shouldn't have told you this, but I did agree that I would let you know as part of our deal, so I am. It is extremely important that you keep it to yourselves as it could risk the lives of my men and possibly members of the public.

'Oh, and Mrs Madison… the Picasso sting was hilarious. He just found out about it an hour ago, and he's really pissed! You must tell me sometime how you did it,' Smithson said.

'For another time, Martin. Thank you,' she said.

Keith Madison did put the Picasso incident behind him for the time being. He made millions anyway, just from being the Cattleman's president. The scams, the bribes, and the blackmails far exceeded a mere couple million bucks. He dressed in the black suit he had carefully selected and practiced a few sad expressions in the mirror. His driver was waiting downstairs, and of course as president, he would have to open the meeting and chair the meeting, so he couldn't be late. He arrived half an hour before the start, and some members were already there offering condolences and wishing him good luck for the position of president.

He poured a large scotch on ice and drank it down in one mouthful. If only he had known that it would be the last drink he would ever have, he may have tried to savour it for a little longer.

He opened the annual general meeting with a request for the previous minutes, which were read out by the secretary. The treasurer was next, with the statement of accounts, which were very healthy of course, due to the amazing job the president had done. Keith asked for any general business but also requested that, unless it was very important, they be brought up at the next meeting in a month's time.

He then stated that all positions of office were now vacant and that a ballot for each had been conducted.

The results were read out, and all positions had been reinstated with an overwhelming majority for the current holders. This was no surprise due to the strong financial position the association was in. Only the president was still to be announced. There was only one man prepared to go up against Madison for the president's job; he was someone who knew well how corrupt Keith was, and had been a victim to his ruthlessness. He was nowhere as popular, as he was a head-down type of person, not the showman that Madison was.

There was a small commotion and chatter as FBI agents appeared at every door of the venue.

Two agents went straight for Jerry Stokes and grabbed him, throwing him to the floor as he went for the pistol he had hidden in his belt. He was held down by four officers, who disarmed and cuffed him before any trouble could get started. Keith stood up and immediately tried to leave, but quickly found himself with an FBI agent either side of him.

Martin Smithson read Keith his rights as he was handcuffed by two agents. Keith wanted to call out that it was just a misunderstanding and that he would be back to take his rightful position as the head of the committee, but he knew there was no point. He would not be back. Jerry Stokes was resisting the arrest and was receiving some heavy-handed responses from four beefy FBI agents; his nose was now bleeding badly. A resolute Keith walked out with his head held high, possibly his last ever moment of fame.

He had almost reached the police car when he stopped, looked to his right, and saw the Dallas Art Security van driver, Mr Benjamin Wall, that man from the cruise who had caught his wife when she had fainted, and of course Mrs Jennifer Madison, alive and well.

He stood there in shock, staring at his deceased wife, the same one that he had just had killed only a week ago.

Agent Smithson was happy for him to take in this scene for as long as he needed. Keith's look of shock slowly turned to a grin, as it all started to make sense. He would have applauded her if he could; it was an outstanding performance. He turned back to the police car and walked towards it, nodding with acceptance of her achievement. She had beaten him at his own game. Before Keith stepped into the back of the patrol car, he again looked over at Jennifer, their eyes met, and he mimed the word, 'Sorry,' before the FBI agent placed his hand on his head and helped him into the back seat.

Jennifer felt a little sorry for him, but he deserved what he got; he tried to kill her over money. She knew he wasn't jealous about her having left him for another man, just that he had lost a beautiful ornament to show off. As the two police cars drove off with each of the two criminals inside, Greg hugged Jennifer and said, 'That part of your life is now over. I want to be the biggest part of the rest of your life.' She hugged him tight; she didn't need to say anything.

Ben wore the black double-breasted suit of Benjamin Wall, and Rebecca, her Art Security uniform, so that Keith would appreciate the whole sting and the effort they had gone to, but to see his wife alive and well must have been a shock that he would have many years to ponder. They all walked slowly back to their hire car as the entire Cattleman's Association gathered outside and watched in disbelief as their president was taken away.

Jennifer was quiet, and Greg knew she would be. It would take her a little while to take it all in. It had been a big couple of weeks.

The next morning, the four of them were having breakfast when FBI Special Agent Martin Smithson called to say he wanted to meet with them before they left the country.

Greg told him where they were, and it was only ten minutes until Smithson pulled up a chair to discuss how the process would go from here for Keith Madison and Jerry Stokes.

He was keen for Greg to explain to him how the Picasso sting had gone down. Greg explained how he swapped the artwork while hiding behind a false wall in the truck and the difficulty of convincing the museum to loan out the original. Smithson applauded them and then asked if he could speak with Ben alone. They both stood up and walked away from the table. Rebecca knew what it would be about and wore a proud smile.

'Mr Woolford, the United States government would like to thank you for the unofficial help you provided at our little Pine Gap complex over there in Australia. As you can appreciate, we can't publicly thank you for the saving of eighteen American lives and millions and millions of dollars we have invested there, but sir, the US government owes you, and trust me, there isn't much I can't make happen for people we owe. You call me for anything, you hear?' Smithson said, shaking his hand.

The two men walked back to the table, and as Ben sat down, Smithson asked if Jennifer felt that she could still be in any danger. Jennifer shook her head. Keith had tried to kill her to shut her up, no other reason, and it was all out now anyway. Smithson thanked them all for their help and left in the black Chevy Suburban that was double-parked waiting for him.

After Smithson had gone, Jennifer said, 'Hey, would you like to come and see my old house? I might just like to take one last look.'

That would be great, they all agreed. Greg looked at Ben in a way that said, 'What was that all about?'

Ben smiled at him and said, 'I'll tell you about it later, mate,' and patted him on the back.

They arrived at the front of the Madison mansion. Jennifer walked up her front steps, knowing it would be the last time. As she opened the door, a surprised Libby screamed in disbelief, her hands over her mouth as if she was looking at a ghost.

'Oh my gosh, Mrs Madison! We were told you had been… we were all so shocked, ma'am,' Libby did her best to say.

Jennifer didn't want to go over the story and just said, 'Libby, I have missed you all,' as she hugged her.

'I have heard what has happened to Mr Madison, ma'am.'

'Yes, Libby, life will be different for us all from now on.' Jennifer went on to explain to Libby that the property would be turned over to Keith's sister and that she and the other staff would most likely not be required by the new owners. 'Libby, finish off the week here and prepare it…' She stopped and turned to Greg.

'Greg, I can't just leave these people and the house like this. I will need to wind things up and meet you back in Adelaide in a week or so.'

Greg nodded in agreement, and then said, 'Would you like me to stay here with you? If you have a spare room somewhere, I can work from here.'

Jennifer hugged him and said, 'I have lots of spare rooms, darling.'

Jennifer showed her friends through the rest of the mansion. Rebecca couldn't believe it, she tried to compare this to anything she had ever seen before, but there was no comparison.

Rebecca turned to Jennifer and said, 'This must be hard to leave. Isn't this just the best of everything?'

Jennifer smiled at her. 'Rebecca, you are still young, and I am sure, to you, this is all very amazing, and it is, but without love— it's just things. Love warms you from the inside out, and as much warmth that money can buy, it just doesn't reach deep enough.'

As Ben and Rebecca departed the Madison property, Rebecca looked back at the massive house; she marvelled at the life Jennifer was leaving for love. It was so different to her meagre existence as a police constable in Alice Springs. She knew she was a different person now and tried to imagine how Ben would change her life from here on. She squeezed his hand, and Ben turned to her and smiled.

Ben sat in the window seat of the Qantas Airbus A380 as the five-hundred-tonne aircraft lifted off from DFW for the seventeen-hour flight to Sydney. Rebecca had her head on his shoulder; her right hand felt small in his left. His right was on her cheek, and his thumb stroked her face. Her beautiful red hair covered his chest. He closed his eyes and thought about the month that had been. He had made some great new friends in Greg and Jennifer, and of course the love of his life that now sat next to him.

She lifted her head as if she knew he was thinking about her and said, 'Where do we go from here, Ben?'

He lifted her head, kissed her lips, and said, 'Let's see, shall we.'

ABOUT THE AUTHOR

Gary Baxter is a highly regarded South Australian, renowned for his lifetime professional career in motorsport and more recently a major contributor to film production. He holds a long list of achievements as a car and motorcycle racer, pilot, movie action vehicle coordination, and stunt driver/rider, and more since the 1980's, with much of this work continuing today.

Gary has been an articulate, entertaining wordsmith since his youth, along with a love for action novels and writing. His long-held desire to write an Australian-based action story to captivate readers has been suspended for years. He has, thankfully, found time to finally fingertip the keystrokes to produce his first novel, 'Ben Designated Marksman.'

Gary is married to wife Lyn and is an attested proud dad to three children and his grandchildren. He resides primarily in Adelaide, and still travels the country as his work takes him.